THE WICKED PRINCE

BY NICOLE BURNHAM

The Wicked Prince

by Nicole Burnham

Copyright 2016 by Nicole Burnham

Cover design by Patricia Schmitt

Edited by Mary-Theresa Hussey

Edition: August 2016

ISBN: 978-1-941828-10-6

For more information or to subscribe to Nicole's newsletter, visit www.nicoleburnham.com

For my grandmother, Dorothy Burnham, creator of the ultimate luxury item: handmade crocheted afghans.

Thanks, Grandma.

CHAPTER ONE

Eighteen Months Ago

Prince Alessandro Barrali wasn't one to consume expensive champagne in feeble sips, but with several hundred people to fool tonight, nursing his drink was a matter of necessity.

Good breeding brought a polite smile to his face as he stood beside the bar at his sister Sophia's annual Christmas party and surveyed the well-to-do crowd. The usual suspects were present. Near the doorway, wealthy patrons of Sarcaccia's national art museum gathered in a knot around British billionaire and adventurer Jack Gladwell. Many of King Carlo and Queen Fabrizia's friends were in attendance, along with a smattering of Sarcaccian government officials and Italian socialites. But Sophia had shaken up the guest list this year, giving it a Hollywood spin by including two A-list British actors and their spouses, an American hip-hop star, three supermodels, and last year's Oscar-winning director. Instead of the usual orchestra, a DJ spun dance music at the far end of the palace ballroom, transforming the atmosphere to that of a youthful, energetic club. Many of Sophia's former college classmates danced under the sparkling chandeliers, one—lucky man—with an up-and-coming pop princess.

It was a setting in which Alessandro was in his element. One that allowed him to spend the night bantering with clever women and dancing with those who most interested him. After a flirtatious moonlight walk through the palace gardens or along one of the island's glorious Mediterranean beaches, he'd take one back to her hotel for a wondrous, no-strings-attached romp.

Unfortunately, tonight he wasn't Prince Alessandro. To all but his immediate family, he was his quiet, contemplative, identical twin brother, Prince Vittorio, the crown prince of Sarcaccia. There'd be no women, no carousing, no adventure. No *fun*. Certainly no second glass of champagne.

He took another paltry taste and cursed himself for creating the situation. Not that he'd have made a different choice, given the circumstances.

Vittorio's former girlfriend, a much-loved Spanish actress named Carmella Rivas, committed suicide in early autumn, shortly after Vittorio ended their relationship. A private, heart-wrenching note arrived for Vittorio only hours after her death. In it, Carmella confessed the many ways she'd secretly deceived Vittorio during their relationship and apologized for her lies. She also claimed that she was pregnant. She said she'd told no one, but felt she owed Vittorio the truth after all she'd done.

Alessandro and Vittorio had been alone in Vittorio's palace apartment when the letter arrived. In the moments Vittorio's eyes scanned the page, Alessandro witnessed his normally stoic brother's complete devastation. The breakup itself had been difficult for Vittorio. Enduring both the heartbreak and scandal of Carmella's suicide while he remained in the public eye—and with the private knowledge she carried their child—was inhumane. Convinced Vittorio needed time alone, Alessandro suggested the switch. Vittorio refused, determined to keep Carmella's secrets and fulfill his duties despite his emotional turmoil, but Alessandro insisted that not only could it be done, it was the best choice for Sarcaccia. He talked his brother into a two-week trial run, during which they'd attended Carmella's funeral as each other.

It had worked. Alessandro urged his brother to leave the country and get his head on straight so he could be the crown prince Sarcaccia deserved.

Unfortunately, what Alessandro thought would be a week, maybe two, had now stretched to ten. There was no indication Vittorio would return home anytime soon.

Not that Alessandro could blame him. Vittorio didn't trust easily and the experience with Carmella had gutted him.

The crowd parted and Queen Fabrizia made her way to Alessandro's side. With her gaze on the guests, she asked, "Are you enjoying yourself, darling?"

He answered with a sidelong glance.

"You're too distant," she warned quietly. "I know you had a long day preparing for your trip to Istanbul, but your brother would circulate. Make casual conversation, dance with a few of Sophia's friends. Ask about their holiday plans."

"Once I finish my drink, I'll do that."

"Thank you. Now smile at your mother."

He did so, then leaned down and kissed her cheek. After a final civilized sip of his champagne, he set the half-empty flute on the bar. He might be the spare, but he'd learned the lessons of the heir. Duty before all else.

For the next hour, Alessandro made his way through the ballroom. He kept his shoulders square and expression placid, as Vittorio did, and commented on only the most mundane topics, such as Sarcaccia's unseasonably warm December weather or the flattering cut of his sister Sophia's glimmering silver gown. As had been the case since Vittorio departed, no one suspected that the twins had switched places. In fact, three separate guests asked if he'd heard from Alessandro, whom the whole world believed was off on another expedition to Nepal, the wilds of Africa, or a similarly isolated location. Or, a few of the bolder guests mused, perhaps he was hidden away at a friend's palazzo with a female or two.

Oh, how he wished.

He thanked each of them for asking, admitted that he hadn't heard from his twin, then repeated what his father recently said in a press conference, explaining, "Alessandro often travels to areas where communication is unreliable. We expect him to return soon, full of stories." He smiled each time he said it, then promptly changed the subject. The entire time, he took care to avoid the single women in attendance. Alessandro had long ago mastered the art of capturing a female's attention with nothing more than an appreciative glance that lasted a heartbeat longer than was considered casual. It had become such a part of him, he wasn't sure he could smother the reflex. It'd give him away as surely as if he wore a name tag.

In his peripheral vision, he caught sight of one of his mother's close friends zigzagging her way through the crowd. Lacking the energy for another round small talk, he shot a meaningful glance at his younger brother, Prince Stefano, then subtly angled his head toward their mother's friend. Stefano took his fiancée's elbow, then guided Megan toward the older woman for an introduction.

Alessandro returned to the bar and ordered what he really wanted: a tumbler of sixteen-year-old Aberlour. Between the hard work he'd done for Istanbul today and the inane chatter he'd endured tonight, he'd earned it.

"Tired of talking about the weather, Your Highness?"

Alessandro looked in the direction from which the question had come. An unfamiliar brunette with wide, jet-black eyes stood a few feet away from him and smiled at the bartender as he handed her a glass of red wine. Her black gown skimmed her trim figure, but wasn't flashy. She showed little décolletage and the gown's leg-baring slit was a modest one. Even her jewelry was demure. She wore nothing but a pair of diamond studs. No necklace, no glittering bracelet. As she turned to face him, he also noticed she wore minimal makeup. Odd, since Sophia's annual party was a night to see and be seen, and this woman dressed as if intent on flying below the radar.

He eyed her curiously. For all her simplicity, she was quite pretty. "The weather is always up for discussion in Sarcaccia, is it not? Our tourist trade relies on it."

"It does. I simply thought that, given your recent pursuits, you'd have other topics on your mind."

Wariness snaked through him. He couldn't put a finger on why, but the woman struck him as highly intelligent, and as the type who could read people quickly. Surely she didn't know of the twins' switch? He resisted the urge to touch the spot under his left eye where a small scar—currently covered with concealer—differentiated him from his twin, and extended his hand. "I don't believe we've been introduced. I'm Prince Vittorio."

"I'm sorry. Francesca Lawrence." She met his greeting with a firm handshake. "I attended the Sorbonne with your sister. Her flat was across the hall from mine during our last year there."

He released her hand to accept his Scotch from the bartender, then turned to her with a smile. "I believe Sophia's mentioned you. Francesca is one of my favorite names. Hard to forget." Sexy. Romantic. A name far more suited to Alessandro than Vittorio. A name that made him wonder if she had racier gowns in her closet.

The woman's dark brows drew together. "I'd be shocked if she referred to me as Francesca. I go by Frannie."

Frannie? Considering the stiff tone in which she corrected him, he revised his assessment of her. She'd be perfect for Vittorio. The woman probably thought he was flirting simply by mentioning that Francesca was a favorite name.

Then again, he supposed he was flirting...by Vittorio's standards.

He raised his glass and said, "Frannie, then," before taking a sip to gird himself for more small talk. "Did you study art history with Sophia?"

"Economics, though I did manage to squeeze in one art history course. Can't avoid studying art in Paris." Her gaze moved over the crowd, then settled once more on him. "I understand you were in Cairo with your father a few weeks ago as part of the Mideast peace negotiations. And that you're traveling to Istanbul soon to continue the talks."

"I am."

"I think that'd be far more interesting to discuss than the weather."

He laughed, both because it came naturally and to buy himself time. Enticing as it might be, talking politics at a party while he acted the role of Vittorio was akin to tiptoeing amongst landmines. No matter how careful one might be, the slightest misstep would trigger an explosion.

From the day Alessandro suggested the switch, he'd spent every minute of his private time studying his brother's diplomatic and charitable work. Despite that effort, there was no way he could remember everything his brother had said and done over the years, particularly since, for many of those years, Alessandro had been out of the country following his own pursuits, none of which would be categorized as either diplomatic or charitable.

Testing his knowledge against Miss Economics wasn't worth the risk.

"It's Christmas," he finally said. "Most people prefer to discuss peaceful topics."

That brought an intriguing curve to her lips. "I see. You're a born diplomat."

"Any talents I have in that area are due to my parents' example, not any natural ability."

She took a thoughtful sip of her wine, then set the glass on the bar. "Your parents do a lot of good work. Sophia and I were just discussing your mother's morning visit to a home for abused and troubled teens."

"It's a cause Queen Fabrizia has supported for many years. She believes their needs are often overlooked." He wasn't sure why, but he got the feeling Francesca—correction, Frannie—was feeling him out for a reason. Perhaps she *did* suspect that he was Alessandro, in which case he needed to change her line of questioning.

The DJ transitioned from the boisterous dance music he'd been playing to a romantic holiday song about peace on earth, then encouraged guests to find a partner. Alessandro set his glass beside Frannie's on the bar and offered his elbow. "Care to dance?"

Her hand flattened against the bar. "With you?"

He flashed his most disarming grin and made a show of looking around. "Does it appear I'm asking for someone else? That wasn't my intent."

He waited. Felt like an idiot holding his arm in front of her. After a few beats, she said, "It'd be my pleasure, Your Highness." She tucked her hand in the crook of his arm and allowed him to escort her to the dance floor.

He assumed her hesitancy came from either nerves or inexperience, but quickly discovered that Frannie was light on her feet, as if she'd danced at soirees like Sophia's dozens of times before. She fit in his arms perfectly, matching each of his steps as if it were second nature. Despite the cautious nature of their conversation at the bar, this felt natural. Easy.

Heads turned their way as he spun her around the periphery of the dance floor. It occurred to him that Frannie's hesitation likely came because *he* hadn't danced tonight. In fact, no one had seen Vittorio dance since he'd been with Carmella. If anyone snapped photos, they'd likely appear in tomorrow's papers.

Well, so be it. Perhaps Vittorio would catch wind of it and decide to return home.

Alessandro glanced at Frannie. She was more self-contained than the effervescent, high-bosomed women with whom he usually danced. Her hand felt small in his, and her touch at his shoulder soft, yet she didn't strike him as fragile.

In fact, she had a good deal of lean muscle, as if she kept fit for a living.

"Did the Christmas party bring you to Sarcaccia?" he asked. "Or do you live here?"

"I came on business, but I have a small flat here in Cateri. My mother is Sarcaccian." She gave him a small smile. "She actually went to school with your mother, though mine was two years behind yours."

Interesting. Since his mother had attended a rather exclusive school, one filled with children of the wealthy and well-connected, it explained why Frannie navigated the party with such ease. Then there was her last name. Lawrence. Though nearly everyone in Sarcaccia spoke English, Frannie didn't have a Sarcaccian accent. "And your father?"

"American. He works in finance and divides his time between London and New York." One of her shoulders lifted, then dropped. "They divorced when I was eight."

"I'm sorry to hear that."

"It was for the best. My mother's a globetrotter at heart and my father's job doesn't permit that. They've remained friendly and I'm close to each of them."

"Divorce doesn't always work that way."

"No, it doesn't. I'm fortunate."

She angled her head and smiled up at him. A hint of playfulness—or subversiveness—twinkled in the depths of her eyes. Perhaps she wasn't as straitlaced as he'd imagined. Or perhaps he was getting desperate after long months of walking in his brother's shoes and saw what he wanted to see.

"You're close to your family as well, Your Highness?"

"Very."

Her dark eyebrows lifted. "Sophia's always said you're a tight group, but that it was a challenge growing up with four older brothers and a younger one. You all wanted to tell her what to do. Even Prince Bruno."

He grinned at that. It sounded just like Sophia. "I wasn't that bad."

That drew a laugh from her. "She claims you're the worst of all."

True, Vittorio was the worst. "I've laid off recently."

"Prince Alessandro apparently pressures her the least. Fascinating, given that you're twins."

"Perhaps because he's around the least." Alessandro moved Frannie closer to the center of the floor, where the crowd blocked them from anyone with a camera who might be lurking around the edges of the room. "What about you? Do you have brothers?"

"Only a sister. She's five years older than I am."

"Are you close?"

"Yes, though we don't see each other as often as I'd like. She's married and lives near London."

The song ended, but the DJ transitioned to another slow tune intended to keep dancers from scattering. Etiquette demanded that he escort Frannie from the floor, as Sarcaccia's Old World customs still meant that dancing with royalty twice in a row indicated romance was in the air, but his curiosity kept him from releasing her.

"You don't mind, do you? I'm enjoying our conversation." Now that they weren't talking about politics or the weather.

She didn't answer, nor did she pull away. After a moment, she said, "Your twin has been gone a long time."

He felt his smile tighten. Before he could give her the same line he'd given everyone else about Alessandro, Frannie added, "I understand he's spent time in the South Pacific."

"The more remote a location, the more it seems to attract him."

"There's a lot to be said for traveling outside one's comfort zone. Seeing parts of the world that are unlike Sarcaccia, understanding a different way of life."

Just like that, he was in familiar territory. "I've learned more from traveling than I have in any classroom. I believe Alessandro has, as well."

"You must travel a great deal as crown prince. Environmental talks, economic summits, that sort of thing." Instead of pursuing the subject of economics, as he expected, she added, "I imagine when you're not in meetings, you're escorted about on carefully planned tours."

"It's not the best way to see a new location, but in those circumstances security concerns often make it necessary."

"I suppose that's true."

The music grew louder as the song hit its crescendo. When it quieted again, she asked, "When your brother's away, where does he stay? Does he stick to luxury hotels, as you must on your travels?"

He scoffed at that. "Alessandro isn't the luxury hotel type. It's not his constitutional role to involve himself in matters of state, which means—fortunately for him—he's not usually tied to those accommodations."

She was quiet for a beat before asking, "Does he pursue charity work when he's abroad?"

The question was asked casually, but he suspected it was a test...though he wasn't sure whether she was testing Vittorio or Alessandro. He spun her away from a couple who'd maneuvered to a spot within hearing distance. "Would it be terribly rude of me to point out that you ask the strangest questions?"

One side of her mouth lifted. "As long as you don't mind the questions, in which case, I don't think you'd have asked me to stay on the dance floor."

"Touché."

Her smile blossomed at that. "Your family has a long tradition of philanthropy. I simply wondered if Prince Alessandro gets involved in local charities when he's away. When he's not, ah, socializing."

Ah, so it was a test. For some inexplicable reason, he wanted to pass, though he still couldn't fathom her reasons for asking, given his reputation for, as she put it, socializing. "Alessandro spends much of his time away either diving or climbing and keeps the details to himself until he returns. The only exception was when he summited Mount Kilimanjaro to raise money for the International Red Cross. That was—by necessity—quite public."

Her gaze lit on a spot behind his shoulder before shifting to him. When he circled so he could see that side of the room, he noticed his mother was watching them. Queen Fabrizia angled her chin in question, but Alessandro ignored her when Frannie spoke again.

"There's an island in the Pacific called Kilakuru. It's rather isolated. No airstrip, so it's only accessible by helicopter or an hour-long boat ride from neighboring islands. Ever heard of it?"

"I have." It was said to be a diving enthusiast's dream, well worth the effort to travel there. He leaned back and gave her a look to say, *You're still asking strange questions.*

She grinned, reading him correctly, but her voice turned serious as she said, "A tsunami recently wiped out much of the island's infrastructure. It seems like the kind of place the Barrali Trust would assist, so I wondered if that's where Prince Alessandro went. That's all." Her gaze darted toward the doors leading to the ballroom's reception area. "Jack Gladwell is spearheading the construction of a shelter for those orphaned by the disaster. He's also funding repairs to the island's emergency services facilities."

"I didn't think Jack Gladwell publicized his donations."

"He doesn't, but he's sailed in that area and felt compelled to help. I noticed him speaking with your father earlier and assumed Jack convinced your parents to finalize—" At Alessandro's open look of surprise, she explained, "I work for

Jack. Well, I do for another two weeks. We spend a great deal of time discussing his charitable objectives."

Jack Gladwell operated a massive business conglomerate. Stefano's fiancée, Megan, once headed business development at one of Gladwell's many hotels. Few people could claim to work for the man directly. Far fewer referred to him by his first name. Frannie intrigued him more with each passing minute. "Why for another two weeks?"

She shrugged. "I was presented with a new opportunity, one that will take me out of my comfort zone. With Jack's blessing, I decided to take the leap."

Though he wondered what she did for Gladwell—and what she planned to do next—he couldn't help but tease her. "It was the fact he acquired an American baseball team, wasn't it? You hate sports. Can't work for a man with a financial interest in such nonsense."

She flashed a dazzling smile, one that made his breath catch. "I happen to love baseball, though the fact he now owns a rival to my Mets is a point against him."

"Rugby would've been a more appropriate British pursuit. Or polo. Baseball is surprising."

"Jack does love to surprise."

The song wound down and the DJ announced he'd play one more slow number before ramping up the beat. Frannie stepped out of his embrace. "Thank you, Your Highness, for allowing me to monopolize your time."

He covered his disappointment with a smile. "I invited you to do so."

"Still, I suspect others wish to dance with you."

He suspected as much, too. Women always flocked to Vittorio, though for different reasons than they flocked to Alessandro. With Vittorio, they hoped for marriage and a happily ever after as the future queen of Sarcaccia. With Alessandro, they simply wanted to get laid. Any woman who approached him tonight would be out of luck on both counts.

Before he could stop himself, he took Frannie's hand and raised it to his lips. "It was a pleasure to meet you."

Her eyes widened momentarily. "And I enjoyed meeting you, Your Highness. Have a happy Christmas."

He returned to the bar, pausing along the way to make small talk with his youngest brother, Bruno, while pretending not to see the women who'd subtly placed themselves in his path. When he finally reached his destination, he discovered his Scotch had been cleared away.

For the best, he supposed. His fascination with Miss Economics and her employment situation was a clear sign he craved a diversion tonight. Alcohol would only make matters worse. He'd been about to dance with her a third time, and he knew better. Vittorio wouldn't have danced with Frannie a second time, and she was exactly Vittorio's type. Intelligent, proper, and lacking flash.

Alessandro turned to face the room and schooled his features into the same placid smile he'd worn earlier. Another fifteen or twenty minutes and he could make a polite exit, claiming matters of state needed his attention in the morning. The fact it was true—and that he was beginning to find the complicated dynamics of the Mideast far more interesting than palace parties—proved he was slowly losing himself to the role of Vittorio, and that would not do. Even if he wanted to jump into the political fray, it wasn't his place.

His place was to show up for the occasional family or charitable event. Otherwise, he need only play backup to his father and twin brother.

The minute Vittorio returned to Sarcaccia and Alessandro was free, he estimated it'd take less than twenty-four hours to find a buxom, carefree woman willing to do absolutely anything he wanted in bed for as long as he wanted to do it. *That* was a role he'd enjoy.

CHAPTER TWO

Today

For a moment, Prince Alessandro thought it was the sway of his family's yacht, the *Libertà*, that woke him. The warm scent of a woman, the silken glide of a feminine thigh against his muscular one, and the pressure of a firm set of breasts against his back indicated otherwise.

He stretched to run his hand along the glorious curve of Sylvie's calf, only to catch the sound of moans coming from the bathroom, followed by running water and a muttered French curse.

"Nothing to worry about," came Sylvie's whisper. "Too much champagne for our Claudine. She will have an aspirin and we will have our moment of privacy. Then, when Claudine returns, we breakfast on the deck and sunbathe together, yes?" A low, carnal growl escaped her before she described exactly what she and Claudine wanted to do once they bored of lounging on the deck. As a preview, Sylvie slid one of her hands under the sheets to give Alessandro an intimate caress, punctuating it with a scrape of her teeth against the curve of his ear.

"That sounds…stimulating." Physically. But why did it leave him hollow on the inside?

After enduring five long months in a gilded cage so Vittorio could manage his personal crisis, all Alessandro had wanted was rest and relaxation. But when

Vittorio opted to make his return public, Alessandro had been compelled to stay put for nearly a year, answering questions from the media and working alongside his brother to assure Sarcaccians all was well. Now that Alessandro finally felt secure enough to leave the palace, the rest portion of his rest and relaxation plan hadn't materialized. He'd enjoyed nights of drinks and rowdy sports betting with his male friends, danced the night away in the see-and-be-seen clubs of the French Riviera, and savored the lush life aboard his family's yachts with stunning women like Sylvie and Claudine.

What he'd delighted in last night was the stuff of most men's deepest fantasies. Typically, he preferred to entertain one woman at a time, but Claudine and Sylvie were unique, always wishing to visit him together. After they'd boarded the *Libertà*, Claudine turned the television to the Sarcaccia F.C. game in time for Alessandro to see his favorite player bury the ball in Real Madrid's net. She'd instructed him to relax on the sofa and cheer on his team while she and Sylvie took turns massaging his shoulders. Performing mind-blowing fellatio. Straddling him at an angle that allowed him to check on the game.

They'd even chastised him when he'd turned his attention to pleasuring them, though it hadn't taken much effort for him to win that argument. Physically exhausted, he'd fallen asleep sometime in the small hours of the morning, one woman on each side. Erotica books that sold in the millions of copies contained stories of nights less titillating than what he'd experienced.

Best of all, the French women preferred to keep their exploits as private as Alessandro did. Claudine and Sylvie were in it for the same reason as he…the sheer, decadent physical pleasure. They didn't give a damn about his family's name or their billions other than what it offered in that moment: a free night on board one of the world's most luxurious yachts as it sailed the Mediterranean off the coast of Sarcaccia.

So why, with Sylvie's hand expertly stirring him to life, did he feel dead inside? He should be rolling over and making the most of the moment. Tasting the soft, salty skin at the base of her throat. Sliding into her warm, welcoming body and satisfying every carnal urge a man might possess.

"Alessandro," Sylvie breathed against him. "You are so big, so hard. I ache for you inside me. Come. Ease my suffering."

He rose on one elbow, smoothed her thick hair away from her face, then did as she asked. Despite her moans of satisfaction and the sound of Claudine entering from bathroom and urging him on in the most ribald language possible, it wasn't pleasurable. Not in the way it once was, before he spent five months walking in his uptight brother's shoes.

Damn Vittorio. The activities that had always excited Alessandro now left him dissatisfied. Purposeless. As if he were an automaton going through the motions of having fun, satisfying the needs of his body, but without *feeling* anything.

It wasn't as if this was the first time. It'd happened last weekend with the amazing Dutch glassblowing artist who'd cozied up to him at a dinner party in Cannes, then joined him at his hotel. And a few weeks before that with the high-profile Italian journalist who'd interviewed him, then bedded him. The journalist had flat-out told him she considered him the ultimate notch in her belt, despite the fact she'd had a long-term affair with a world-famous actor. He'd attributed his blasé attitude that night to her mention of the actor. But when it'd happened again with the Dutch woman, then again with Sylvie and Claudine....

Sylvie and Claudine were his go-to women for hedonic thrills, guaranteed.

Ninety minutes later, while the gorgeous French women bathed topless on the foredeck, he stepped out of the shower in his suite, used a towel to scrub his dark hair harder than usual, then stared at himself in the mirror. The face staring back was virtually indistinguishable from Vittorio's. He flung the towel in the direction of the heated rack as an epiphany hit him: stepping into his twin's shoes might've given the crown prince a much-needed break from duty, but it had the opposite effect on Alessandro. Months of fulfilling a government role, working with heads of state on solutions to the humanitarian crisis in the Middle East, and hosting affairs at the palace—all while ensuring no one knew he wasn't Vittorio—served as a monumental challenge.

Freedom now bored him. There was no *challenge* in it.

He stepped into his boxer briefs, then pulled on a pair of freshly laundered slacks and a sharp button-down shirt. He needed to get out of town. Not on board the yacht, and not to nearby Italy or the French Riviera. He needed to return to Nepal. Or Zimbabwe. Explore little-known corners of the globe with nothing more than a backpack to weigh him down. Climb a mountain rather than a woman. Learn something. Expand his mind. Then, once he'd had his fill, maybe sex would feel exhilarating again. Stimulating. *Fun.*

He'd promised to stay close to Sarcaccia to ensure all remained stable at home with Vittorio's return. Well…it'd been long enough. More than long enough. He'd done his duty. He'd made himself available to the media, answered all their questions. Proven that the work he'd done in Vittorio's absence was all with his father's and brother's blessings. He shouldn't be expected to hang out in southern Europe waving the Sarcaccian flag at parades for the rest of his life.

"After breakfast, we're returning to Cateri," he informed the women once he dressed and made his way to the deck. "Unexpected business. I'll ensure you're provided transportation from the port to wherever you wish."

The women made all the expected protests over the change in plans, but shrugged into their clothes and made their way to the breakfast table. He didn't miss the amused look they shared when they thought he wasn't paying attention. Within hours, they'd be on to their next escapade and they believed he'd be on to his.

For some inexplicable reason, their attitude galled him.

Decision cemented, he spun on his heel to inform the captain.

* * *

Frannie perched on the edge of a brocade chair in the Barrali family's private library, her gaze moving back and forth between Queen Fabrizia and Prince Vittorio. Try as she might to keep her focus on the business at hand, she couldn't stop mentally cataloging the differences between Prince Vittorio and his twin, Prince Alessandro.

When the crown prince asked her to dance at Sophia's Christmas party, she'd been caught off guard. At the time, the entire country had been consumed by the tidal wave of gossip that followed the suicide of Vittorio's ex-girlfriend, Carmella Rivas, a few months before. Some newspapers attributed the actress's tragic death to career pressure, others directly to the breakup. Certainly the Spanish papers had blamed Vittorio, despite the fact he'd spoken passionately at Carmella's funeral service about her talent, her kind heart, and her beauty, and had followed up by announcing he'd established a fund in Carmella's name to help those struggling with thoughts of suicide.

No one expected him to dance at the Christmas party. When he'd kept Frannie on the dance floor for a second song, she'd nearly stumbled in shock.

Of course, a few months later she learned the truth. The man with whom she'd danced wasn't Vittorio, but his twin, Prince Alessandro. The one Barrali known for his wanton ways. If ever there was truth to the axiom that people would see what they wanted to see, that was it.

When he'd untangled himself from the well-heeled crowd and come to stand beside her at the bar, she'd heard a simmering frustration in the way he voiced his Scotch order. Then she'd caught a glint in his eye, one that indicated an active mind hid behind his proper exterior, and she thought she'd found a kindred spirit. Someone whose mind was far away from the Christmas party. It was what made her open her mouth to ask if he had anything to discuss aside from the weather. When they'd danced, she'd also sensed he was a man who believed in *noblesse oblige*. A man cognizant of both his blessings and his responsibilities, who believed in living life to the fullest even as he frowned at the propriety of her questions about his work in the Middle East or his twin's exotic travels. She thought she'd discovered that the proper, responsible prince known for his practicality had a secret side, one that appealed to her desire to grow beyond the fortunate circumstances of her upper-middle-class life and take on a new adventure.

How wrong she'd been. He had a secret side because he was living a lie.

While Alessandro had held himself formally that night, there'd been a consciousness about his carriage she didn't see in the crown prince today. Vittorio's posture and quiet charisma came naturally. Alessandro, on the other hand, had seemed an actor in a role, mimicking his brother's erect spine and squared shoulders as he'd surveyed the ballroom before taking his leave.

But she'd seen what she wanted to see.

In her own defense, she hadn't met either of the brothers before that night. Looking at Vittorio now, she wondered how anyone who knew the pair could confuse them. Kind and intelligent though he was, Vittorio lacked the stifled look of wickedness she'd noticed in Alessandro's amber eyes. And Vittorio was more than willing to discuss philanthropic work with her today, with all the seriousness the topic deserved. She couldn't imagine Prince Alessandro doing the same.

"How long do you anticipate the shelter on Kilakuru will be needed?"

Frannie's attention snapped to the queen. "For the tsunami survivors, another year, at least. However, if I can secure the funds, I'd like to keep the shelter running permanently. No similar facilities exist on the island or on any of its neighbors. I'd hate to see the investment made in the infrastructure go to waste."

"I agree, if there's truly a need," Vittorio said. "Otherwise the buildings should be turned over to the local government and used for other purposes."

The queen glanced at her son, then asked, "Where did orphaned children go before the tsunami?"

"Relatives or neighbors usually took them in. However, with the economic impact of the tsunami, it's a burden on those families, which means the children often feel unwanted at the very time they most need love. We observed several cases where children as young as nine or ten attempted to support themselves. You can imagine how that goes. Aside from the orphans, there are a number of children whose parents simply can't care for them right now, given their financial situation. Until they can rebuild their businesses or permanently relocate, those families need our assistance."

Queen Fabrizia turned to the man she'd introduced as Mikhail, the chief financial officer of the Barrali Trust. "What are your budget concerns?"

"The shelter's employees aren't highly paid, and several are volunteers. It may not be a sustainable staffing model."

"That was a conscious decision in order to devote more funds toward the facility itself," Frannie explained to the queen. "There are a number of locals who volunteer, though we never know how many hours a week we'll have them. For others, we pay a little over minimum wage and provide room and board at the shelter if they wish to stay there. For those who aren't local, we also cover the cost of transportation to and from Kilakuru, plus we'll provide one trip home per year if anyone stays over twelve months. So far, foreigners have been on three- to six-month cycles."

"Do you have a full staff now?"

"We're shorthanded, but managing." It was a hard admission to make. If she had to come up with funds to pay larger salaries on top of covering employees' housing and food, it could break the bank. "It's important to me that the people who come are dedicated to the community. The island is a diver's paradise, so we keep an open dialogue with Kilakuru's tour operators about their regulars. We hope to find people who are familiar with local conditions and willing to come work for several months if it means they can dive to their heart's content. It's how we found our staff nurse."

"Resourceful." The queen looked to Mikhail. A silent message passed between them.

"Full operational support?" Mikhail asked. At the queen's nod, he said, "The Barrali Trust contributed a half million euros toward Jack Gladwell's rebuilding efforts on Kilakuru eighteen months ago. Much of that went toward the shelter's construction. However, if Ms. Lawrence's budget is accurate, enough remains in the discretionary fund to dedicate to the shelter's operations for five years."

"In that case, please allocate the funds for one year. Ms. Lawrence shall discuss progress with you at the nine-month mark and if all appears satisfactory, we shall extend funding for an additional four years." She turned to Frannie. "If that's acceptable to you?"

Frannie stifled a gasp. She hadn't expected an answer today, let alone such a generous one. "That's more than acceptable, Your Highness, it's extremely kind. Your family's donations have made a world of difference already. Knowing we can maintain a stable environment for Kilakuru's children for the next five years is nothing short of a miracle."

"One year to start. Four more conditional on progress during the first year," the queen reminded her. "We're happy to do it. In fact, I may know a potential volunteer or two. I'll have Mikhail notify you if so."

"That would be very helpful, Your Highness."

The queen stood and Vittorio followed suit. Frannie shook both their hands and promised to use their donation as efficiently as possible.

"I have every confidence in you." The queen's warm smile went all the way to her soft green eyes. Though in her sixties, the Barrali family matriarch could pass for a woman in her forties. Her soft pink dress accentuated a lean figure, and she kept her hair in a modern cut that suited her heart-shaped face and delicate features. Sophia had complained to Frannie on more than one occasion that her mother could run farther and faster than she could, no matter how diligently Sophia exercised. More than her dedication to fitness, however, it was the queen's confidence that gave her the glow of youth.

"Thank you."

"Mikhail will work out the financial details with you. Then I believe Sophia is planning to take you to lunch?"

"She is. She told me she'd meet me here in twenty minutes."

"I'm so glad the two of you have maintained your friendship over the years. It means a great deal to her."

"And to me."

Once the queen and Prince Vittorio took their leave, Mikhail went over the logistics of the disbursements with Frannie, then left her to explore the spacious library until Sophia arrived. The long, rectangular room was spectacular. Soaring windows overlooked the palace's famous gardens, where wide gravel paths snaked between low boxwood hedges surrounding beds of roses in full bloom. Benches tucked into the boxwood offered quiet spots for reflection. In the center of the garden, a fountain sprayed jets of water.

Tempting as it was to linger by the windows, Frannie's attention was drawn to the library itself. Opposite the windows, elegant shelves held thousands of books. She trailed her fingers along the polished wood and studied the spines. Though the expected leather-bound classics were present, works from contemporary authors occupied most of the space. Mysteries, romances, and thrillers appeared to be the royal family's favorites. Biographies and well-thumbed travelogues also occupied several shelves. The magic of the library rested in its wondrous Impressionist paintings displayed in the gaps between the bookshelves, the colors so vivid Frannie put a hand to her chest as she looked at them one by one. She paused in front of a work she'd noticed when she'd first entered the library, a smaller canvas of a young girl reading in the grass. A wildflower tucked behind her ear shone in a lively yellow against her dark hair. Her shoes lay off to the side and her stockinged feet were stretched behind her. The girl looked utterly at peace.

Frannie's mouth dropped into a soft sigh as she stepped back and admired the artist's technique. "You look like a Berthe Morisot! Amazing."

"It is a Morisot."

Frannie whipped around at the sound of the rich male voice. "Prince Vittorio. I'm sorry, I didn't—"

Her heart dropped to her stomach as she got a good look at the man leaning against a windowsill behind her. He wore gray slacks and a blue shirt in the same shade as the sky behind him. A silvery-blue tie was partially hidden by his arms, which he'd crossed over his chest...a rather firm chest. He'd entered the library so quietly she hadn't heard him, yet his presence permeated the room. "My apologies, Prince Alessandro."

"You're observant. Even our parents confuse us on first glance now and then."

"Your brother was here a few minutes ago and he was in a suit." There were other differences—the tousle of his dark hair, for starters—but she wasn't about to enumerate them.

One side of his mouth lifted, then she caught the same wicked glint in his eye he'd had the night of the Christmas party. This time, he made no effort to hide it. "You knew anyway. I'd suspect you'd know who was who if we both stood here naked."

She shrugged, not trusting herself to respond. Definitely not picturing him naked. The man was devastatingly attractive. All firm jaw, rich olive skin, and broad shoulders. Problem was, he knew it. His stance radiated the confidence one only encountered when face-to-face with an extremely good-looking man, one who needed only to enter a room for women's heads to turn and pulses to leap.

Looking at him now, it bothered her all over again that she'd danced with him while hundreds of people watched and secretly snapped photos, all the while believing him to be Prince Vittorio. Even if he had a good reason for pretending to be his brother, she felt—betrayed wasn't the right word—insulted. Belittled.

"I thought you didn't like art. Yet you recognized an unsigned Morisot."

"I never said I didn't like art. I said I managed only one art history class while at the Sorbonne." She remembered their conversation at the bar as if it had taken place yesterday. It surprised her that he did, too, given that it'd taken place a year and a half ago. "And I wasn't positive it was Morisot. I simply thought it was her style."

"You thought accurately." He rose from the windowsill and closed the distance between them. His gaze went to the painting, then to her. For the first time, she noticed a light scar under his left eye. The lights weren't so dim at the Christmas party that she wouldn't have seen it, yet she didn't remember it.

He caught her looking. "Did you know it was me at the Christmas party?"

"No."

He studied her for a beat, then his dark brows knit. "Why did you ask Vittorio so many questions about me?"

"Your family has a long charitable tradition. You have a predilection for far-flung travel. Given those two facts, I thought you might be interested in doing some real, hands-on philanthropic work. I wanted Vittorio's impression of your suitability for such a task. Apparently, you aren't. Suitable, that is."

He moved another step closer. She could feel the heat of his skin and see the golden striations in his rich brown eyes. She wanted to look away, but sensed that doing so would be a mistake.

"I don't believe I've ever heard the words predilection, philanthropic, and suitability used all in one breath," he said. "Enlighten me. Why am I unsuitable for philanthropic work?"

"First, because you lied to me."

His eyes widened in mock offense. "Lied, Francesca?"

"You claimed to be Vittorio. And you know it's Frannie." He'd called her Francesca on purpose. Again, she wasn't sure whether to be honored he'd remembered or galled at the way he used the information.

"It wasn't personal. I lied to everyone. In the end, my brother and I explained to the world what we'd done and why. He's a better crown prince for it, and Sarcaccia is better for it."

"That doesn't explain why you danced with me twice. You knew what people would think."

A smile reminiscent of the Cheshire Cat lit his features and he laid a hand on his heart. "Now I see. It's not the lie that's the problem. You thought Vittorio might be interested in you. You were embarrassed."

She shook her head, but before she could get a word out, he added, "Are you the charity case? If so, you should know that I'm very good at hands-on."

CHAPTER THREE

"You're abominable." Shock at what he'd said—and then at what she'd said, right to the prince's face—had her forming fists at her sides. It took her a moment to add, "Your Highness."

"You're lying to yourself. You were dressed to blend in that night, but when you stood beside me at the bar, something motivated you to speak up."

"Altruism."

"Attraction."

He was too close, infringing on her personal space. Then his mouth was on hers, quick and hot and lush. Instinct made her gasp and step away, but his arm at her back prevented escape. He grinned, then kissed her again. This time, his tongue darted across the seam of her lips, urging her to open to him and respond in kind. All at once, she remembered what it was like to be in his arms. The pressure at her lower back as he'd spread his palm there when they'd danced. The warm, masculine scent of him teasing her senses. The daring attitude. The way they fit so perfectly.

He kissed her like he meant it. As if his entire approach had been building toward this. As if he *had* been attracted to her that night. Because he was right... she had been attracted to Vittorio. To *him*. He'd appealed to the part of her that said it was okay to take a risk, to reach beyond her comfort zone and do something unexpected.

And she was attracted to him now, despite everything common sense told her.

She pressed her hands to his chest to push him away, but faltered as he smiled against her lips. A sudden, painful wave of desire made her want to open to him, to return the kiss—

He released her at the same time she heard a female voice in the next room say, "I'll find my mother after lunch. Thank you, Umberto."

Sophia.

Alessandro stepped back, then gazed at the wall behind her with the same studious expression a man might have while strolling through an art museum on a quiet afternoon. Frannie put a hand to her cheek, certain her face burned.

"Attraction," he whispered before Sophia breezed into the library. The princess stopped short when she saw them and smiled.

"Alessandro! I didn't know you were here."

"I came to see Massimo." He leaned against a nearby chair as he turned his attention to his younger sister. "Fortunately, I ran into Ms. Lawrence and we were able to catch up."

"You two know each other?" Sophia's brow puckered, then she remembered. "The Christmas party you attended as Vittorio." To Frannie, she said, "I still feel bad about not telling you afterward who it was you'd danced with."

"You shouldn't. You were protecting your brother." She didn't note *which* brother.

The princess's gaze went past Frannie. "Were you looking at the paintings? That's one of my favorites."

"It's beautiful."

"She recognized it as a Morisot."

Sophie grinned at Alessandro's comment. "I'm not surprised. Frannie's one of the most observant people I know."

"I'm discovering that."

Frannie's throat couldn't constrict further if Alessandro had wrapped his hands around her neck and squeezed. Thankfully, Sophia saved her from speaking. "Shall we go? I have a patio table at Ristorante Villa Enrica and a driver ready to take us."

"That sounds divine. I love the view of the Mediterranean from there and haven't been in years." A glass of wine and the wash of a sea breeze across her face wouldn't hurt, either.

"Have a good afternoon with Massimo," Sophia said to her brother before turning to lead the way out of the room.

Frannie moved to follow, but Alessandro shifted as she passed, causing Frannie to brush against him. She didn't miss his mischievous wink.

She nearly made it to the door before a shiver ran through her. It only took a split second for his laughter to reach her ears.

* * *

Alessandro knocked on the door to Massimo's palace apartment a second time. A low *woof* sounded from the interior, then nothing.

"Gaspare, where's Massimo?" he asked through the thick door. Alessandro had called when the yacht arrived at the marina to see if his younger brother would be available for lunch. Massimo had been out of the army for two years, but continued to run on military time. It wasn't like him to miss an appointment.

Alessandro pulled his phone from his pocket to check for messages. Sure enough, Massimo had begged off after receiving an urgent call from the veterans' support center he and his wife, Kelly, had recently opened. They'd left to tend to the emergency.

Great.

The apartment door was unlocked, so Alessandro opened it and knelt to greet his brother's dog, a massive Sarcaccian Shepherd. He massaged Gaspare's dark head for a moment, then said, "Okay, boy, let's find your leash. I'll take you to the garden."

Alessandro had planned to ask Massimo how he'd found his footing in Sarcaccia after returning home from years abroad. Until he'd been injured in the line of duty, Massimo had been driven. *Challenged.* Off in foreign lands, intent on his mission, with allies at his side. The king had forbidden both Vittorio and Alessandro from entering the armed services in any capacity in which they might face combat conditions. Alessandro had secretly envied Massimo's position...even as he feared for Massimo's safety.

When Massimo's life had been upended, he'd found a new purpose at home. It'd taken time, but he'd done it. Now Alessandro needed one.

Instead, he'd gone and kissed Miss Economics in the palace library.

He never treated women—anyone—the way he'd treated Frannie. He might be a hellion at times, carousing with friends at all hours, but he wasn't rude. Ever. What had possessed him to needle her, intentionally using her full name and teasing her about her formal vocabulary when it was obvious he'd made her uncomfortable?

Then to *kiss* her?

He swore aloud, then dropped to one of the benches in the empty garden and tipped his face toward the midday sun.

When he'd entered the library on his way to Massimo's apartment and spotted the slender brunette, it had caught him off guard. Rarely were guests alone in the palace. She stood in profile, staring up at the Morisot painting. Her hair was drawn into a businesslike bun at her nape, and she wore a modest navy dress and low heels, but there was an electricity about her that drew him. It had taken him only a moment to place her. Frannie-Not-Francesca, the woman from the Christmas party. The one who'd grilled him about Alessandro's travels, believing she was speaking to Vittorio. The one with whom he'd shared two dances. He'd later uttered the phrase "stick-in-the-mud" when describing her to his twin as a great candidate for Vittorio's future bride...before Alessandro realized that Vittorio had already met Emily, the woman of his dreams.

A few heartbeats later, Alessandro realized that Frannie was oblivious to the fact she was no longer alone in the library. Her expression changed from intense concentration to rapture as she continued to study the painting. Intrigued, he'd moved to the windowsill, waiting for the right moment to make his presence known. When she identified the artist and gasped, he couldn't help himself. She'd spun to face him, and he couldn't stop the grin that had leaped to his face when she recognized him.

Then he saw it. The tightening of her features and flattening of her gaze that said she didn't trust him. She'd sized him up, judged him, and found him lacking. A fraud. *Less than Vittorio.* She'd topped it off with a declaration that he wasn't good enough to do philanthropic work.

Like she was out doing "real, hands-on philanthropic work?" If attending swanky fundraisers or—how had she phrased it at the party? Oh, yes—discussing charitable objectives with Jack Gladwell counted, he supposed she did.

Her timing was as terrible as when he'd met her at the Christmas party. Then, he'd been attracted to her because he'd been without female companionship for so long. Today, he'd come off the yacht frustrated by his lack of direction. Her critical words hit their mark.

He'd egged her on. She pushed back. Then he challenged her with the most reliable weapon in his arsenal.

What in the world possessed him?

Worse, he'd enjoyed it. And so had she. She'd been about to return his kiss when he'd heard Sophia. He'd bet his favorite Suunto climbing watch that when she'd put her hands on his chest, it wasn't to push him away. She'd been about to curl those sweet fingers into the fabric of his shirt. If that wasn't proof enough of Frannie's attraction, he'd seen it in the shiver that made her stutter step on her way out of the library. It'd made him want to kiss her all over again. Instead, he'd laughed.

His sister's friend! Sophia would shred his innards with her bare hands if she knew what he'd done.

Gaspare nosed Alessandro's knee, jerking him back to the present. The prince leaned down and unclipped the leash. "Go on, boy. Run."

The dog didn't need to be urged a second time. He bounded along the wide gravel path toward the garden's large fountain, but stopped at a feminine, yet brisk command to stay away from the water. Alessandro leaned forward to see his mother approaching from the direction of her palace apartment. She wore a soft pink wrap dress and a pair of wedge heels. Her fingertips trailed over a budding rose as she neared him.

"Mother." This couldn't be good. Her busy schedule precluded her from wandering through the gardens in the middle of the day.

She turned a brilliant smile on him. "Good afternoon, my dear. Such a surprise to see you here. Mind if I join you?"

He scooted to make room for her on the bench. "No Daniela?" he asked, referring to her ever-present assistant.

"She's organizing my wardrobe for tomorrow's state dinner. The French president and her husband will be here."

"I see. And you decided a stroll through the garden was in order?"

"I was completing my correspondence when I saw you with Gaspare. I decided to take a short break."

"With a purpose, I assume."

A bubble of laughter escaped her. "You know me well."

He shifted to face her. In the summer sun, the creases along Queen Fabrizia's brow and at the corners of her bright green eyes were apparent. Given that she'd raised six children and watched over an entire nation at her husband's side, they were lines crafted both by stress and by joy. She loved fiercely and completely. Much as she tried to micromanage her children, Alessandro wouldn't have her any other way.

"What is it you wish to share, Mother?"

"I think this time, it's you who have to share." She brushed her hands over her lap, then angled her head to study her son. "You've been to Nice. Out on the yacht. In the clubs. Anywhere but here at the palace. And your company has been…questionable. When I heard you'd returned to shore a few hours ago, I knew there must be a reason."

"I'd hoped to see Massimo." His mother remained silent, her eyes locked on his face, waiting for the rest. She was a master at compelling people to reveal their innermost thoughts with nothing more than a look, and he wasn't immune. Finally, he admitted, "I wanted to talk to him about his adjustment to civilian life."

Her brows raised a fraction. "You're having difficulty readjusting to your position after fulfilling your brother's duties for so long."

He whistled for Gaspare, who'd escaped from view. "I wouldn't say it's difficulty readjusting. It's…I suppose I'm bored. I hate saying that, because it sounds ungrateful. I'm well aware of how fortunate I am."

A mischievous smile danced at the edges of her lips. It was a look he'd seen in numerous photos of his mother, much to her chagrin, as she considered the look unbefitting a member of the royal family. However, it captured her true personality.

"This is serious. I don't believe you've ever asked your younger brothers for advice."

"Mother—"

She raised a palm. "You received little credit for all you did while Vittorio was away. You cut off contact with your friends for months in order to convince the world you were away. You moved into your brother's palace apartment. You wore his clothes and literally walked in his shoes. You made hundreds of public appearances and did a great deal of diplomatic work on behalf of our country."

Alessandro shrugged. "The family gave me all the credit I needed. Besides, it wasn't much work. Most of what I did was follow Father's lead."

She surprised him by placing one hand on his knee. "No, you did the work. The creation of the safe zone around Abu Kamal was entirely your doing. It was a new idea, and effective one. It's saved thousands of lives. Doctors Without Borders is operating there now. The Peace Corps. Children are being educated rather than torn from their families or worse, trafficked. It's not their home, but it's a start."

He acknowledged her point with a nod. Abu Kamal was a success story. "I couldn't have done it alone."

"Nothing that effective is accomplished alone, but I know how much study went into that proposal and the effort it took to convince others that it could be accomplished." She withdrew her hand from his knee as Gaspare plodded back to the bench. "You need a new purpose. After the months you spent handling your brother's role, then staying here to deal with the media, I didn't wish to push. I certainly didn't begrudge you taking off for the past few months. However, now that Vittorio is marrying, it's high time you found a permanent role here in Sarcaccia. Eventually, your brother will be the monarch. You need to be here when that happens."

"Father's in wonderful health. I suspect he'll be on the throne for some time."

"Nevertheless, you need to find your place."

He shrugged. His mother was right, but what was left to him? The constitution kept him from representing the government internationally. The local government was jammed with talent, and most charities were covered by his siblings, parents, and other wealthy Sarcaccian patrons. His contributions wouldn't make much difference.

Climbing had satisfied his need for accomplishment for years, but how many mountains could one man ascend before it felt pointless? And the parties, even those in glamorous settings, had become repetitive. *Boring.*

"There's no need to speak to Massimo and risk hearing about it for the rest of your life," the queen said. "I'm happy to help. There are dozens of projects where I could use you. It'll be a good start."

"Such as?"

"The new children's library. It's scheduled to open next month. If you were to make a few appearances, it'd go a long way toward raising awareness of the toddler and after-school programs it will provide...oh, never mind. I can see from your face that the idea doesn't appeal."

"It's a worthy cause—"

"But not you."

No, not him at all. "I'm not exactly a role model for children."

She laughed and reached down to pet Gaspare. Her smile faded as her fingers connected with his fur. "This dog is wet! He went in the fountain against my express command."

"Not everyone follows your commands? Shocking."

"They should." Gaspare had the intelligence to look remorseful as the queen withdrew her hand. "I wonder, Alessandro...perhaps it's not children that are the issue, but which children."

"What do you mean?"

"Children here in Sarcaccia are fortunate. Even if their home situation is difficult, there are basic support systems in place. That's not true in the rest of the world. For instance, think of the children who are living in Abu Kamal. While they're safe now, their world view is different from that of children here. They've seen war up close and endured hardships that forced them to grow up quickly. What if you could help children such as those who live in the safe zone you created in Syria?"

"Children in that situation don't need fundraising as much as they need diplomacy and the ability to return to their homes. That's Father's role, and Vittorio's. I don't want to overstep, especially given the questions raised when I took Vittorio's place."

"Not every child who's endured hardship has faced it due to war. Natural disasters can be every bit as devastating. You've traveled. You've seen it."

That was true. When he'd last visited Nepal, the effects of multiple earthquakes were apparent. Buildings destroyed, villages cut off from supply lines. Families uprooted. He'd filmed a video during his trip that was used for the Red Cross's fundraising efforts for the area, but it felt small in comparison to the need.

"Helping children in a situation like that would give you purpose, Alessandro, though if you wanted to go beyond fundraising and awareness campaigns, it would require leaving Sarcaccia, at least in the short term. Getting your hands dirty, putting in hard work. I'm not sure that's what you want. But perhaps there's a good compromise. For instance—"

"No. I'd like that." Miss Economics and her holier-than-thou dismissal flashed through his mind. Maybe she'd seen his Red Cross segment and concluded that a quick film pitch was all he was capable of doing. "I can be hands-on."

The queen was quiet for a moment. "Have you heard of Kilakuru?"

"Pacific island. Tsunami devastated it a while back." Miss Economics alluded to it the night they met. Hearing his mother mention the place now struck him as quite the coincidence. "How do you know of it?"

"The Barrali Trust contributed to Jack Gladwell's construction of a children's shelter there."

"Let me guess. Sophia's friend Francesca Lawrence was responsible for your contribution?"

"Your father worked directly with Jack. However, Ms. Lawrence used to manage his charitable giving, so she likely had a hand in the process. You're in touch with her?"

Not unless *in touch* meant kissing her in the palace library, then watching her leave.

"I've only spoken to her once or twice," —precisely twice— "so no."

"Yet when I mentioned Kilakuru, she was your first thought." His mother eyed him. "You danced with her twice at Sophia's party. Given Vittorio's situation at the time—"

"You'd encouraged me to mingle and dance with Sophia's friends, remember?"

"So I did."

"Some of us follow your instruction on occasion," he said, aiming a look at Gaspare. "She mentioned Kilakuru that night, and that she worked for Jack Gladwell. Neither is a common topic of conversation, which made it memorable." Never mind that his idiocy in dancing with her so publicly made the conversation memorable.

The queen continued to scratch Gaspare's head as she studied Alessandro. "They could use extra hands at the shelter. I could use eyes and ears to ensure that a continued investment from the Barrali Trust is money well spent."

"You want me to work at a shelter? With children?" He wasn't sure what he imagined himself doing, but going to a Pacific island to babysit a bunch of kids wasn't it. Then again, part of him burned to prove Frannie wrong…even if only to himself.

"I understand if you feel it's beneath you."

"It's not that—"

"It's more of a challenge than you'd imagine," his mother said, as if reading his mind. "If you want to be hands-on, as you say, Kilakuru is a good place to start. We could spare you here for three months. That's the typical time that foreign volunteers stay. If you enjoy it and feel you're making a solid contribution, perhaps you can extend your stay a month or two. That should give you time to consider how you'll make an impact here. You need to find your passion, such as Massimo's work with veterans or Stefano's conference center and transportation upgrades. Mikhail can make the arrangements. You'd be doing me a favor. I need to ensure our contribution is used effectively."

He mulled over the idea. It held more appeal than the children's library. And there was the opportunity to explore a diver's paradise. "I'd need to return in September for Vittorio's wedding."

"I doubt they'd begrudge you a week's leave."

Alessandro leaned against the bench and blew out a long breath. It was as far away from palace life as he was likely to get. Wasn't that what he wanted when he'd finally stepped out of Vittorio's shoes? Three months doing charity work near surf and sand would be easier than the five months he'd endured pretending to be his straitlaced brother.

One thing was for certain: on an island so remote it lacked an airstrip, he wouldn't encounter women talking Morisot, enticing him into a kiss.

"In that case…I believe there's an island in the South Pacific calling my name."

"You're off again?" a familiar voice said from behind the bench. "I heard you just arrived."

"Yes, Vittorio, I'm off. If you need me, Mother will know how to reach me."

Alessandro stood and gestured for Gaspare to follow him, then leaned over and gave the queen a kiss on the cheek. In a voice meant for her ears only, he said, "If this goes horribly wrong, I'm blaming you."

"I can't wait."

She waved Alessandro away, then patted the bench for Vittorio to join her. "We need to discuss your wedding plans. Daniela brought me the updated guest list this morning."

Alessandro couldn't help but punch his twin on the shoulder as he passed. Talking wedding plans with Queen Fabrizia was far worse than anything Alessandro might face on Kilakuru. He didn't envy his brother that one bit.

CHAPTER FOUR

"You've got to be shitting me."

Frannie stopped in the midst of stacking freshly washed towels inside the nursing station's linen cabinet when she caught sight of two men walking through the open courtyard of the Sunrise Shelter compound. She managed a pleasant smile as she waved out the open window to Tommy Solofa, a local auto mechanic who'd worked at the shelter since it opened, but her stomach pitched at the sight of the man walking beside Tommy. Much as she wanted to believe that Kilakuru's bright, early afternoon sun was playing tricks on her eyes, her gut knew the truth.

"Frannie? What's wrong?" Chloe Robinson, the shelter's nurse, finished tucking a fresh sheet around one of the room's two beds. Alarm etched her features as she turned to look over her shoulder, following the direction of Frannie's gaze.

"It's all right." Frannie took a deep breath and stacked the final towel before using more force than was necessary to close the cabinet door. "When Mikhail called from Sarcaccia to say that the Barrali Trust found a highly qualified volunteer, this isn't who I was expecting."

"How all right can it be? I've never heard you swear before." Chloe's eyes widened as the men drew nearer. "Oh, shit! I've seen him before. Is that…?"

"Prince Alessandro Barrali."

"Here? To volunteer with *us*? That can't be right." Chloe stared for another beat before her forehead creased into a frown. "Wait…how can you tell? He and his brother look exactly alike, don't they?"

Oh, Frannie could tell. It was in the smooth arrogance of his walk, the carefree wave of his hair. Even the devilish grin that lifted the man's cheeks as he spoke to Tommy made it clear he was Alessandro rather than Vittorio. But to Chloe, she said, "The paperwork I received listed the volunteer's last name as Barrali, first initial A. That'd be Alessandro."

"And you didn't tell me?" Chloe smoothed her hands over her sun-streaked blond hair. "I look awful! I probably smell awful." She wrinkled her nose and sniffed her armpit. "Okay, well, not too bad. But Frannie! What's wrong with you?"

"I assumed it was a mistake, that the person who filled out the forms mistook the Barrali Trust for the name of the volunteer." Either that, or a cruel joke. She'd kissed the man—well, *he'd* kissed *her*—two short weeks ago. There'd been an intensity to the simple act of having his lips meet hers that rattled her all the way to her bones. She'd tried to act unaffected, but he knew better. She'd left the room with his teasing laughter ringing in her ears.

Her only saving grace was the certainty she'd never see him again.

He couldn't be so intent on humiliating her he'd fly halfway around the world. He had better things—better women—to do with his spare time. He'd had debutantes, actresses, and models throwing themselves at him since he was old enough to date.

Frannie slid the empty laundry basket under one of the beds, then made her way out of the nursing station and across the compound toward the cinder block building that housed her office and living quarters. Her heart beat in her throat as she walked with Chloe close at her heels. Was Alessandro really planning to stay for three months, living and working within the spare confines of the shelter? He'd claimed not to need luxury hotels, but this was the land of squat toilets, solar showers, and sketchy Internet. It was a huge leap from one world to the other.

She chewed her lip as she approached her office. Was it possible she'd misjudged him? Could that have been why he happened to be in the palace the same day she'd made her pitch to Queen Fabrizia?

She instantly dismissed the thought. If Alessandro Barrali was as upstanding and as focused on humanitarian causes as the rest of his family, he wouldn't have pinned her to the wall and kissed her in the middle of the palace library, then mocked her on her way out the door.

Which brought her back to where she started…what in the world was he doing here?

The deep rumble of Tommy's laughter met Frannie as she stepped into the office. He greeted her with a broad smile on his face. "This is our new volunteer, Prince Alessandro."

"Please, call me Alessandro. This isn't the place for formalities," he told Tommy, then turned and extended his hand. He hesitated, then blinked, his honeyed eyes reflecting genuine shock. "Frannie Lawrence. I didn't expect to see you here. Are you on assignment for Jack Gladwell? I didn't think you worked for him any longer."

"I don't. I run the Sunrise Shelter now. Welcome. We're thrilled to have another volunteer." Her heart thumped a million miles an hour, but she managed to keep her voice even and her handshake quick and professional before she gestured toward Chloe. "This is Chloe Robinson, our nurse. You've met Tommy. Tommy's sister, Irene, works primarily in the nursery. She lived in the United States for several years and worked as an EMT, so she does a lot to help Chloe. The four of us are here twenty-four hours a day, along with four of the six teachers."

"They have rooms in the bunkhouses with the older kids," Tommy added. "Brave souls, those four. The other two teachers and the kitchen staff think they're crazy."

Alessandro laughed, then greeted Chloe with a smile and a warm handshake. Chloe's eyes appeared glazed as she mumbled a greeting. It wasn't often that good-looking men made their way to the shelter, let alone good-looking, wealthy, royal men, and Chloe was young and single.

"You have quite an operation here," Alessandro said. His statement encompassed everyone, but Frannie felt there was a question in it meant for her, as if he couldn't quite believe she was in charge and living here. "It looks like every tree and building on this side of the island was flattened. Hard to believe it's been over a year and a half."

"I took him on a loop around the island when we left the marina," Tommy said. "He was able to see how far the tsunami wave reached and get a sense of the devastation."

"Good thought. Thank you," she told Tommy, then turned to Alessandro. "In a spot this remote, rebuilding is slow. It took over a year to clear away the debris from the damaged homes and businesses and to deal with hazardous items like propane and gas tanks. But now we have this" —Frannie swept her arm to encompass the shelter— "and it's been a godsend for the fifty-six children who live here. We owe our donors a huge debt of gratitude for their support, Jack Gladwell and your family in particular."

"I'm glad the funds are being put to good use." He glanced out the window, toward the center of the compound. "I spent some time reading up on the financials. I was stunned when I learned how many kids live here. I had no idea the tsunami left so many orphaned."

"Thankfully, not all of them are orphans," Chloe explained. "Fewer than twenty, in fact. But the tsunami forced a lot of parents to leave Kilakuru to find work on other islands. Since the shelter was designed with classrooms, they opted to have their children stay here until they can either rebuild or permanently relocate."

Alessandro blew out a hard breath. "That has to be difficult for both the children and their parents. Even if the kids are old enough to understand the logic of why their parents made that choice, it must leave them with a sense of abandonment."

The insight surprised Frannie. She knew Alessandro was intelligent, but she hadn't expected him to be sensitive to the emotions of those around him...not unless he saw an advantage. Her experience in the library being prime evidence.

"We work very hard to overcome that. Our focus here is on supporting the kids emotionally as much as on addressing their physical needs."

Alessandro slid a large, well-worn gray backpack off his shoulder and set it under the front window. "Then let's get started. I have no idea what I'm doing, but I can take direction."

"I like him already," Tommy said, clapping Alessandro on the back as if they were old friends. The prince's title and wealth didn't appear to affect him as it did Chloe, who still gazed at Alessandro as if she didn't quite believe he was real. Then again, any gorgeous male would impress Chloe, and Alessandro was nothing if not gorgeous.

"I'm going unload the supplies that came on the boat," Tommy added. "I should be finished before school lets out."

"Thanks, Tommy. Yell if you need a hand." Frannie turned her focus to Alessandro and gestured toward the center of the compound. "I'm happy to give you a tour. If you need to rest first, or use the facilities—"

"I'm fine. Ready to go."

"Do you need to get your things from Tommy's truck?"

"I have them."

"That's it? One backpack?" It was a large backpack, but still…Alessandro was a prince. Frannie couldn't imagine Sophia traveling with one bag.

"The more I read about the shelter, the lighter I thought I should travel. I assume I won't need many personal belongings. However, I have a shipment coming with my dive gear, as well as medical supplies and dry goods Mikhail said you'd likely need in the coming months, based on your past orders. Laundry detergent, paper towels, items of that nature. Plus two boxes of what I'd consider luxury items."

"That's so thoughtful. Thank you." She sounded as astonished as she felt. The staff was efficient with their use of supplies, but knowing another order was on the way gave them breathing space. Knowing the supplies came from Prince Alessandro…well, that was a shock unto itself. Then again, he looked the part of shelter volunteer today. He wore lightweight, cargo-style pants that could take a beating, along with a short-sleeved casual shirt and a serviceable pair of shoes similar to Tommy's.

If she didn't know his reputation and hadn't seen him in the formal environment of the palace, would she be as surprised by his foresight?

"I'll finish sorting the linens in the nursing station," Chloe told Frannie, though her eyes remained on Alessandro. Before Chloe ducked out, she told him, "We're glad to have you. Every set of hands is a big help."

Frannie didn't miss the skip in Chloe's step as she crossed the compound.

"How long have you been here, Frannie?"

Frannie's attention snapped back to Alessandro. His arms were crossed over his chest and he was studying her as if she were an exotic animal in a zoo. Not in a hostile manner, but a curious one. It sent a skitter of awareness through her that gave her gooseflesh, despite the heat of the day. "A year and a half. Ever since I left my job with Jack Gladwell's organization in London. Why?"

"Does my mother know?"

"Of course. That's why I was at the palace. She wanted to meet in person after I'd sent a proposal for additional funding to the Barrali Trust."

The dark slashes of his brows knit, as if he were contemplating the answer to a puzzle. "I thought you were there to have lunch with Sophia."

"I was…after I met with your mother. Much as I adore Sophia, I didn't travel halfway around the world to have lunch with her."

Alessandro absorbed that. "Your meeting with my mother went well?"

"The Barrali Trust now supports a huge percentage of our day-to-day operation cost, so yes, it went wonderfully." She angled her head. "Really, I should be asking you the questions. Why are you here?"

"Hands-on philanthropy."

"Not with me, you aren't."

His soft laugh made it clear he remembered every word exchanged during their encounter in the library. "That's not the type of hands-on I had in mind. Besides, I had no idea you'd be here."

"Not with Chloe, either. Or any of the shelter's employees." That was the last thing the kids needed.

"Again, not what I had in mind. Believe it or not, I'm truly here to work."

"But...why?"

He leaned against the cinder block wall and scrutinized her. Her hair was up, off her neck. Not in the polished bun she'd worn at the palace two weeks ago, but in a messy ponytail. White sunscreen streaked her jawline where she'd failed to blend it completely. She wore tennis shoes, olive green shorts, and a gray tank top. A black bandana hung in a loop around her throat, rolled so she could push it up on her head if needed.

Though it showcased her long legs and lean, sculpted arms, Frannie's outfit was meant for practicality, given the tropical environment. He'd bet anything she hadn't known he was coming, though he was certain his name would've been on the paperwork Mikhail had e-mailed ahead to the island when Alessandro boarded the plane for the long flight from Sarcaccia.

He uncrossed his arms and shrugged. "Why not?"

"Because you're...you're a prince. You don't do this kind of thing. You know we only have one phone here, right? A landline, on my desk. I mean, everyone has cell phones, but the coverage is terrible. Our Internet is intermittent at best. A lot of days I take my laptop to the police station to check my mail. And wait until you see the size of our cockroaches. They're big enough to—"

"When we met, I told you that I'm not the luxury hotel type."

"With all due respect, Your Highness, I don't think you're the food-slinging, floor-sweeping, math-tutoring type, either."

"Yet you asked Vittorio—or so you thought—about my travels for the express purpose of finding out whether I'd be suited to helping you here."

That caught her for a moment. Her voice softened. "I asked him—you—because I'd just accepted this position, it was on my mind at the party, and the opportunity presented itself. I've since discovered the error in my thinking. Even then, I never pictured you here as a full-time volunteer. At most, I was hoping you'd bring attention to the project and assist with fundraising efforts in Europe. Given your travels, I thought you could speak to a crisis like Kilakuru's. Make it feel immediate to people who have the ability to help."

"In other words, once you met me in person you changed your mind." He pushed away from the wall. Her opinion shouldn't bother him—he'd been judged all his life and let it roll off his back—but in this case, for some reason, it did.

"I flew a long way to come here. You need help. The residents here need help. I know I'm privileged, I know I'm wealthy. I have a reputation for socializing when I'm in southern Europe. I'm perfectly willing to speak to the crisis and raise awareness if that's what you want. But I've also lived in harsh conditions and done so willingly. I spent a month in Nepal sleeping on cold floors and in tents and using squalid facilities—or the outdoors—when necessary. I've hiked through rough terrain with heavy gear. I've lived for days at a time on rice and beans. Certainly the world knows I've gone for long periods without access to phones or the Internet. Though I can't say I enjoyed every minute, I've managed. It keeps my brain and body active."

"That's why you're here? For an adventure?"

He'd come to prove to himself that she was wrong about him. He'd come for the challenge. He'd come because he was bored out of his mind. None of those reasons was what she wanted to hear. He suspected any reason he gave would prove insufficient; even his mother's hope that this experience would serve as a springboard to a long-term pursuit at home.

Rather than answer the question, he said, "Given what you've told me of your parents' backgrounds, and the fact you attended the Sorbonne and worked for Jack Gladwell, I imagine you could live a pampered life, too, if you wished. Yet here you are. So how about you show me around and put me to work. If, in a week or two, you find that I'm not what you require in a volunteer, I'll go. I'll tap my resources to find a replacement you consider worthy. In exchange, I'd appreciate it if you'd refrain from insulting me further. Deal?"

He extended his hand and waited. Her lips twitched with a mixture of frustration and embarrassment, but she accepted his handshake. Instead of letting go, she held his gaze and wrapped her other hand around his. "These children are my world, Your Highness."

Even as he admired her protective streak, he hated that she felt the need to say it. Mostly because, given his reputation and his behavior in the library, he couldn't blame her.

"Understood."

"Then we have a deal."

She released his hand, but he didn't let go. He'd done a lot of questionable things in his life; this, however, he'd get right. "I'll hold you to it."

CHAPTER FIVE

Frannie felt like the emotionally constipated schoolmarm cast as the villain in every preteen television movie. In other words: an evil, grouchy, judgmental shrew.

How could Alessandro make her feel that way with a few simple words?

Probably because she *had* been judgmental. But dammit, in choosing to leave Jack Gladwell and run this place, she had taken on a role akin to a schoolmarm's. She had to protect the kids, even if it didn't make her popular. And, frankly, she had to protect herself. Alessandro Barrali knocked her off her game like no one she'd ever met.

"Let's start over, then." She released the prince's hand, surprised to find she'd gripped it so tightly in both of hers. "I'll take you on the grand tour. You can leave your pack here until we find you a bunk."

Once they were in the center of the Sunrise Shelter compound, she gathered herself, then pointed out the various buildings. "The nurse's station is key," she told him. "Chloe has her own room and bathroom in the back, so unless she's diving, she's available. Not a day will go by when you don't have to escort a kid there with a scraped knee or sore throat. Chloe's great with them all. She's even convinced most of them that shots don't hurt."

Alessandro gave the station a long look. "Bet there were a lot of tetanus shots administered after the tsunami."

"Yep. And those leave little arms sore. Come on, I'll show you the dining hall now that it's quiet."

"How many buildings do you have?"

She swung in a circle to count. "Nurse's station, schoolhouse, two bunkhouses, a nursery for the kids under age five, and the dining hall. Plus my office makes seven. If you count the gazebo at the far end of the complex between the bunkhouses and the nursery, we have eight." She indicated the spacious grass-roofed structure, which was fitted with a circle of thick wooden benches. "We use the gazebo on weekends and in the evenings for games, meetings, stories, you name it. Teachers will sometimes hold class outdoors if the weather is nice and the kids are behaving. Tommy plans to install a grill behind the gazebo…though that's going to be a surprise for the kids. He's using parts of other grills he's salvaged from tsunami wreckage. Tommy owns an auto repair shop and can fix just about anything."

"So he works both here and at the shop?"

She shook her head. "The shop sustained a lot of damage in the tsunami. He's done most of the repairs himself and has plans to reopen once there are more cars on the island. Until then, the shelter provides a reliable income."

Alessandro squinted against the bright sunshine as he took in the layout of the compound, with its brightly painted cinder block buildings set around a dirt-packed central area. She could almost see him trying to imagine what it would be like once the kids were out of school.

"Normally, there would be more shade, but between two-thirds and three-quarters of the palm trees in this area were either flattened or so damaged they had to be taken down as a matter of safety." She pointed to the mountain behind the shelter. Dense rainforest covered it, though there was a gap near the top where one of the island's Catholic churches stood. "See the tree line? That's where the tsunami wave reached. Everything above it was safe. Everything below was damaged or wiped out. We've transplanted a few trees and hope to do more in the coming months, but the buildings were the priority."

He surveyed the hill, then angled his head to face her. "I'm more impressed by what you do have than what you don't. Until I read the budget report and understood the scope of this project, I'd pictured the shelter as a single building."

She smiled at that. "A little over a year ago, you wouldn't have been wrong. There was only one bunkhouse—that yellow building—and the dining hall when I arrived. Both of them were unused storage facilities that survived the tsunami. The gazebo was here, too, but lost its roof a few years before the storm and had been unused for a decade. When we first opened, my office was in a corner of the kitchen and we held classes in the dining area. Having the funds from Jack and from the Barrali Trust enabled us to update both buildings and to complete the rest of the compound with materials shipped from Australia and New Zealand. We used local labor to keep the money in Kilakuru's economy. The shelter's residents have put in a lot of work, too. All the interior painting was done by the kids and the shelter's employees."

Frannie moved ahead of Alessandro to open the screen door to the dining hall. At this hour, the tables were empty, though animated chatter and the sound of pots and pans being scrubbed in the kitchen area at the back of the building was audible. Large fans circled overhead and a breeze carried through the space thanks to screened windows that ran along both sides of the hall. Alessandro stood under one of the fans and pulled his white shirt away from his chest.

She pretended not to see the tanned skin revealed when his top button popped free. One glimpse and her mind immediately jumped to the sensation of his mouth moving against hers and his hands pulling her body flush to his. Worse, she completely forgot what she'd been about to tell him regarding the dining hall.

She bit the inside of her lip and tried to regain her train of thought. "I'm afraid we don't have air conditioning."

"I wasn't expecting it. The fans feel great." He let go of his shirt and walked to the wall where trays, napkins, and utensils occupied a long metal table. "The kids eat all their meals here?"

"Yes," she answered, glad to have a distraction from the smooth skin at the base of his throat. "The school-aged kids use it in the afternoons and evenings as a homework hangout, and we have meetings and game nights here when it's too cold or windy to be in the gazebo." She tried to envision the long tables and benches through the prince's eyes. Would he be comfortable eating here for all his meals? Would he tire of the noise and chaos of several dozen children eating at once?

"It reminds me of boarding school, but better. Not so stiff." His eyes sparkled as he turned to face her. "I bet they're not forced to sit in assigned seats or wait for the headmaster to pick up his utensils before they can eat."

She couldn't imagine a young Alessandro sitting still, waiting for an adult to eat before he could pick up his own fork. "No, we're definitely more laid-back than that. However, the kids clear their own trays, and we do stick to a daily schedule. It's posted by the doors of the school, the dining hall, and the bunkhouses each morning."

He turned to follow the direction of her gaze to the sheet posted beside the front door. "That's it?"

"It keeps everyone on the same page. Literally, I suppose," she added. "The kids do best when they know what to expect each day."

She urged him to follow her to the kitchen, where she introduced him to the staff. All three women were locals, one of whom, a dark-haired woman in her early twenties named Pearl, handed Alessandro a cookie and gave him a bashful smile while Frannie showed him around.

Once they left the kitchen and headed toward the boys' bunkhouse, Frannie explained, "You'd never know from her positive attitude, but Pearl's husband was killed in the tsunami. She was a newlywed and devastated. Her sister and brother-in-law lost their home and business and ended up putting their kids here in the shelter while they work temporary jobs in Australia. Pearl lives in a tiny place and doesn't have the resources to care for her niece and nephew, but working here gives her a modest income and allows her to keep her sister informed about the kids."

Alessandro glanced over his shoulder toward the dining hall and kitchen. "Bet it makes all the difference in the world to the kids to have her here."

Frannie smiled at that. "It does. Pearl's wonderful."

She opened the front door to the yellow bunkhouse. A long, cinder block building with high windows, it stayed cool thanks to its location under a stand of trees that had been transplanted following the tsunami.

"I see why you chose this building for a bunkhouse," Alessandro said as he looked up and down the rows of bunk beds. "Lots of ceiling space for bunk beds without feeling claustrophobic."

"It took a lot of work to make it habitable. Thanks to Jack Gladwell, we were able to salvage flooring from damaged homes and use it here. He also arranged to have the bunks shipped from Australia. As soon as the crates arrived at the dock and we assembled the beds, we filled them."

"Where did the kids stay before that?"

"Outdoors. Tents. Whatever shelter wasn't lost in the tsunami. The lucky ones were able to stay with relatives or friends on the other side of the island, which didn't have as much damage. The churches all opened their doors, too. I first visited Kilakuru a week after the tsunami and was stunned by the conditions." She thought back to that visit. What she'd witnessed changed her life. "I was impressed with the islanders' resourcefulness and optimism. Would you believe that more than one person apologized to me for not being able to host me in their home? That's how generous Kilakurans are."

"You were working for Jack then?"

She nodded. "He'd just returned from a sailing trip through this area when the tsunami struck and he wanted to help. I headed the company's charitable works division, so I offered to lead a team here to assess the situation."

Alessandro ran a hand along the wooden frame of one of the bunk beds. "You ended up moving here permanently."

"This place has that effect." On the flight home, she'd struggled while writing her report to Jack, uncertain she could accurately convey the power of what she'd witnessed. She wasn't sure she could convey it to Alessandro now. "A week after I returned to England, I went out to tea with a few girlfriends. It was a picture-perfect day in central London—sun shining, leaves falling from the trees in the park across the street, tourists smiling for photos—and as we sat around our table, all I could think about was the contrast between my life and what I'd seen during that assessment visit. I had a secure job working for an honorable man. A flat in a great neighborhood. Friends who'd meet me for drinks or go out to dinner whenever I wished. Good health. The love of my family. The survivors on Kilakuru had only each other, yet they'd apologized to me for their lack of hospitality. I couldn't get this place—these wonderful people—out of my mind."

"That's when you decided to return?"

She nodded and leaned one hip against a bunk bed. "The next time I saw Jack, I told him that if the shelter I'd recommended in my report became a reality, I'd head it myself. He laughed and told me it was the oddest resignation he'd ever heard." A grin leaped to her face at the memory. "I knew then he'd find the funds to support the shelter. I had the sensation I'd stepped off a cliff."

His gaze narrowed. She felt he could see right through her. "It sounds like you wanted a challenge."

"I don't know about a challenge. Maybe what I wanted was meaning. A sense of belonging to something larger than myself." She shrugged. To a prince who'd seen and done it all, the passion that brought her here likely sounded clichéd. "I had moments of doubt on the flight here, but once I stepped onto this property and started working, I knew I'd made the right decision. It's more rewarding than anything I've ever done." She straightened, realizing she needed to finish the tour before school ended for the day. "I hope you'll come to feel the same way."

"Time will tell, but I hope so, too." The sincerity in Alessandro's voice surprised her. Then his forehead puckered and he strode to the head of one of the beds and crouched to look at the lower bunk. "There's a camel here."

Frannie laughed at the familiar, long-lashed eyes staring at her. "That's Humphrey. The rule is that he stays tucked into bed during school hours. Otherwise Remy—that's the boy who sleeps here—would take him to class. He's quite attached to Humphrey."

"Humphrey? That's a mouthful for a kid."

"He wanted something with 'hump,' then realized the humor in Humphrey." At Alessandro's raised brow, she added, "It's because he's not hump free. His full name is Humphrey, the Ironically Named Camel."

That elicited a burst of laughter from Alessandro. "That's awful. How old is Remy?"

"Seven. Remy's father ran a dive operation here on the island and one of his regular clients sent the camel from Dubai. It arrived the day after Remy's teacher discussed the concept of irony. Remy was quite pleased with himself when he came up with the name."

"Bright kid."

"He is."

Alessandro studied the camel, whose tawny nose and ears poked out from the bunk's neatly arranged sheets. "I hate to ask, but what brought Remy to the shelter?"

"His mother died of a cerebral aneurysm when he was an infant, so it was just Remy and his father. His father was out to sea when the tsunami hit. He never returned." Just thinking about all Remy had been through made her heart ache. "Remy's the sweetest boy, but he's had a rough time. He was at school when the tsunami warning came. The teachers evacuated the kids to a grocery store on higher ground. After the waves subsided, the kids in Remy's class were picked up as their parents made their way to the store. Remy was the last one there. He stayed with one of his teachers for a few days, then the Red Cross took care of him until we opened. His parents were originally from Marquesas Islands, so he doesn't have any other family here on Kilakuru."

"His family from the Marquesas didn't come for him?"

"Unfortunately, no." Not that she hadn't tried. She'd finally located his mother's family, but they were less than interested. "On the other hand, it'd be tough for him to make the transition to joining a family he doesn't know at this point, and he knows that he's loved and valued here."

She showed Alessandro the adults' rooms at the rear of the bunkhouse, then the restrooms and the solar showers that were located behind the bunkhouse. After that, they proceeded to the girls' bunkhouse and the nurse's station. Chloe gave Alessandro a quick overview of where to find emergency supplies in the event he needed to provide first aid. When Chloe finished, Frannie led the way to the nursery.

"Overwhelmed yet?" she asked.

"Fascinated."

"Good." If anything at the camp would overwhelm him, though, the nursery would be it. "What's your experience with infants and toddlers?"

"I've made visits to orphanages and children's hospitals on behalf of my family. Usually I play cards with the kids or tell stories, but that's the extent of it," Alessandro admitted. "I've never been responsible for any."

She didn't miss the hesitancy in his voice. Gently, she said, "You'll learn fast if you end up helping in the nursery. Eight of our kids live here, all between the ages of two and five. They're all wonderful, which makes caring for them a joy." The scent of antibacterial hand gel tickled her nose when she opened the door and crossed the threshold. In the center of the tiled floor, a little girl with dark, glowing skin and a ribboned bun at the back of her head bounced on a green plastic worm with bright red wheels.

"Why, who's on inchworm today?"

"Miss Fwannie! Miss Fwannie is he-yah!" the little girl yelled before stumbling off the worm and racing for Frannie. Frannie scooped the girl into the crook of her arm before turning to Alessandro.

"Hello there." Enthusiasm and genuine warmth radiated from the prince as he wiggled his fingers at the toddler in greeting.

"Hi!" She giggled, then buried her face in Frannie's shoulder.

"This is Juliette, but we call her Julie," Frannie said. "Her mother works here in the nursery."

"And tries to keep her out of trouble," a voice said from the opposite side of the room.

Frannie looked over at Julie's mother, Mira, who was crouched near the sink to wash a toddler's face. The boy was the youngest of the group, having just turned two, and he squirmed under Mira's washcloth.

"All going well today, Mira?"

"Organized chaos, as always. Wouldn't have it any other way."

Frannie introduced Alessandro to Mira, then to Tommy's sister, Irene, who supervised a game of toddler Twister on a padded mat. Alessandro flashed an over-the-top look of mock horror at the group playing Twister, which sent them into a fit of laughter before they all tumbled to the ground.

"Mira and Irene alternate day shifts with two other women," Frannie explained as the kids scrambled to start a new round. "You'll meet them tomorrow. Irene and Tommy live in rooms behind the nursery and take turns covering the night shift."

Frannie set down Julie, who ambled off to join a friend playing with the nursery's doll house, then she showed Alessandro the small dining area and toddler sleeping rooms at the back of the nursery. "The little ones eat most of their meals here, since they're on an earlier schedule than the school-aged children. Once they hit school age, they move up to the bunkhouse. In the meantime, the little ones join the older kids at the gazebo in the evenings and for special projects in the dining hall from time to time. The interaction is good for both groups. For instance, at Christmas we had a cookie decorating party. The kitchen staff had the older kids make the dough, then the younger kids cut out the shapes. The kids from the nursery school did the decorating."

As they let themselves out of the nursery, the room behind them erupted in screeches, no doubt from the kids playing Twister. Alessandro glanced over his shoulder. "They love those kids."

"The kids know it, too. Mira and the two women who are on duty tomorrow each worked at day care facilities on the island before the tsunami. I was lucky to get them. They'd likely make more money on one of the other islands, but they opted to stay here and—"

A loud bell kept her from finishing the thought. Alessandro turned in the direction of the sound. "Is that an alarm?"

"School's out. Time for the onslaught." A beat later, students began to pour out of the schoolhouse and a chorus of happy voices echoed across the courtyard. She cast a sideways look at Alessandro. "Think you can handle supervising homework time? That's where I've been most desperate for a volunteer. I know it's not what you're used to—"

"Of course. It will give me a chance to get to know the children."

"You're not too tired from the flight?"

"I slept on the plane. I'm here to work, so I may as well get started."

She exhaled. How he handled this afternoon would say a lot about how he'd adapt. "Then we'll head to the dining hall, I'll introduce you to the kids, and leave you to it."

He shot a grin in the direction of the horde, but Frannie didn't miss the doubt clouding his eyes.

"Hey, everyone!" she called over the din. Once faces turned her way, she waved her arm. "Come to the dining hall! There's someone new for you to meet!"

She made a mental bet with herself. Five days. That's how long he'd last. Not due to physical exhaustion—the man certainly had the physique to handle life at the shelter—but due to the mental load necessary to care for the residents. This wasn't like a quick hospital visit, such as those he made for his family. Or even like a hiking trip to Nepal, where he was only responsible for himself. At the five day mark, he'd make an excuse. Say he was needed at home. Or that there were volunteers who'd do a better job with the kids.

As long as none of them got attached to the prince, it'd work out fine. In the meantime, she'd keep her distance so *she* didn't get attached.

CHAPTER SIX

Alessandro suspected his temple would hit the table hard enough to split the wood if he didn't keep his head propped firmly on his fist. He'd never been so exhausted in his life, and that included the dissolute week he'd spent in Thailand with his college friends following their graduation. Or when he'd summited Kilimanjaro with a badly strained muscle and managed to hide it from reporters.

When Frannie said, "time for the onslaught" this afternoon, she'd meant it. Four dozen school-aged kids had descended on the dining hall in a riot of laughter, elbows, and backpacks. Once the kids had taken their seats, Frannie had stood near the doorway and introduced him to the group as Alessandro. She gave no indication of his royal status, but said that his family had contributed the money that helped build the Sunrise Shelter. After a big round of applause and effusive cheers, the kids queued up for snacks and settled at the long wooden tables to tackle their homework.

After an hour, they'd taken a scheduled break. Some played kickball in the center of the compound, others lounged in the bunkhouse, and one small group sat and chatted in the gazebo. Later, they'd returned to the dining hall to have dinner and wrap up homework before heading to the bunkhouse to shower, read, and prepare for bed.

He'd caught a few glimpses of Frannie while he'd umpired the kickball game. Once when she'd crossed the compound with Tommy, and a second time when she'd entered the nurse's station with a clipboard in one hand and a box under her other arm. Then he'd spotted her at dinner, sitting with the youngest of the elementary school children. He had no idea what was said, but the giddy expression on Frannie's face as a little girl stood and jumped in a circle in a strange imitation of a rabbit made it hard for Alessandro to focus on the kids at his table. Frannie had disappeared after that; he had no idea whether he should find her or if she planned to come to the dining hall to find him. Either way, he needed a bed.

"The first day's always the hardest," Irene Solofa told him as she gathered a stack of papers at the end of the table Alessandro occupied. "I can't believe you're still awake. Tommy said you haven't slept since you arrived."

"Haven't you noticed? I *am* asleep."

His response garnered a snort of laughter from Irene. Though she spent most of her day in the nursery, Irene often helped during homework time. The two of them had kept the older kids on task, though Alessandro quickly realized he'd need to do some studying himself if he were to assist with schoolwork. It'd been ages since he'd cracked a book other than a thriller, and he'd been compelled to do a quick geometry textbook review in order to help one of the girls understand her assignment.

Picturing the girls working on their homework reminded him that he'd meant to ask Irene a question. "There was one girl at the end of the table in a pink dress who didn't seem to talk to anyone. Who is she?"

"Long black braid, adorable cheeks?" At Alessandro's nod, Irene said, "That's Naomi Iakopo. She doesn't speak."

"Not at all?"

Irene shook her head. "Not since her parents left. They took her baby brother with them when they went to Papua New Guinea to find work. We thought they'd have returned by now, but her father's had trouble getting a position. Naomi was a quiet girl anyway—at least according to her mother—but the separation has been difficult. She smiles and pays attention during social time and school, and her grades are top of the class, so we continue to treat her as if she's part of the conversation and hope that someday she decides to speak."

"I wondered." The little girl seemed both part of the chaos in the dining hall, and yet separate from it. "Sounds like she might benefit from time with a counselor."

"A lot of the kids would. We do our best—Chloe and I each have some training—but we always wish it could be more."

"Your best is outstanding. I have a lot to learn if I'm going to keep up." Alessandro marshaled the remains of his energy and pushed to stand. "Frannie mentioned that both you and your brother live here in the compound?"

Irene gave a slight nod. "We have rooms at the rear of the nursery, near the little ones. We rarely get a full night's sleep, but those kids" —she put a hand to her bosom and sighed— "well, there's a whole lot of love in that building. Wouldn't trade it the world."

At that moment, Frannie breezed into the dining hall. "Kids are in the bunkhouses getting ready for bed. You need anything, Irene?"

She paused when she saw Alessandro at the other end of the table. Her eyes widened in surprise, which, for some odd reason, made him notice that they curved upward at the outer edges. Had he ever noticed the shape of a woman's eyes before? Perhaps that's why he remembered how unusually dark they appeared as she'd turned to face him after studying the Morisot. He'd been drawn into their depths by that alluring little curve.

"You're still here?"

"You expected me to leave?"

Pink suffused her cheeks and Irene laughed at Frannie's obvious embarrassment.

"Of course not. I thought you'd have gone to bed by now. Except" —she put a hand to her forehead and groaned— "I haven't given you a bunk yet. I'm so sorry. It completely slipped my mind."

"It's all right," he assured her. "I was talking to the kids and discovering much I don't remember about geometry. Or chemistry."

"You helped with chemistry?"

"Only for a few minutes," Irene piped in, her eyes bright with amusement. "I sent Johnny to Alessandro with a trick question, just to see how Alessandro would react. He was perfectly calm on the outside, but I could tell he was panicked on the inside."

"You're lucky I appreciate a good prank," he told Irene. When he'd realized he was the butt of a joke—and that Irene had majored in chemistry in college—it'd fostered a good laugh all around the table. "Just wait until I send him to you with an obscure European history question."

"I'd be in trouble there, for sure. Unless it's about the Tudors. I've read every book I could find about that family. So much intrigue and murder!"

He gave her a quick wink. "Royal families and their intrigues. You'd think they'd know better."

That brought laughter from both Irene and Frannie. Frannie started to say something about finding Alessandro a bunk when the door to the dining hall swung open to admit a scrawny boy in aqua blue pajamas with a Thomas the Tank Engine logo on the chest.

"Remy? What are you doing out of bed?" Frannie asked.

The youngster sucked in his lower lip. Alessandro figured this must be the Remy of Humphrey fame. Judging from the boy's abashed expression as he looked at Frannie, he'd counted on the dining hall being empty.

"I, um, thought I left something here during homework but I can look in the morning."

Irene scrutinized him. "You took your backpack and all your papers with you. What do you think you forgot?"

"It's okay. It's nothing."

He backed toward the door, but not before Frannie crossed her arms and pinned him with a look. "Did you bring Humphrey to homework time?"

Remy paused for a moment, as if debating what to say, then visibly deflated. "I know I'm supposed to leave him in bed during school and homework, but he was sad and he needed me. It was a long day and he got hot."

"Camels are built to take the heat," Frannie said. "They're tough."

"Yeah, I know, but they still get lonely," he replied. "I'm sorry, Miss Frannie. I promise to leave him in my bed next time."

As Remy spoke, Alessandro scanned the floor underneath the tables. On the far side of the room, where Irene had been supervising the elementary school students, a spot of color stood out against the dark wood of the floorboards. Alessandro crossed the dining hall and plucked the camel from underneath a table, then turned and held it aloft. "This camel looks lonely."

"Humphrey!"

Remy crossed the room at a run, then grabbed the camel from Alessandro's outstretched hand. He hugged it to his chest, then looked at Alessandro through the type of impossibly dark, curly lashes that only seemed to be found on children. "Thank you."

"You're welcome." Alessandro lowered his tired body to the bench before cocking his head at Remy. "Miss Frannie told me all about Humphrey this afternoon. I think his name is perfect."

A bashful smile flitted across his lips, then he buried his face in the top of Humphrey's golden head.

"I'm glad to meet you, Remy. I'm going to work with Miss Frannie here at the shelter for a few months. If you'd like, I can check on Humphrey while you're in school to make sure he's not lonely. Would that help?"

The little boy nodded, though only his eyes showed above Humphrey's tawny head. Irene came and put a hand on Remy's shoulder. "How about I walk you to the bunkhouse? I was about to head there to give some of the boys their papers. You weren't the only one who left things behind today."

"Okay," he mumbled before turning to leave with Irene.

"Thank you," Frannie said once they were alone. "That's exactly what Remy needed to hear. With a little luck, he'll feel confident enough to leave Humphrey in bed next time."

Alessandro leaned back, resting his spine against the edge of the dining hall table. "I didn't get the chance to meet him during homework time or kickball. He was with Irene's group. From what I saw, he gets along well with the other kids."

"Like foxhole buddies, this bunch. They've endured a lot together. Fortunately, they're all great kids. I suspect they'd get along even in a normal situation." She held out her hand. "Come on. Up. I'll get you a place to sleep before you turn into a zombie on me."

He allowed her to help him stand, then followed her out of the dining hall. Night had descended. Lights strung to the eaves hummed as they illuminated the compound. Giggling came from the direction of the girls' bunkhouse. Otherwise, all was still. He expected Frannie to turn toward the boys' bunkhouse; instead, she led him toward the office where he'd met her at the start of the day.

"I assumed I'd be with the teachers in the boys' bunkhouse," he said as she pushed open the office door and clicked the overhead bulb to life.

"Your backpack's still here," she said.

"Oh." He was more tired than he'd thought. All he'd envisioned was a bunk and his head hitting a pillow.

She shouldered his backpack before he could grab it, then took a step toward him. "You all right?"

"Fine." He glanced up as a fly circled the bare bulb. "Tired."

Her hand went to his elbow and he jumped at the touch. She didn't seem to notice him start, though. Instead, she led him toward the rear of the office and through a set of wooden doors that smelled of fresh stain and into a barren hallway with four doors, two on each side. She walked to the door on the near left and pushed it open. "It's not much, but it's clean and there are fresh sheets."

"Ah...all right." His brain was getting fuzzy. Hadn't Frannie said she stayed behind the office? "This isn't your room, is it?"

"I'm across the hall. There's another empty room next to mine, but the bunk has a leg that needs to be repaired. The bathroom is next to you. It's simple—just a toilet and small sink—so you'll need to cross the compound to the shower house if you want to clean up. I left towels at the end of your bed."

"That's not...I don't want special treatment."

"What you want and what you need are two different things." Her hand went to his arm again, her fingers curling around the area above his elbow as she looked up at him. Her tone mellowed as she added, "You're so exhausted your eyes are glazed over. You didn't walk a straight line when we left the dining hall. If I put this pack on your back, you'll tip over. Stay here your first week, where it's quieter. Get a good night's sleep until you adjust to the routine and get over your jet lag. Then, if you decide you'd rather be in the boys' bunkhouse, you can move. In the meantime, the teachers there have it handled."

Propriety made him want to argue, even as his inner voice said, *Frannie, I could kiss you right now.* He inhaled deeply to steady himself, then took his backpack from her and turned the knob on his bedroom door. "What time do you need me in the morning?"

Her hand dropped to her side. "Breakfast is at seven, but don't worry about it tomorrow. Everyone knows you've had a long flight and—"

"I'll see you at seven."

He face-planted on the bed without bothering to change clothes or brush his teeth. His last coherent thought was that a bunch of kids would not get the better of him. Nor would Frannie Lawrence.

CHAPTER SEVEN

"So, you never told me…does Prince Charming snore?"

Chloe softly hip-checked Frannie as they walked along the main dock at Kilakuru's marina. When Frannie received a call just after dinner notifying her that a shipment of supplies had arrived, Chloe had volunteered to drive with her to the dock to collect the boxes, claiming she needed to get out of the compound for a while and stretch her legs.

Given that Alessandro had been the topic of conversation from the moment Frannie slid the key into the ignition of Tommy's truck and turned onto the road that led from Sunrise Shelter to the island's marina, Frannie suspected Chloe's main purpose was to grill her about Alessandro.

"I wouldn't know," Frannie said as she paused to adjust the boxes she carried.

"Oh, come on! You have to. You were practically sleeping with him!"

Frannie pinned Chloe with a look of annoyance, mostly in the hope she could stop herself from blushing at the mention of sleeping with Alessandro. "First, he spent less than a week in my building before he moved to the boys' bunkhouse. Second, his room was across the hall from mine and through two doors. He'd need to snore at the volume of a blue whale for me to have heard him. If you consider that 'practically sleeping' with me, I have to question your nursing credentials."

Chloe huffed out a breath. "Well, damn. Can't you give me anything to work with?"

Frannie raised a brow in question as the nurse balanced a box against her knee and opened the back of the truck. Chloe slid her box inside, then reached for the two Frannie carried. Given that they'd already loaded the largest boxes, little space remained.

"I was hoping you'd tell me that he snores so loud he shakes the floorboards. Or that you spotted him in the hallway with the world's worst case of bedhead and drool running down his chin. Maybe that he leaves used dental floss hanging off the side of the bathroom sink."

"Why in the world would I say that?"

"So I won't find him attractive. It's a nuisance having to see that much male perfection every day, knowing that it's not for me."

As they returned to the boat to see if there were any small boxes that could fit in the truck's remaining space, Chloe added, "He's been great with the kids, though. Between us, I didn't think he'd last a week. It's been three and I haven't heard him complain once. Well, other than when Johnny vomited on him."

"I didn't think he would, either." Frannie paused to thank the crewman who'd moved the rest of their boxes from the boat to the dock, then looked at Chloe. "Wait. Johnny vomited on him?"

"Right after last week's pizza dinner. Johnny stopped in the middle of a flag football play, put his hands on his knees for a second, then turned to race for the bathroom. Crashed into Alessandro and spewed all over his shirt."

"How dare Alessandro complain about that."

Chloe laughed as she and Frannie each picked up boxes. "He told Johnny it wasn't fair to take the last slice of pizza if all he was going to do was waste it. Well, then Alessandro complained about the fact the laundry detergent hadn't arrived yet and Mira used the last scoop for the nursery linens. He'd hoped to use the washing machine and detergent for his shirt instead of the sink and a bar of soap."

"He'll have his detergent now. Lots of it, judging from the weight of these boxes."

Chloe huffed in agreement. "Do you remember what else is supposed to be in here?"

Frannie thought about what Alessandro had said the afternoon he'd first walked into her office. She'd been so distracted by the fact he was there, standing before her, halfway around the world from where she'd last seen him, that she'd almost forgotten. "I'm not sure. Laundry detergent was what stood out to me. His diving gear. And medical supplies. He said he looked over a list of our regular orders and used that. Oh, and he said something about luxury items."

"Oooh...he did, didn't he?" They managed to put two more small boxes in the truck, but Chloe held the tailgate without shutting it. "Should we look?"

"The kids will probably be in bed by the time we're done, given that we're going to need to make a second trip. Better to look after we've unloaded." She didn't want to risk waking the kids by driving into the compound any later than necessary.

"Wonder what a prince considers a luxury item?" Chloe asked once they were on the road leading out of the marina.

"Guess it depends on whether he was thinking about Sarcaccian standards or island standards when he arranged the shipment."

Curious as she was about the contents of the boxes, Frannie didn't intend to find Alessandro to ask. It had taken all her discipline to keep a professional distance since the prince arrived. Not that he'd been improper—in fact, if she hadn't been the one in the palace library with him, she'd never have believed that incident occurred. She'd put him on maintenance duty with Tommy during school hours, then assigned him to the older kids for homework and recreation time in the afternoons. More than once, as he'd crossed the compound with Tommy or monitored a game, she'd caught him watching her. Then, yesterday, he'd glanced her direction while carrying garbage from the kitchen to the roadside Dumpster and nearly tripped over a downed palm frond.

She'd been sorely tempted to mouth the word *attraction*, just to irk him. Instead, she'd kept her attention on her conversation with Irene and pretended not to see. God forbid he realize that he'd been correct when he'd made that accusation in the library. Or worse, that she was growing more attracted to him every day. It wasn't even his physical attributes, though when he'd stripped off his shirt and climbed on top of the gazebo to help Tommy repair a loose section of the roof last week, she'd had trouble averting her gaze.

It was the little things she'd observed, like the geometry textbook he regularly carried to his room at night. The times he sat beside Naomi at dinner and spoke to her in a manner that didn't require a response. The fairness with which he refereed the kids' afternoon sports. His knack for treating everyone on the staff as his social equal. The way he checked on Humphrey's well-being and gave Remy a discreet report each afternoon during homework time.

More than once, she'd caught herself daydreaming about the prince as if she were a teenager with a celebrity crush. It exasperated her.

"I'm still not used to the fact we have a prince working with us," Chloe said, cutting into Frannie's thoughts. "He acts like any other bloke. At the same time, I feel like there's something about him" —she sighed audibly, then let her head drop against the headrest— "I don't know. An aura."

They turned off the road and into the parking area in front of the compound. Frannie cut the headlights and turned to Chloe. "Would it be weird if I said that I know exactly what you mean? It's as if he's, I don't know, alone. On a separate plane from the rest of us."

"Exactly."

They climbed out of the truck, opened the back, and carried the shipment to the office for sorting in the morning. "Let's put the biggest boxes along the wall, then stack the smaller ones on top and around them," Frannie said. "If we run out of space in here, we can store the smaller ones in the empty bedroom."

Chloe nodded. Once they finished unloading, they drove back to the marina for the rest. The boat's crew had taken the time to place the remaining boxes in the marina's main office, alongside the parking lot, making the second load much quicker to retrieve. They'd returned to the shelter and stacked the final boxes in the office when a piercing scream echoed through the compound, the type to set the fine hair at the back of Frannie's neck on end.

A second scream quickly followed the first.

"Boys' bunkhouse," Chloe said as Frannie whipped open the office door, already headed toward the horrific sound.

* * *

Bloodcurdling.

It was the only word that leaped to mind as Alessandro sat up, ramrod straight, his heart beating as fast as if he were stranded on a mountain face with an avalanche bearing down on him.

He sucked in a deep breath and listened. Was the pained cry a dream, or real? The past few nights, exhaustion caused his mind to play tricks on him. In his dreams, the perpetual island breeze morphed into a wild wind that carried the roof off the bunkhouse. Typical night sounds—the occasional giggles of kids as they whispered between their bunks in the main room, or the high-pitched squawk of Kilakuru's nocturnal birds—transformed into squeals of kids in pain.

Alessandro forked his hands through his hair, still damp from the shower he'd taken to cool off before bed. A glance at his bedside clock told him he'd only been in his room for half an hour. Most of the boys probably hadn't even nodded off.

Then he heard it again. An anguished scream pierced the stillness. This time, it was followed by a low moan.

He flung back his sheets and jogged, barefoot, from his small bedroom into the hallway that connected the adults' space to the main room of the bunkhouse. Behind him, he heard the math teacher's bedroom door open.

"Sounds like Remy," Walter Tagaloa said, his voice low as he followed Alessandro. "He hasn't had a nightmare like this in a long time."

It took Alessandro mere seconds to spot the terrified child. Just enough light streamed in from the room's high windows to illuminate the tangle of bedding around Remy, who was curled up in a ball at the head of his bed, shaking.

"He doesn't know where he is," Johnny whispered from a nearby bunk as Alessandro passed. The older boy was sitting up, his covers pushed to his waist. "I told him it was okay, but I think he was still asleep. He screamed again and then started crying."

"Thanks, Johnny."

"I'll get the other boys settled if you can handle Remy," Walter said in a low voice, his gaze sweeping the room. Several of the other boys were sitting up or propped on their elbows, their attention focused on Remy.

"You sure? He doesn't know me that well." Alessandro had never dealt with a child in such a state.

"He knows you like Humphrey. He trusts you. He'll calm down if you sit with him for a few minutes. He might be embarrassed afterward, but the other kids won't tease him. They understand."

"All right." Alessandro hadn't spent much time with one-on-one with Walter, but Alessandro's instincts told him Walter was trustworthy when it came to matters regarding the kids. Everyone at the shelter liked Walter a great deal, and given that Walter taught math—a subject many of the kids claimed to hate—their affection for him spoke volumes.

"Hey, Remy," Alessandro said as he approached Remy's bunk. "Did you have a nightmare?"

Remy stared at Alessandro with wide, panicked eyes, but said nothing. Slowly, so he wouldn't upset the boy, Alessandro sat on the bunk's edge. Remy tucked his feet even closer to his body, then his jaw trembled.

"I had nightmares when I was your age, so I know how real they feel. Like you can't catch your breath and your heart is going to explode. But everything's fine now, I promise."

Tears filled Remy's eyes and his jaw shook harder. Not the reaction Alessandro was hoping for. Remy's gaze went to the neighboring bunks and he seemed to shrink into his bedding, as if he wanted to disappear.

Alessandro leaned in closer and whispered, "If you're worried about the other boys, I guarantee, they've all had nightmares, too. Everyone does, from time to time."

"They think I'm a baby. I didn't mean to scream."

The blanket muffled the words so Alessandro barely heard them, but they made him smile. "Let me tell you something. I have four brothers, a sister, two half-brothers, and a half-sister. I know a bit about what other kids think, and they don't think that."

Remy said nothing, but looked miserable. Alessandro tried again. "I have a twin who's four minutes older than I am. When we were kids, he lorded it over me all the time, as if being older automatically made him smarter and stronger. His teasing could be vicious. Worse, because I was a daredevil, I was always the one who got into trouble at home and in school, which meant everyone believed he was better...me included. But when I had nightmares, he was the first to come to my bed and tell me it was okay. He knew how scary they can be, and how real they feel. If a boy who took every opportunity to make fun of me did that, I have to believe that the boys here—who all are your friends—will act the same way."

Remy didn't look convinced, but he relaxed enough that Alessandro could see Humphrey's tawny head jutting out of the sheets near Remy's shoulder.

"Well, look who's here." Alessandro rubbed the camel's head. "He looks like he didn't sleep very well, either."

"He's a stuffed animal. He doesn't sleep."

"You know him better than I do, so I'll take your word for it." Alessandro sat back, unsure what to do next. Remy wasn't going to sleep anytime soon, that was certain. Around them, the room had quieted. No sounds came from outside the building, though he assumed Frannie was still up and about. She hadn't stopped by the dining hall at the end of homework time as she usually did, but she always seemed to be the last one to turn in at night.

He put a hand on the lump that was Remy's foot. Heat radiated through the blanket. "Want to take a quick walk around outside and get some fresh air? I think it'll help me sleep. Since you're awake, it'd be nice to have you to keep me company."

"We're not allowed out after bedtime. We have to follow the schedule."

"I'm going to give you a pass. If Miss Frannie stops us, I'll take the blame. I'm good at taking the blame." He put his hand alongside his mouth and in a conspiratorial tone said, "Humphrey can come, too."

Remy sucked his lower lip into his mouth, thinking. After a few breaths, he whispered, "I'm in my jammies."

"So? I am, too."

"No, you're not."

"I'm in shorts. Close enough."

"You don't have a shirt."

"I'll get one." Alessandro frowned. "Are you going to come or not?"

Remy nodded, then slid from the bed and wiggled his toes into his slippers, which were nestled beside the bunk. Alessandro wasn't sure what he'd say to Remy, but figured a stroll around the compound might help the boy forget whatever images populated his sleep. Alessandro signaled Remy to stop and wait, then retrieved his shirt and shoes from his room. As he led Remy outside, he noticed Frannie standing to one side of the bunk room's entrance, her back against the wall. Walter was by her side, surveying the room. She gave Alessandro an understanding smile before leaning over to confer with Walter.

She must've come when Remy screamed, but Alessandro had been so focused on Remy he hadn't noticed. Nor had he seen Chloe, whom he spied walking away from the bunkhouse, in the direction of the nurse's station, as he and Remy began their loop around the compound. Once the door closed behind Chloe, the night stilled. Only the low calls of nocturnal birds and the distant wash of the Pacific could be heard. Lights strung under the eaves of the buildings provided enough light for walking, but didn't interfere with the glorious display of stars overhead.

He wanted to comfort Remy, but wasn't sure what to say, so he kept quiet.

"Chloe says that you're a prince. A real one, not like the movies. Is that true?"

It wasn't a question Alessandro expected. He glanced down, but the boy's gaze was focused straight ahead.

"She told you that?"

"I heard her talking to Mira about it." He kicked a dried up piece of palm frond that'd made its way into the compound. "Is it true?"

He glanced at Remy and wondered just how many of the adults' conversations the kids overheard, given their tight living quarters. "It's true. But I'm not a prince on Kilakuru. Here, I'm no different than anyone else."

Remy shifted Humphrey from one arm to the other as he contemplated that. After they passed the nurse's station, he asked, "If you're a prince and you have a lot of brothers and sisters at home, why'd you come here?"

Alessandro shrugged. Since his arrival, he'd asked himself the same question a dozen times a day…though not quite in the way Remy did. "I wanted to do something different."

"If I had a bunch of brothers and sisters, I don't think I'd leave. I think it'd make them sad."

The little boy sounded matter-of-fact, but Alessandro's heart broke for Remy. The kid had no one. No parents, no siblings, and apparently no uncles or aunts… at least no uncles or aunts who wanted to take him in. "You know, families don't have to be related. It might not feel like it, but you have a family here."

"No, I don't. Not like most of the other kids. My dad died. He drowned."

The force of that simple statement struck Alessandro like a hammer blow to the chest. It took effort to keep his voice steady as he replied, "I heard about your dad. I'm sorry. He sounds like he was a good man and he loved you more than anyone else on Earth. Miss Frannie told me that lot of people liked to dive with him. They came from all over the world."

"He was really good at it," Remy said. "He used to take me on his boat sometimes. We'd go snorkeling and he'd find sea cucumbers for me to hold. He could always find them."

"You like sea cucumbers?"

"They're weird. They feel all bumpy. You can't tell which end is the head and which is the rump."

Alessandro smiled. "Maybe Miss Frannie will let me take you snorkeling with the other kids one of these days. I'm probably not as good as your dad at finding sea cucumbers, but if I do, you can show everyone how to hold them. You think?"

"Maybe."

Alessandro heard the *no* in the polite response. Remy wanted his father or no one. Alessandro understood, but it frustrated him, too, knowing he couldn't do anything to make Remy feel better.

They passed the gazebo and approached the boys' bunkhouse. "Ready to go inside?"

Remy shook his head.

"One more lap, then. Any more than that and you'll be too tired for school tomorrow." Alessandro feared he'd also be too awake to fall asleep, no matter how exhausted his body and brain.

"Why do you have so many brothers and sisters?"

Alessandro laughed. "That's a question I'd have to ask my parents. I didn't know about my half-sister and two half-brothers until recently. Even if I didn't count them, six kids are plenty for one family."

"I bet when you were little your parents got real tired."

"They probably did. But they love us all, just like the teachers here love you and the other kids." He looked sideways at Remy. "That's what I meant when I said that you have a family here."

Remy didn't hide his skepticism. "I think we make you tired."

Alessandro gave Remy a quick rub on top of the head. "Yes, you do. But it's a good tired. Like when you're tired after kickball or when you've played a long game of tag."

Remy frowned but said nothing more as they circled back toward the bunkhouse. They entered silently to keep from waking the others, then Remy carefully placed his slippers beside his bunk and crawled under his sheets with Humphrey gripped tightly to his chest. The camel's nose poked over the top of the sheets and its big eyes appeared to survey the room.

Noting that Johnny was watching from his bunk, Alessandro didn't tuck in Remy—he sensed that Remy wanted the older boy to see him as tougher than that—but raised his hand to wish the little boy good night and turned toward his own room.

Alessandro smoothed his hand over his jaw as he entered the rear hallway, frustration twisting his gut. He felt so powerless to help the boy. So incompetent. He couldn't bring back Remy's dad. Couldn't stop Remy from having nightmares. Couldn't stop Remy from believing that the older kids were judging him.

And Remy was right about Alessandro's exhaustion level. It bothered him deeply that it showed.

How could he adapt to the rigors of climbing in the Himalayas or manage the lack of sleep that accompanied long weeks carousing in Cannes and Ibiza, yet struggle to adjust to life at Sunrise Shelter?

The night he'd entertained Sylvia and Claudine on board the *Libertà*, he'd awakened feeling unsettled. He'd realized that he missed the feeling that he could rise to a challenge. That he could make a difference. He'd never experienced it while showing up for charitable events with his family; he'd only experienced it while standing in for his brother.

He'd agreed to come to Kilakuru not only to prove that he could, but to recapture that feeling of accomplishment. But now...now he felt both unsettled and useless.

What the hell was he doing? He didn't make a difference to these kids. Not a meaningful one.

"How's everything?"

Alessandro started at the sound of Frannie's voice. He drank in the sight of her standing in the bunkhouse's back hall, steps from his bedroom door. A few tendrils of hair had escaped her ponytail, tempting him to smooth them away from her cheeks. She was so close he could see the glint of the tiny gold studs in her ears.

"Alessandro?"

His exhaustion fell away and his heart thundered in his chest. "Better."

CHAPTER EIGHT

A slow, alluring grin lifted Frannie's cheeks at his delayed response.

"I didn't mean to startle you," she said, hooking her fingers into the front pockets of her shorts. "Walter and I came here to talk so we wouldn't disturb the boys."

"Walter went back to bed?"

"Just now. I was about to leave." She angled her gaze in the direction of the main room. "Remy hasn't had a nightmare like that in a long time. It scares some of the boys when he howls like that."

"It scared me. Believe it or not, I was dead asleep."

Alessandro leaned one shoulder against the wall and folded his arms. His Old World Sarcaccian upbringing put him in the habit of being well-groomed when in female company, yet as disheveled as he knew he looked right now—unshaven, in shorts and a T-shirt, with his hair still damp—her presence relaxed him. He wasn't sure why, and it bothered him.

Even more disturbing, in the three weeks he'd lived at the shelter he'd discovered that Frannie was as much a stickler for rules and schedules as he'd suspected. He'd always been one to chafe against rules—the prime reason he escaped the palace whenever he could—but here in Kilakuru, Frannie's regimented system didn't bother him in the slightest. In fact, as he studied her now and realized it was the first time in days he hadn't seen her with a clipboard within arm's reach, he found that he was beginning to appreciate her methods.

"Walter said you were great with him."

He huffed. "Walter's extremely generous."

"From what I saw, Remy was agreeable to the notion of a walk."

"I doubt it helped. In fact, I may have made it worse." Especially if Remy lay in bed contemplating their conversation, though he supposed it was an improvement over whatever plagued the boy's sleep.

"I don't believe that." She placed her hand on his forearm and smiled in encouragement. In the semidarkness of the hallway, the heartfelt reassurance took on an air of intimacy. Frannie must've sensed it, too, because she quickly withdrew her fingers. "I'm sorry I was delayed. If I'd been here, I'm sure I would've agreed with Walter's assessment of the situation."

"Whether that's true or not, it's nice of you to say."

"I heard enough of your conversation with Remy to know you said exactly what he needed to hear. Especially regarding the attitude of the other boys."

"You heard my bullied-by-Vittorio story?"

"Most of it."

Frannie's index fingers flexed in the front pockets of her shorts, then she glanced in the direction of the now-silent main room. He realized that she was nervous. Instead of saying she would've agreed with Walter, she'd had to add *assessment of the situation*. And before that, it was *agreeable to the notion*. Just as when she'd spoken to him in the library, she covered by using more words—and bigger words—than necessary.

What struck him was that *he* had a case of nerves, too. He'd had little time with her since his arrival, and they hadn't been alone since she took him on the tour of the grounds that first day. He frequently caught glimpses of her throughout the day as she moved from building to building, checking in with Chloe, the nursery attendants, and the teachers. Each day, he looked forward to her evening pass through the dining hall, when she inquired about the kids' homework or participated in board games and the little ones' story time. It was the one occasion he could guarantee he'd speak to her each day.

Tonight he'd caught himself stealing looks at the door every time it opened, wondering when Frannie would arrive. A wave of disappointment flooded through him when Tommy told the kids to pack up their belongings and head for the bunkhouses to prepare for showers and bed.

He couldn't remember the last time a woman's failure to appear left him disheartened. If he'd ever felt that way.

Now that he stood alone with Frannie in the hallway, everything about her seemed magnified. The soft skin along her cheekbones. The sweet upward curve at the outer edge of her eyes as she studied him.

"You must have had a busy day," he said. "I didn't see you after dinner."

"The marina called. Your shipment arrived, so Chloe and I made a couple of runs to pick up the boxes. We just unloaded them in my office."

He closed his eyes for a moment and sent a silent prayer of gratitude skyward. "That's the best news I've heard all day."

"Something essential in there?"

She had no idea. "You wouldn't mind if I opened one of those boxes now, would you?"

"I don't see why not, as long as you have—"

He was out of the hallway before she finished the sentence.

* * *

Frannie couldn't answer Chloe's question about whether or not Prince Charming snored. She was fairly certain, however, that Chloe would agree that it didn't matter, given that the man had a torso worthy of a Renaissance sculptor's chisel. Any woman awakened by his snoring would be rewarded by the view.

When Frannie spotted Alessandro working shirtless on the gazebo roof last week, it had been at too great a distance to observe the perfection of his olive skin or the dips and curves that defined his shoulders. She hadn't noticed the subtle ripple of muscle that crossed his abdomen. She'd seen the lean waist, the breadth of his shoulders, the way his back worked as he swung the hammer. But when she'd entered the bunkhouse and saw Alessandro sitting on the edge of Remy's bed with the moonlight angling over his upper body like a heavenly spotlight, she'd nearly gasped out loud.

Beside her, Chloe had gaped at Alessandro, shook her head, then uttered, "Remy's in capable hands…I'm going to take a cold shower," before she slipped out the bunkhouse door.

Chloe's timing was impeccable, because if she had waited a minute longer, she would've seen Alessandro stand and cross the bunkhouse in nothing but a pair of shorts to fetch his shirt and shoes.

For her part, Frannie found herself frozen in place until Walter Tagaloa approached to let her know he'd told the other boys to stay in bed, shattering the spell Alessandro had cast over her. She'd nearly pushed the image of the prince's flawless torso from her mind when she'd come face-to-face with Alessandro in the back hall as he returned from his walk with Remy.

Even in his white T-shirt, shorts, and a pair of athletic shoes, Alessandro oozed sexuality. Worse, she could smell his shampoo and see that his hair still held the dampness of a shower. How could she be attracted to a man's *shampoo*?

How could it make her wish he'd kiss her again, as he'd done in the palace library?

It'd be the worst thing that could possibly happen. As it was, he'd been so focused on the shipment, he hadn't even waited for her to finish speaking before he bolted for her office.

She heard footsteps, then he frowned at her from the hallway door, said, "You're coming, right?" and disappeared again.

She yanked her fingers from her shorts pockets and followed, stopping only to glance at Remy's bed to ensure he was asleep. Alessandro crossed the compound at a breakneck pace. Whatever was in those boxes, he wanted it badly. Given that he hadn't mentioned the shipment since the day he arrived, she couldn't imagine what had him so fired up.

"I hope you have a knife or box cutter. There's not one in the office," she said to his back. A well-muscled back that his shirt did nothing to hide. And those shoulders. Her gaze locked on them as he walked in front of her. It seemed impossible for a man's shoulders to be so perfectly sculpted. Strong, firm, but not obnoxiously large....

Francesca Lawrence! Stop!

Ogling the man would only give him an opening to flirt if he caught her, and that...well, that would lead down a road she couldn't travel.

She stopped short as she entered the office behind Alessandro. He was already crouched in front of the stack of boxes, mumbling to himself.

"Is this everything?"

"According to the cargo slip I received at the marina. It's in the truck if you want me to get it." The shipment was one of the largest ever received at the shelter, aside from those of furniture or building supplies. She couldn't imagine how anything more would've fit on the boat, let alone in her office.

He began lifting from the top of the stack to reveal one of the two large boxes that had been placed along the wall, then pulled it toward the center of her office floor as if it weighed nothing. "No, I'm fairly sure this is it. You have a knife?"

She knew it. He hadn't heard a word she said. "Give me a few minutes and I'll grab a box cutter from Tommy's toolbox."

"Don't bother." He filched a pair of scissors from a jar on top of her desk and wedged them under the side of the box to create enough space for his fingers. Once he forced his fingers inside, he grunted, then pulled at the top until it gave.

"What's so important that you can't wait until morning? Or for a box cutter?"

"You'll see."

When he finally lifted the thick flaps, his expression brightened. "You'll love this. It's not the box I thought, but—" He waved her over. "Come here."

She approached slowly, wondering what brought such a broad smile to his face, and pulled back one of the flaps. She looked at him in amazement, then at the contents of the box. "Oh, Alessandro! This is fabulous!"

At least a dozen kaleidoscopes lay pillowed in bubble wrap. Alessandro moved them aside so she could see what lay underneath: brand-new board games and two boxes labeled as magic kits. He looked up, gauging her reaction, then lifted out the games and magic kits to reveal a plain carton at the bottom of the box. He lifted the lid slightly, then raised a brow at her as if to say, *take a guess.*

"I haven't a clue."

"Dress up clothes for both boys and girls. They're sized for the nursery school kids. All up to the highest safety standards, I promise."

He opened the lid the rest of the way to show her princess outfits, cowboy outfits, and a Robin Hood type costume.

"There are more of these in another box," he added. "Star Wars costumes, mostly. The other box also has art supplies. Watercolors, crayons, art paper. There's at least one deflated *fútbol*, several volleyballs, and a pump tucked in with the laundry detergent. I imagine we can scrounge something to use as a volleyball net. I hope that's all right?"

Frannie put one hand to her chest. Her eyes welled up at the thought of the kids' reaction when they saw it all. They'd be ecstatic. Alessandro's gifts would tap into the one thing the children had in abundance: imagination.

"It's more than all right," she told him. "The little ones will die when they see the clothes, and you've seen how the older kids spend their free time. This is right up their alley." The board games would be welcome for the older kids, who'd worn out most of the games they already had. Some of what Alessandro provided were familiar favorites, but others were entirely new. The kaleidoscopes would be popular with the children Remy's age as well as the younger ones. And all of the kids would have fun with the magic kits and art supplies. She could imagine Johnny, in particular, volunteering to put on a magic show for the little ones at the nursery school.

While she sorted through the games, Alessandro pulled out the other large box and used the scissors to wedge open the side. He bent to peek inside. When Frannie looked over to check on his progress, he surprised her with a playful wink that made her feel beautiful, despite the fact she'd spent the evening loading supplies. "Hit the jackpot. The box I really wanted to open."

"What is it?"

"Comfort items. This time, they're all for the grown-ups. There's even something for you, Miss Uptight Sorbonne Economics graduate."

She straightened and put her hands on her hips. Uptight? "Is that what you think of me?"

How uptight could she possibly be, standing in the middle of a South Pacific island in shorts and a tank top with dust from carrying the boxes all over her arms?

"You're the one who wanted to talk world politics at a Christmas party, remember? If that doesn't scream uptight, I don't know what does."

The man knew how to deflate an ego. "What'd you put in there, back copies of *The Economist*? A political biography or two?"

Not that she wouldn't love to sink into a great political biography in the moments she had to herself each night before drifting off to sleep, but it bothered her that when Alessandro looked at her, he saw a stiff, boring, scheduled schoolmarm. Not a woman with a range of interests, one who'd taken the leap to travel around the world, alone, to build and manage a shelter.

Not the woman he'd kissed in the library. Though he'd mocked her, even laughing as she'd stumbled while leaving the room, part of her wanted to believe he'd found her attractive.

Alessandro ignored her question, grunting as he forced the top of the box. When it opened, he reached in, pulled out bubble wrap and tossed it in the general direction of her desk, then withdrew a small packet and lobbed it at her. She recognized what she held at nearly the moment she caught it. "Verveine soap!"

"Too girly for you?"

Her throat tightened. This wasn't a gift for an uptight, staid type. It was a gift that spoke to her heart.

"Verveine is my favorite. How'd you know?" She turned the package and read the handwriting on the brown paper, which described the soap as handmade, organic verbena soap from France. The fresh, light scent made it obvious this wasn't a cheap, grocery store bar, but one that had been made with pride, in small batches. It reminded her of springtime walks in the hills of Sarcaccia or southern France. Of nosing around tiny European shops that had been owned by the same families for generations, and of meeting craftsmen who spoke with passion about their ingredients and methods.

"I asked Sophia what she'd take to a remote island, one with no luxuries." He shot a look at the box. "There's more soap, plus plenty of lotion, shampoo, and conditioner. Enough to share with everyone. I had the shop add a few other items they thought you could use. Of course, Miss Economics, if you'd prefer back copies of *The Economist*, I'm sure it could be arranged."

She raised the bar to her nose and closed her eyes. *Heaven.* "Much as I love a good opinion piece on supply-side economics, this is too decadent to resist. Just smelling it makes me feel spoiled. Thank you."

"After a long day with the kids, the adults here deserve to spoil themselves a bit. You, especially."

A tender note in his voice made her look at him, but he quickly averted his gaze to dig through the box. "Ah, good for the shop. This should make you feel pampered after a long day."

He pulled out a sumptuous white robe, sized for a woman, complete with a waist tie for modesty and a hood for warmth, then withdrew a pink card that had been packed on top. Frannie recognized the logo at the top before Alessandro mentioned the name.

"It says there are more being shipped separately, compliments of the shop owner's cousin, who's a bedding designer based in Nice. Apparently, he just came out with a line of robes and wanted you to have some of the first. There will be a separate shipment soon arriving with one for each of the shelter's employees. Even the men." Alessandro's eyes lit with delight. "Can you imagine Tommy lounging in a fluffy robe like this?"

She couldn't believe the lavishness of it. Islanders weren't familiar with this level of luxury, even before the tsunami. The nearest place to buy robes like these would be in one of the fancy shops in Australia or New Zealand. Even if they could travel there, no one on the island had money to blow on such an extravagance. "These are too much, Your Highness. I couldn't possibly...*we* couldn't possibly—"

His brow furrowed. "We're back to Your Highness? I thought I was Alessandro here at the shelter."

"This isn't a run-of-the-mill bedding designer. Most people here couldn't afford one of his pillowcases. He may be the shop owner's cousin, but he's a household name."

"It's a gift. Accept it in the spirit in which it's given."

Frannie set the soap on her desk and met Alessandro's look of consternation with a steady gaze. She hadn't intended to put his title between them, but in this instance it was probably a good thing. "You know there wouldn't be pricey robes if it weren't for the fact a member of the Barrali royal family placed the order for the soap. The robes aren't for the benefit of the shelter, but to impress you."

"I doubt that's true. There are always kind people who want to help where they can. If a high-end designer wants contribute by making those who do the hard work at a shelter more comfortable, why not?"

"Alessandro, you know I'm right. Why would he—"

He waved the pink card in exasperation before dropping it into the box. "If he did it because he wants to gain my future business, is that so bad? Companies give away free samples all the time in the hopes they'll gain new customers."

She took a step toward him and fingered the plush fabric of the robe. She didn't hide the doubt in her tone as she pointed out, "Freebies are rarely the equivalent of a month's worth of meals."

"Frannie." His voice was soft, pleading. "It's a small thing, given all you do. For all everyone here does. It'll make the designer feel good to know his robes are being worn all the way in Kilakuru."

"It would feel wrong to me. I can't possibly—"

"Yes, you can. He wouldn't have sent them if he didn't want you to have them." Alessandro placed the robe in her hands. Standing this close, she could see the pattern of gold flecks in his soft brown eyes...eyes that searched hers with an intensity that made her throat constrict. "Yes, it's luxurious. Yes, it feels out of place to have something so pleasurable in a place that's seen so much heartbreak and horror. That's what life is, though, isn't it? Finding the joy in every situation and appreciating it? Accept this. Take joy in it. It hurts no one. Next time my mother replaces bedding in the palace, I'll suggest she order from him, all right?"

Frannie let out a long, slow breath. Maybe this was a lesson she needed to learn. "All right. But I want to send a thank you note to the designer. And to the soap shop."

"Of course."

"And thank you, Alessandro." She curled the robe to her chest. "I didn't mean to sound ungrateful. This is extremely kind. Not just the soaps and the games and the kaleidoscopes, but that you thought of doing all of this in the first place."

"You haven't seen the laundry detergent yet. Or the ice packs and first aid supplies. I'll have you falling at my feet for those." His tone was deliberately provocative. "And I can only imagine Chloe's reaction if I were to whip out a roll of bandages and—"

"Don't you dare!"

His eyes widened a notch, then amusement settled in.

"Uh-oh. Are you worried I might flirt with Chloe?"

Frannie could smack herself. She was never the type to speak without thinking. She tried to cover with a lighthearted, "I didn't mean—"

"You're afraid I'll kiss her under the nursery school's art wall the way I kissed you under the Morisot."

Her mouth went bone dry at the suggestion. "Alessandro."

His name emerged in a rasp so breathless she didn't dare continue. She suspected anything she said would only dig her into a deeper hole.

"Or…is it that you think I'm flirting with *you*? By giving you a robe, soap, and other" —he stepped closer— "intimate items?"

The seriousness in his tone rooted her in place, affecting her as powerfully as when she'd witnessed the moonlight striking his bare torso earlier. Her breath turned to lead in her lungs. Why was he doing this to her? "Are you?"

CHAPTER NINE

He let her question hang in the air for a long beat, then another. Frannie thought she'd go out of her skin. She should've changed the subject. Backed away. Asked an entirely different question.

"You're still learning the difference between altruism and attraction." A muscle at the corner of his mouth jumped, then he straightened. "In this case, I'm making sure you're cared for. Just as you've been caring for me."

She forced herself to exhale slowly. "That's kind of you to say, but I haven't been caring for you. Telling you what to do, sure, but I tell everyone here what to do. It's my job."

He shook his head, though his expression remained serious and his gaze locked with hers. "I had only a vague notion of what to expect when I arrived. You made sure I had a comfortable bed and quiet during my first week so I could adjust. You gave me important details on everyone's background so I'd know the best way to make friends. You told Irene to help me if I needed it during homework time—don't deny it, I know you did—and when you introduced me, you did so in a manner that ensured neither the kids nor the adults would treat me differently due to my heritage. That's taking care of me. I appreciate it. No one's done that for me before. Not like you have."

Never in a million years would she have expected such a speech from Alessandro. From Vittorio, sure. Vittorio was the epitome of graciousness and always knew the right thing to say to make those around him feel valued.

Coming from Alessandro…the rarity of such a compliment made it more meaningful.

And, to her endless frustration, made her want to reach out, cup his cheek in her palm, and pull his mouth to hers.

"You're supposed to say thank you," he prodded.

Her face heated. "Thank you."

"People should compliment you more often. You'd handle it better."

He'd left her so dumbfounded, she merely clutched the robe and stared at him instead of responding. Then again, better not to respond at all than to kiss him. She managed a small smile. "I'll endeavor to express my gratitude more appropriately."

Her stomach seized as he continued to hold her gaze. He had to realize how the expression on his face—one that was both appreciative and piercing in its intensity—would affect her. If this wasn't flirting, she wasn't sure what was.

"You'll…endeavor to express your gratitude?" His mouth split into a grin as if she'd told a colossal joke. "I'll keep it in mind."

In an effort to take the tension down a notch, she directed a glance at the open box and asked, "What was it that had you so anxious to open the boxes? I assume you didn't forgo a bit of joy for yourself."

"Never." His smile had the very devil in it as he spun to reach inside the box. Frannie took the opportunity to turn away from him and set the robe on the seat of her chair. Her cheeks still burned and it galled her that Alessandro elicited such a reaction with nothing more than a look or a teasing reminder to say thank you.

She was as bad as the women who fawned over him at every public event in Sarcaccia. If he realized how easily he affected her, he'd probably consider her equally airheaded. Or as easily manipulated. Sophia had complained to Frannie more than once that Alessandro could get a woman to do anything he wished with nothing more than a look. The princess considered it an affront to the intelligence of all women.

He'd been the epitome of respectability since his arrival on Kilakuru. On the other hand, he'd proven he wasn't above attempting to manipulate her that afternoon in the library.

She wished she knew which was the real Alessandro, the true personality beneath the can't-look-away physique and devastating charm.

"Here we go. Heaven. Care to share?"

She took a calming breath, then spun and raised her gaze to his. Alessandro held two bottles aloft, one in each hand. "There are more where these came from," he said. "I figured six would do. Not one of them arrived broken, which is a miracle."

"Is that--?"

"Aberlour. Scotland's finest. A good burn of this at the back of your throat each evening and you'll find you can tolerate anything. If you're wrapped in a sinfully soft robe while you indulge, all the better." He set both bottles of Scotch on her desk, then strode to a nearby steel cabinet, turned the key that rested in the lock, and opened the double doors. "Tell me you have some glasses here so I don't have to break into the dining hall. They don't even need to be actual glass. Paper cups will do. Anything to take the edge off after tonight's disaster with Remy."

"It wasn't a disaster." Her heart sank. "And I hate to burst your bubble, but—"

"Not a glass in sight." He shut the doors on Frannie's stash of office supplies. "We'll just drink out of the bottle tonight. I'll grab glasses from the dining hall for tomorrow."

He started to open one of the bottles, but Frannie put her hand over his. "Alessandro, you can't."

His brows lifted as his eyes met hers. "Can't what?"

"No alcohol is permitted at the shelter."

One side of his mouth lifted in a wicked grin. "Not to worry. I'd never let the kids have this. Vittorio would be shocked to know I'm sharing with you. I take my Scotch seriously."

"Adults either."

He stared at her. As realization set in, his expression went rigid and his fingers flinched under hers. "You're joking."

"I'm not." Suddenly self-conscious, she withdrew her hand. "I'm sorry. I know you had it shipped all the way from Europe and that you've had a difficult day, but—"

"Not even after the kids are in bed?" He released the bottle and gaped at her. "What harm is there? We're responsible."

"First, it's not a good example for the kids. Second, one of the reasons parents who've been forced to leave their children in our care are comfortable doing so is because they know we're going to be stone cold sober every minute of the day and night while we're here at the shelter. They've learned the hard way that an emergency can arise at any time. They want their kids protected."

His jaw worked. "One glass of Scotch doesn't render me insensible."

"I never said that." Gently, she picked up both bottles and put them on the floor of the steel cabinet, then walked to the box and took the rest of the bottles out of bubble wrap and started putting them in the cabinet.

"You're confiscating them as if I were a teenager caught with a cigarette in class?"

His voice held a bite she didn't like and she straightened her spine in response. Holding a bottle in each hand, she said, "You're welcome to take a bottle to the beach or marina during your off hours, when you're away from the kids. Until then, I'm putting them away. They aren't permitted here."

"Scotch is a nightcap. Not a beach drink."

"Regardless, the kids shouldn't see these and you shouldn't be tempted by their existence."

"There's temptation everywhere. That's the real world. It's never hurt me to indulge…in any of it. I know my limits, in all things."

"Unfortunately, your limits and the shelter's limits aren't the same." She set the last two bottles in the cabinet, then turned the key. Hated that she felt like an uptight schoolmarm once more. Having him accuse her of treating him like a teen didn't help. "I'm sorry, Alessandro. I feel awful—I do—because I understand how stressful this place can be—"

"You never show it."

Oh, she was ready to show something, but she didn't have the luxury of releasing the rage that occasionally welled within her. She had to tamp it down and act like a reasonable adult. Even now.

"Alessandro, there's a reason I held that bar of soap like it is made of gold. I'm sure you feel the same about your Scotch. It's a respite." She sighed, then picked up the robe from the chair and set it on the desk. Slowly, she ran her hands over its plush loops. "It's not easy. It'll never be easy as long as there are kids living in this compound. I may not show it, but I understand the desire for a moment of peace and comfort. It's a deep, palpable craving some days."

He eyed the cabinet. Frustration rolled off him in waves. She could tell he didn't see the harm in a simple pour. She wished she could make him grasp that it wasn't a matter of controlling his consumption. It was the fact that drinking was breaking the rules.

Kids needed rules. Kids needed stability. Parents needed confidence in their children's environment. It made the world safer. *Predictable.* Her parents' divorce could've devastated her if her father hadn't been so stable, so reliable.

The tsunami had taken the predictability from these kids and their families. The shelter was a rock to them now, so long as everyone adhered to the rules that kept the environment stable.

"How do you do it? I've only been here three weeks, yet it feels like three months."

"Does it feel that way because you don't like it, or because you're tired? Believe me, I drop into bed every night exhausted to the bone."

"Because it's *hard.*" He interlaced his fingers and put his hands on top of his head, causing his biceps to pull the fabric of his T-shirt. His eyes drifted closed, and he blew out a hard breath. "I have a comfortable life in Sarcaccia. I know that. I'm grateful for it. Given my family's wealth, I could kick back and do nothing.

Instead, my parents instilled in me the sense that life isn't worth living without goals. I worked my tail off at university to finish at the top of my class, even if it didn't matter to my future. International relations fall to my brother, not me. I've gone out of my way to do physical work. No one can climb a mountain on a whim. It takes months of training, months of pushing myself in a gym and outdoors. Above all else, it takes mental fortitude. When I'm not climbing, I do martial arts training to build that. But here" —he opened his eyes and met her gaze— "here I'm at a loss. I don't know how to reach the goal. I'm not even sure what the goal *is*. I certainly don't know how to translate what I'm doing here into a productive goal I can pursue once I'm home."

He dropped his arms and started to pace the tight confines of her office. "None of my training stops the overwhelming urge I have to grab Naomi's parents, drag them here from Papua New Guinea, and show them how much she needs to be with them. It doesn't stop me from wanting to punch Remy's relatives on the Marquesas for failing him just because they had issues with his parents."

She frowned. "Wait. How could you know there were issues?" She'd only told Alessandro that Remy's relatives didn't come for him.

"I asked Irene one night after homework time. She told me that when you contacted them, you learned that there was a falling out between Remy's parents and the rest of the family after the wedding. The relatives said that if Remy was alone, it was his parents' fault for not making arrangements. Irene also told me that they didn't return your follow-up calls. He's such a wonderful boy. How can you not feel angry about that?"

"I do." If she hadn't, she wouldn't have griped about it to Irene, Tommy, and Chloe, who adored Remy as much as she did.

Alessandro's jaw worked as he sat on the edge of her desk. Frannie circled the desk to sit beside him. "Every single adult at the shelter feels that aggravation. It's basic instinct to want the kids to be happy and to rebel against whatever stands in the way, even if that seems to be the kids' own families. But allowing that anger to overtake us doesn't help the kids. At the end of the day, that's all that matters. Helping them."

He cast a sideways glance at her. "Problem is, I have no clue how to help them. Johnny acts tough, but I can tell he's unsure of his future after high school. I can't draw Naomi out of her shell. And I don't have the foggiest idea how to handle Remy or his nightmares."

Deep dissatisfaction filled his voice as he spoke. Much as she knew she shouldn't, Frannie took one of Alessandro's hands in both of hers and gave it a squeeze. "It may not feel like it, but you are helping them."

He started to respond, but she cut off his argument. "Since you found Humphrey in the dining hall on your very first day, Remy has trusted you. Remy told us he brought the camel to homework time because it was lonely. You didn't tell him that Humphrey is only a stuffed animal and that it would be fine in his bed, which is what a lot of people would've said. Instead, you promised to check on Humphrey during the day. It was a great response, one that acknowledged his feelings. And tonight, when you took Remy for a walk around the compound, it gave him time to shake his nightmare so he could sleep. It was the right thing to do. When we left the bunkhouse, he was sound asleep."

Alessandro looked at her hands, wrapped around his. "If any of that worked, it was dumb luck. I'm tired. I'm irritable. I'm not a natural like you or Tommy or Irene. Even Walter's a lot better than I am at this, and he's a math teacher. Not exactly the type of person known for making kids comfortable."

That made her smile. She didn't imagine Alessandro compared himself to others often, and when he did, he didn't find himself lacking. "None of these kids have dumb luck on their side. If they did, they wouldn't be here in the first place."

"I'd say they're plenty lucky. They have you."

The words were said with a tenderness that surprised her. She let go of his hand and smiled at him. "Thank you."

"Ah, she remembered how to take a compliment."

Frannie laughed. "I'm a fast learner. I just…I hope you understand about the Scotch."

"I do." He pushed to stand, then made a point of eyeing the cabinet. "But I don't have to like it."

"Understood."

She expected him to turn and head for the bunkhouse. Instead, he paused in the doorway, crossed his arms over his chest, and asked, "Other than getting a good night's sleep, which clearly isn't going to happen tonight, do you have any practical suggestions for how I might deal with the kids? Whatever you do seems perfect."

"I'm not anywhere close to perfect." At his openly skeptical look she said, "I want to scream at the world some days. I dream about the morning I wake up to see the entire island fixed…with all the roads repaired, with homes rebuilt, with people back to their lives and jobs and families. With the schools and shops open again. So my practical advice? Keep in mind that that's what the people of Kilakuru are dreaming of, too, and that they're doing their best to make it happen. Much as you might want to throttle Naomi's parents, try to remember that they're frustrated, too."

His mouth formed a grim line. "Does Naomi realize that?"

"On a practical level, yes. Her parents write to her often and tell her how much they want to see her and promise that they're working very hard to find jobs. They're trying to help her understand that it's best for her if she stays in school, and that they can't enroll her elsewhere until they're employed. But in her heart? No, I don't think she understands why this is happening to her."

"It's heartbreaking to see her at meals. Her eyes follow everyone around the room. She doesn't look sad, but she doesn't speak, either. When she plays kickball, she doesn't cheer for her team or celebrate when she makes a great play. She just… watches. Walter and the other teachers say she's the same in class."

"I know. But you're doing the right thing. You include her, you act as if she *does* speak. You treat her like the intelligent girl she is." Frannie exhaled, long and hard. "Miracles don't happen overnight. I tell myself that as often as I feel like Sisyphus, endlessly rolling a rock up a hill only to watch it roll down again, I'm not. There's progress here. With Naomi. With Remy. With all of them. And with the island. A year ago, the marina was nothing but a pile of battered wood and twisted metal, and the dock was nonexistent. Nine months ago, there was no Internet. Three months ago, our nurse was leaving for a new position and we hadn't yet found Chloe."

"You're saying things will work out."

"This civilization has been here a thousand years. It will rebuild. Parents will find jobs. Children will find homes."

He leaned against the door frame, but didn't open the door to leave. "I'm used to seeing more progress when I take on a task."

"You're used to things that are within your control. This place isn't."

"Yet somehow, you seem to have it within yours. At least, you make the kids think you do."

"That's because I love them."

His smile was slow and sexy. She got the strange sensation that he was looking right through her...as if he knew something about her, but wasn't going to share.

"What?"

"You love them *and* you keep everything on a schedule. You said it yourself, the kids do best when they know what to expect. You bring order to their lives."

If she had something handy to throw at him, she would. "Is that a jab at my rules? Because it won't get you the Scotch."

His laugh rolled right through her, making her smile in return. "I'm not talking about the Scotch, though I'll take that any way I can get it. A good nightcap brings order to *my* life." He straightened, then pushed the door with his hip. "Good night, Frannie. Sleep well."

"You, too."

He paused. "We could toast our new understanding of each other."

She made a show of rolling her eyes. "Alessandro? Get out."

CHAPTER TEN

Alessandro grimaced at the raw spot on the side of his hand, then used the back of his arm to wipe the sweat from his brow. He shifted his grip on the sandpaper block and attacked the final remnants of rust on the large piece of metal that would become the bowl of the shelter's new grill.

The school bell had declared the end of the day more than an hour ago, but Irene had assured Alessandro she had homework time covered, affording him the opportunity to continue working with Tommy. If they were going to pull off their plan to surprise the kids with a cookout next weekend, they'd need to use every spare moment to finish.

And—Alessandro bit back a curse as he scraped the heel of his hand—he'd need to find a pair of gloves.

Despite the abrasions he'd incurred from aggressive use of both the sandpaper block and a wire brush, the afternoon of physical labor served as a welcome change from poring over books with the kids. He'd spent more hours studying calculus, chemistry, history, and proofreading papers in the month since his arrival on Kilakuru than he had since college. The amount of material the kids covered in comparison to what he was assigned years ago astounded him. The drive they had to understand the material and succeed astounded him even more. None of them—from the youngest preschoolers to the oldest teens—took their education for granted.

Tommy put his hands to the base of his spine, then stepped back to survey the freshly painted section that would be used as the barbecue grill's lid. A few weeks earlier, Tommy had spread rusted metal parts across newspapers in the empty area where they now worked, well behind the gazebo and out of sight of the compound. Whenever possible, Tommy escaped here to sand down the metal, figure out what was salvageable, and weld the useful pieces together to create a new grill. Two days ago, Alessandro followed and offered to help. Now that they'd nearly finished, Tommy started tackling the welded pieces with spray paint.

"The kids will smell the paint," Tommy muttered. "I hope Irene can keep them from wandering back here."

Alessandro flipped over the piece he was sanding so he could tackle the other side. "I don't think that'll be an issue today. Frannie couldn't get an Internet connection this morning and walked to the police station to use theirs. One of the officers had a volleyball net and offered it for the kids. She and Chloe planned to set it up at the far end of the compound from the gazebo while we worked on the grill. Once Irene lets the kids out of the dining hall for recreation time and they see a net and balls, they'll race that direction."

"I might race that way, too. I love volleyball." Tommy grabbed a can of black spray paint to hit a spot he'd missed. "It's the national sport of Kilakuru. Did you know that when you packed the boxes?"

Alessandro shook his head. It'd been almost two weeks since his shipment arrived and Frannie had been doling out the gifts to the kids a little at a time. The volleyballs hadn't yet made an appearance. "It was my sister's suggestion to send deflated balls and a pump. She pointed out that kids can play at any age and that volleyball doesn't require safety gear or special shoes."

"Smart sister."

"She often is. Not that I'd admit it to her." Now that he thought about it, he realized that Sophia likely got the idea the same afternoon he'd seen Frannie admiring the Morisot. It would've been natural for the two of them to talk about life at the shelter when they'd gone out to lunch.

It was only a couple of days later when Sophia had knocked on the door to his palace apartment and asked to borrow a book on Tibet. He and a palace staffer were in the midst of loading the boxes for Kilakuru, and Sophia took an interest in both his trip and the shipment. Not only had she suggested the balls, she'd shared her thoughts on the list of board games he'd selected for inclusion. Then, when he asked her opinion on luxury items that could withstand the journey, she'd suggested the soap. She'd specifically mentioned the verveine.

Given his sister's enthusiasm, Alessandro had to wonder whether Sophia was in league with his mother. Both of them knew he was heading to Kilakuru to work at the shelter, yet neither mentioned Frannie's presence. Nor could it be coincidence that Sophia's soap suggestion happened to be Frannie's favorite.

The question was: why?

"If I told Irene how smart she is, I'd never hear the end of it," Tommy said. "It's bad enough she's older than I am and thinks she knows best."

"It's the same with my sister and she's younger. When Sophia made the suggestion, I pretended to have to think about it. I finally told her that deflated balls would work well as packing material for the laundry detergent. I'm sure she thought I was an ungrateful, pompous jerk, but it was better than having her know I thought her idea was brilliant," Alessandro responded, which drew a laugh from Tommy.

Alessandro blew dust off his piece. At the same time, a series of whoops and cheers followed by, "me, me, me!" echoed from the compound.

"They discovered the net," Tommy said as he capped the spray paint. "The balls were worth shipping, packing material or not."

A few minutes later, Tommy finished inspecting the painted pieces and wiped his hands on a rag. "I need a break. Time to show those kids my volleyball skills. Care to join me?"

"I have another section I'd like to finish today. You go ahead."

"Your loss. Don't overdo it on your hands, okay? Too much sanding and your joints will scream tomorrow. I speak from experience."

Alessandro waved him off. "I'll be fine. Have fun, but no spiking at the kids."

"No promises. I'll see you at dinner."

Tommy disappeared, taking a circuitous route to the compound so the kids wouldn't know where he'd been. Alessandro bent his head to focus on the task at hand.

It was slow, painstaking work, sanding section after section of the pieces Tommy had collected, then either welding the pieces or finding the proper size screws to assemble them into a functioning grill large enough to cater to the entire shelter. In the aftermath of the tsunami, every piece of metal that had been hit by the massive waves had rusted. Tempting as it was to order a new grill and have it delivered, Alessandro appreciated the environmental need to repurpose what was already present. Retrieving and repairing lost items also gave the residents the sense that the tsunami couldn't defeat them. That sense of pride outweighed any benefit a new grill might offer.

A bead of sweat ran down the side of his temple. Another dripped from his forehead, hitting the hard-packed dirt near his feet. When he finished sanding the next section, he'd head directly to the shower house. Eating dinner in his current state was out of the question.

Of course, the shower house made him think of the soap he'd delivered to each of the women working at the shelter. Ever since he'd opened the boxes in Frannie's office, he'd caught whiffs of it on Chloe, Irene, Pearl, and—though he tried not to—on Frannie. The worst was yesterday, when Frannie walked behind him in the dining hall while he was seated at dinner with Naomi and some of the other girls.

He didn't need to look to know that it was Frannie, rather than one of the other women. The airy lemon seemed part of her, a natural extension of her optimism and sunny attitude. It spoke to her ability to focus on everything good and right, rather than on the millions of wrongs in the world.

Crazy, he thought as he attacked the metal. He'd always been one to admire the scent of a woman, but never had he caught himself daydreaming about the scent of a particular woman, let alone contemplated the ways it reflected her personality.

He closed his eyes, remembering the joy that radiated from Frannie's face as she read the handwritten label, then raised the bar to her nose. It was a simple action, yet one that sent a wave of yearning through him. When he'd told her she deserved to be spoiled, she'd looked at him with such heartfelt emotion in her eyes he'd been forced to turn and dig inside the box once more, for fear she'd see the ache in his.

A scuff behind him made him pause. He turned his head, expecting to see a bird or a snake. Instead, Naomi stood near the base of a palm tree. She held her hands behind her back and watched him. Her stance made him suspect she'd been there a while.

He smiled in acknowledgment, then turned to his task. As if she'd said hello, he told her, "You caught me daydreaming when I should be working. You're welcome to help if you'd like. There's a grate propped against that rock that could use some cleaning. You don't have to, though."

It took Naomi a full ten seconds to move, during which time Alessandro kept up his rhythmic sanding. When he dared look at her, she'd taken a seat on the rock where the grate rested. She whipped her hands to her lap, making him suspect she'd been holding something behind her back when she'd approached him and had hidden it behind the rock.

"The bucket next to the grate has soapy water," he told her. "There's a pile of rags at the edge of the newspaper. Use those to clean the grate, but be careful not to touch the black metal pieces that are on the newspaper. They're covered in wet paint."

Naomi located the rags, dipped one in the bucket, then took a seat on the rock and started washing the grate. It was slow work, but didn't seem to bother her. When Alessandro finished the piece he was sanding, he walked to Naomi's side and used one of the wet rags to wipe away the dust he'd created. He placed the piece near those Tommy had painted, then grabbed another section to sand. His hands ached and he was ready to be done for the day, but it was the first time

Naomi had approached him, rather than the other way around, and he wanted to see where it went.

Several minutes later, cheers came from the compound. Tommy's ebullient voice carried over those of the kids, though the words were unintelligible.

"Didn't feel like playing volleyball?"

Naomi shook her head. She was such a beautiful girl. She had the soft, rounded cheeks typical of the South Pacific, glowing black hair pulled into a long braid, and dark, intelligent eyes framed by thick lashes. Despite the silence that evidenced her pain, he sensed that Naomi possessed a deep well of inner strength. Her grades were good, she kept her bunk area scrupulously clean, and Alessandro noticed that she took the time to put away her dishes after each meal. Even now, she concentrated on cleaning every nook and cranny on the grate. She cared about the quality of her work.

What he wouldn't give to see her with her family.

"I love volleyball, but even I'm happy to sit out the game today. It's hot." He glanced at Naomi. "It's hot back here, too, but at least we have a few trees for shade. And there's no running involved."

Naomi gave him a small smile and nodded. He kept her gaze for a beat, then focused on his sanding. His mouth grew tight and chest ached. It was the first time he'd ever seen her smile. Knowing he'd broken through that barrier was the most rewarding moment he'd experienced since his arrival.

"Any kids see you come here?"

She shook her head.

"What about the adults?"

She shrugged one shoulder.

"Maybe Tommy?"

A nod.

"That's good. If he knows, he'll make sure no one comes looking for you. All of this" — he waved his sanding block in the direction of the newspapers— "is a surprise. Tommy wants to have a barbecue next weekend for everyone. He's lined up the food, so all we need is the grill. I can trust you to keep a secret, right?"

"I won't tell anyone."

He nearly dropped the block at the softly spoken words. It took him a second to regain the rhythm of his sanding and say thank you.

He ached to tell her that she had a lovely voice and should speak more often. To ask her questions about her parents and baby brother. To tell her she wasn't alone. He restrained himself, knowing he was far more likely to scare her than reassure her if he said the wrong thing.

"When you're done cleaning the grate, we should head back to the center of the compound. I need to take a shower before dinner."

She nodded. A few minutes later, while he stood and stretched, she located a clean rag and used it to dry the grate, then she set it next to the freshly painted items.

"That really shines in the sun," he told her. "Good job."

She smiled again, this time more broadly than before. She turned away and picked up her rag. He suspected she wished to hide her reaction, but the set of her shoulders was as much evidence of her pride in a job well done as her smile had been.

He put away his sanding block and organized the rest of the materials before covering them with a small tarp Tommy had left behind. He turned to see if Naomi was ready to return to the compound and was surprised to see her crouched behind the rock.

"Is everything all right?"

She stood, but kept both her hands behind her back. An odd expression danced across her face.

"What are you hiding, Naomi Iakopo?"

Her dark eyes twinkled with mischief at his question. She withdrew one hand from behind her back, flashed her empty palm, then slowly withdrew the other... which held a bottle of Aberlour.

He couldn't have been more shocked if she jumped on top of the rock and sang at the top of her lungs.

"Naomi, did you take that from Miss Frannie's office cabinet?" At her shrug, he asked, "Why?"

He expected her to shrug again, but in a voice scratchy from disuse, she said, "It's your special treat."

"What makes you think that?"

"I heard Miss Frannie tell Chloe that she 'put away Alessandro's booze' and that you weren't happy about it because you like to have it before bed." She shifted the bottle in her grasp. "My mom and dad have whiskey sometimes before they go to bed. They call it their special treat."

The kids heard a lot more than they should around this place. Still, it touched him that Naomi wanted to do something for him. Not only that, she cared enough to explain what she'd done after having gone months without speaking at all. "When I had it shipped here, I didn't know it's against the rules. So no, I wasn't happy, because it is my special treat. But that doesn't make it right to take it."

Her face fell. "You don't want it."

Oh, he wanted it. He suspected she'd taken quite a risk to steal it, too. For *him*. It was probably the first thing she'd planned and done for another person since arriving at the shelter.

His jaw tightened as he debated what to do. "I'll tell you what, Naomi. I'll put this somewhere safe. When your parents return to Kilakuru, I'll take it outside the shelter and drink a toast with them to celebrate. Then I'll give the rest back to Miss Frannie to put away. I don't think she'll mind that. But no more sneaking into her office, all right? We have rules in place for good reason. All of us need to follow them."

Her look was solemn as she nodded her agreement and proffered the bottle. He accepted it, then told her to scoot back to the compound. When he was alone, he raised the bottle to inspect it. She hadn't opened it.

Sweat trickled down his back as he ran one finger over the familiar gold print identifying the sixteen year-old single malt and tried to ignore the siren's call of the honeyed liquid inside. Frannie would kill him for keeping it, but he wasn't going to blow it with Naomi. If he spilled her secrets, she might never develop the confidence to speak with others.

She needed to know her trust wasn't misplaced.

He tucked the bottle under his arm, circled the compound, then entered the boys' bunkhouse by the back door.

CHAPTER ELEVEN

"Hands out flat, the way I showed you." Frannie waited for Julie to spread her palms before placing the half-filled plate in the toddler's chubby hands. "Now use your thumbs to hold the edges. Got it?"

"Got it, Miss Fwannie!"

Julie toddled toward the blankets where the other nursery school kids ate, her steps slow and deliberate so she wouldn't upend her plate. When she sat, she looked to see if Frannie had been watching. Of course, she had. Frannie gave Julie a thumbs-up and was rewarded with a proud grin.

Chloe, who stood beside Frannie at the end of the food line, mouthed a, "thank goodness" to Frannie before turning to help the remaining nursery school kids with their meals.

The sizzle of grilling chicken and pork filled the air, along with the scent of Tommy's ginger, honey, and coconut marinade. Pearl had provided a delicious, tangy potato salad, Irene made her special coleslaw, and several of the older children contributed by slicing and seasoning taro root for the grill. Papaya chunks topped with freshly squeezed lime juice were being consumed faster than the dining hall staff could bring new trays from the kitchen. Later, there would be banana cake, and Tommy promised the kids that when the stars came out tonight, they'd have the opportunity to make s'mores at the fire pit.

All in all, it was a perfect Saturday afternoon. Even the breeze was soft, blowing just hard enough to keep insects at bay without carrying the kids' plates or napkins across the compound or lifting the hems of the sundresses most of the women wore for the occasion.

Frannie brushed the front of the cotton fabric of her yellow sundress. It was the most comfortable item she owned and perfect for Kilakuru's weather, but the nature of her job meant she rarely had the opportunity to wear it. Pulling it over her head this afternoon felt like a kickoff to the celebration.

"I think I want to marry that man," Chloe whispered. She turned away from Frannie to hand a stack of napkins to Mira, who'd escorted the toddlers through the line and was about to join them on the blanket. When Chloe turned back, she added, "He's amazing."

Frannie didn't hide her confusion. "Marry who?"

That earned her a frown. "Tommy, of course. Have you tasted the pork or chicken yet? Where has he been hiding this talent?"

"I haven't had a chance yet, but the smell alone is enough to make me weep."

"Even the kids who usually avoid chicken and pork are eating it. How many parents would love to have the ability to make chicken that even picky eaters will try?"

Frannie looked around the gazebo and saw that Chloe was telling the truth. To a child, they were devouring their food, Tommy's grilled meats included.

"What are you saying, Chloe? Are you trying to find out if Tommy snores? Or if he walks out of the bathroom with floss hanging out of his teeth?"

Chloe shushed her. "All I'm saying is that the man can cook. I was impressed with his work on the grill itself. The cooking, however…I'm stunned. Is there anything he can't do?"

Frannie grinned, but kept further comments to herself. Chloe was a fantastic nurse and loved both her work and the kids, but Frannie suspected that part of Chloe craved the opportunity to spend her evenings in a bustling city, barhopping with friends and flirting with single men, rather than sleeping in a small nurse's station on a remote island. Barhopping on Kilakuru was impossible and the bustling atmosphere of the shelter had nothing in common with downtown Melbourne. On the other hand, Chloe claimed the nearby coral reef offered her idea of nirvana. Which reminded her…Chloe had gone out early this morning, returning to the shelter about an hour after breakfast ended.

"How was your dive?"

"Spectacular." A broad smile lit the Aussie's features. For the next few minutes, as they continued to keep the food line organized, Chloe waxed poetic about the fish and coral formations she'd spotted. When she mentioned that Joe Papani, one of the island's policemen, had gone out with her dive group, Frannie prepared herself for another round of isn't-he-amazing talk. Instead, Chloe said Officer Papani had heard an out-of-season tropical storm might be heading their way.

"I received a weather alert last night," Frannie told her. "Most of the meteorologists' computer models predict it'll turn north along the usual storm track, but I'm not sure we can consider ourselves safe yet."

"That was my impression, too. I'm set at the nurse's station, but you may want to ask Tommy what we have on hand to board up the windows that don't have storm shutters."

"Already did. There should be enough wood left over to ensure the generator shed's better protected, too."

Chloe's lips thinned. "Hadn't thought about that. Probably a good idea to reinforce it, no matter what. Even if this storm doesn't hit us, eventually one will."

"Agreed." Though new, sturdier power lines had been installed on the island following the tsunami, they both knew a strong storm could mean days without electricity. Neither of them wanted to risk losing their supply of refrigerated food and medicines.

Chloe stooped to pick up a stray fork and Frannie's eyes moved to Johnny, who stood nearby chatting with Tehani, one of the few girls his age. Johnny grinned, then accepted Tehani's plate and walked to an open spot near the side of the gazebo while Tehani went to get drinks for each of them.

"Don't let him catch you watching," Chloe warned.

Frannie quickly averted her gaze. "Something going on there that I should know about?"

"Not if you keep watching."

Frannie laughed. "That makes me think I should watch more closely."

Chloe smiled, then her expression turned serious. "A few days ago, Tehani asked Walter if he could arrange for her to take college entrance exams in September. She also asked if he knew what it would take for her to get financial aid."

Frannie handed a plate to one of the toddlers, demonstrating the safest way to carry it, then turned back to Chloe. "What did Walter tell her?"

"He said that he'd make arrangements for the entrance exams, and that he'd be happy to give Tehani practice tests in the meantime and help her research financial aid." Chloe angled a look at the teen. "I don't know her that well. You have any clue what she's planning?"

Frannie shook her head. Tehani was seventeen and nearly done with high school. By all accounts, she was a bright girl. "She has a brother in Fiji, but he's only nineteen or twenty. He left Kilakuru after his high school graduation, just before the tsunami. He works in the kitchen at one of the hotels in Suva. He'd planned to return to work in his parents' restaurant after saving enough from the Fiji job to get his own place."

"Too young to support her, then," Chloe said on an exhale. "But maybe she wants to join him? Go to the University of the South Pacific in Suva?"

"Perhaps." Tehani was one of the few orphans at the shelter, having lost both parents when the family's beachfront restaurant washed away in the tsunami. Her brother was the only person she had left. "I'll talk to Walter. In the meantime, it's good she's spending time with Johnny. I know he plans to attend university once his parents get their feet on the ground again."

"Even if he's a year behind Tehani in school, he'll be a good sounding board."

Frannie nodded. Despite their unique circumstances, the teens at the shelter had the same emotional wiring as adolescents everywhere. They often felt more comfortable working through problems with each other than turning to adults.

Once the older children had their food, the adults took turns serving themselves. The teachers and dining hall staff elbowed each other and joked around as they filled their plates. Tommy stood at the far end of the line from Frannie and Chloe, manning the grill, laughing with everyone as they complimented him on his pork and chicken. Across from the gazebo, Irene set up a speaker and encouraged the kids to dance once they finished eating, then joined the adults in line, swaying her hips in time with the music as she walked. It was as joyous as Frannie had seen the adults in a long time.

Finally, Frannie's eyes lit on Alessandro. He stood behind Tommy, deep in conversation with Remy. She couldn't tell what the discussion entailed, but Remy's mouth was going a mile a minute. Alessandro seemed transfixed, leaning in to ensure he caught every word. His hair gleamed with dampness, as if he'd showered before joining the party.

"Wonder if he can cook?" Chloe whispered, her gaze following Frannie's. "Not that it'd matter. Alessandro has other attributes."

"Tommy *and* Alessandro? Your hormones have officially gone into overdrive."

"That's never been in doubt, but you misunderstand. I was wondering about Alessandro for you."

Frannie waved off the idea. "Forget it."

"You haven't seen the way he looks at you."

"Since I locked up his Scotch, you mean?"

Chloe pulled another packet of napkins from under the table and unwrapped them for the adults who were coming through the line. "Surely he's over that by now."

"I imagine it crosses his mind every time he sees one of us walking from the shower house to our bunks wearing a white, fluffy robe."

Chloe tipped her head, conceding the point. "I do love my robe. I've never felt as self-indulgent as when I'm wrapped up in it, and that includes when I'm home in Melbourne, cuddled in a blanket in my favorite chair."

"Bet the shower is better at home, though."

"Even with those fancy soaps Alessandro gave us, it's no contest."

Tommy waved for Frannie and Chloe to fill their plates now that everyone had gone through the line at least once. Frannie nearly groaned aloud at her first bite of the pork. Chloe was right; Tommy was a master.

"Told you," Chloe said as she took a seat next to Frannie on one of the gazebo benches.

"Was Frannie wrong about something? Please, share."

Frannie jumped as Alessandro's rich voice came from behind them. He had a paper plate balanced on one hand and held a fork in the other, a chunk of potato lanced by its tines. His soft gray shirt skimmed his chest and arms, highlighting his tight, muscular build. She'd started to think of the shirt as her favorite, specifically for its fit. Today he'd tucked it into crisp black shorts, a pair she'd never seen before. She wondered if he'd saved them for a special occasion.

"She's never wrong," Chloe said, then shifted away from Frannie to make a spot for Alessandro between them on the gazebo bench. "I just told her that Tommy's a miracle worker with chicken and pork."

"He's a miracle worker, period," Alessandro said. "That grill looks professionally manufactured. No one would guess that it's cobbled together from recovered metal parts. As long as the shelter has food worth grilling, that will do the job."

Frannie and Chloe murmured their agreement around bites of chicken. Two nights prior, while the kids were occupied playing board games in the dining hall, the adults had taken turns walking to the area behind the gazebo to admire the finished product. They'd been shocked by how much Tommy had accomplished. Pearl instantly declared that she'd do her best to find the ingredients to make banana cake because no party on Kilakuru was complete without it.

Walter had whimpered aloud at the words *banana cake*, earning him a ribbing from everyone gathered around the new grill. He'd told them that he could take the teasing as long as it meant he got the first slice. Pearl had promised it to him on the spot. In exchange, Walter called in favors from friends to secure the necessary ingredients.

"Tommy told me you put in a lot of work, too," Chloe told Alessandro. "I'm sure he appreciated the help."

"I liked talking with him. He's a fascinating guy. I can see why his auto shop did great business." Alessandro leaned forward. Keeping his voice pitched so only Frannie and Chloe could hear, he said, "I also had a helper of my own. Last week, the day you two set up the volleyball net, Tommy left me to work alone so he could join the game. Naomi wandered behind the gazebo and saw what I was doing. I put her to work cleaning the grill grates."

"She knew about the grill? That little stinker," Chloe said, then frowned. "How did I not notice she was missing?"

"You had two kids in the nurse's station, so it wasn't on your watch," Frannie assured her. "Tommy saw Naomi walk that direction and told me. I kept waiting for her to come back to play volleyball, but she didn't show up until dinner."

"She helped on two other days after that," Alessandro said. "I didn't want to say anything. I got the impression she didn't want anyone to know."

"I wish she wouldn't sneak away," Frannie said, "but it's good for her to feel like she's contributing."

Alessandro opened his mouth to comment, but his gaze shuttered and he merely nodded.

Before Frannie could think much of it, Chloe polished off her chicken, then stood. "I'm going back for seconds. Any requests?"

"No, thank you," Alessandro said, while Frannie shook her head no.

It took only seconds for Frannie to realize that Chloe wasn't coming back. After she helped herself to more chicken, Chloe filled a plate for Tommy and insisted he sit and eat with her in the gazebo, which left Frannie alone with Alessandro for the first time since they opened the boxes together in her office.

Alessandro's forehead creased in thought as he watched Chloe and Tommy. "I imagine, being Australian, that Chloe's used to cookouts. Did you do anything like this when you were a child?"

Frannie shifted to face Alessandro. She wondered if he sensed the same tension between them that she did whenever they spoke one-on-one. "With my Sarcaccian mother? Never. Even if she'd wanted to, we never lived where there was the space for it. What about you?"

"With my Sarcaccian mother? Never."

His rolling laugh had her smiling in response. "No, I can't picture your Sarcaccian mother eating barbecue from a paper plate."

"Queen Fabrizia standing behind the palace holding a paper plate full of potato salad would be a sight," he admitted. "Though she's missing out. The first time I attended a cookout, I was as an adult. It was in Tanzania, during my trip to climb Kilimanjaro. I loved it. There's something about eating outdoors that makes food taste better."

Frannie took another bite of chicken and nodded her agreement.

"Where were you raised?" he asked. "At Sophia's party, you mentioned that your parents divorced when you were eight. You never said where you lived before attending the Sorbonne."

She couldn't put a finger on why, but he wasn't asking to be polite. He was genuinely interested.

"I was born in New York, just outside the city, and lived there until my parents divorced. My mother moved back to Sarcaccia and my sister and I went with her."

His brows lifted. "I didn't realize you grew up in Sarcaccia."

"I was only in Cateri for third and fourth grade. But before that, we always spent our summers in Sarcaccia, visiting my mother's side of the family. Even though my father's family is scattered throughout New York, Sarcaccia always felt more like home to me than the States."

"As it should…and I say that with no bias whatsoever." Alessandro stretched one arm along the back of the bench. "What about after that?"

"It was difficult for my father to visit us regularly when we were in Sarcaccia. Not many direct flights from New York, limited time off work…you can imagine the challenges. My sister and I missed him terribly. The summer before I started fifth grade, he requested a transfer to his firm's London office. My mother agreed to buy a flat a block from his. My sister and I had rooms at both our parents' places and went back and forth all the time. My sister was starting tenth grade then, so she was old enough to take me to school on the Tube. London was an adventure. We felt so independent."

"You must've loved that."

"I did." Frannie couldn't help but smile at the memory of those days. "Whenever my mother was in town, she tried to walk us to the station, which horrified my sister. She didn't want her new friends to see her mother walking with her to the Tube, even if it was because of me. For the first week or two, my mother stayed about fifty meters behind us. When she finally realized my sister and I would be safe as long as we stuck together, she let us go. I suspect she watched from the window, though."

"I can understand that." After a bite of papaya, he frowned. "You said whenever your mother was in town. She wasn't there all the time?"

"She was at first, but she never acclimated to life in London. She had as hard a time there as she did living in the New York suburbs."

"She missed Sarcaccia?"

"I'm sure that contributed. Truthfully, though she's never been one to settle. When she met my father, she was working at the United Nations as part of the Sarcaccian delegation. The pace of the job and the travel made her happy. She continued to work there after my sister was born, but by the time there were two of us, it was too difficult. It didn't take long for her to realize that life with two kids in a three-bedroom house in the suburbs wasn't for her. She needed outside engagement to keep her mind active. About a year after we moved to London, she accepted a job escorting study abroad students around Europe. She'd travel for a few weeks at a time and sit in on some of their classes. It made all the difference in her mental health. When she returned to London at the end of those trips, she was always so much happier."

"It had to be difficult for you and your sister."

Frannie shook her head. "My dad was great when she was away. He was always so organized, so reliable. Everything you'd expect of a finance guy. The stability he offered made the divorce much easier for my sister and me. He was our safety net. But as I've gotten older, I've come to understand my mother, too."

She'd never before uttered those words; saying them brought her a sense of wonder. How had it taken her so long to realize this? "In fact, it was my mother's example that gave me the confidence to leave Jack Gladwell to come work here. From the time my sister and I were young, she told us that no matter how comfortable or secure life may be, a person can't grow without embracing change. And what's life if one doesn't grow?"

Frannie took another bite of her chicken, then realized Alessandro hadn't responded. She paused to study him. His mind seemed a thousand miles away.

"And now I've officially bored you."

"Not at all. You've made me think." His gaze sharpened, as if he'd ferreted out the answer to a puzzle. "You never felt abandoned while she was away? Or when your father was busy with work?"

"Not at all. They made sure we knew we were loved. It wasn't a traditional upbringing, but it worked for me."

Alessandro said nothing, but his expression was one of skepticism.

"It wasn't so different from your upbringing," she pointed out. "You might have lived in a palace, surrounded by hundreds of staff members and government officials, but I mean in regard to your parents. Their positions require a great deal of travel. When you were a child, did it ever make you feel abandoned?"

"No, it never did." Surprise edged his voice. "It's who they are. I never knew anything else."

"Neither did I." She couldn't help but smile at him. "I imagine it's why you like to travel. It helps you understand how others live. Their traditions, their unique perspective on the world, what they hold sacred. I'm sure you've learned a lot about yourself and your capabilities over the years."

The dancing ramped up behind them as everyone finished eating. Toddlers paired up with the older kids, and the result was heartwarming. A few of the teenagers followed Tommy and Chloe to the volleyball net for a game. Walter and Pearl chatted as they covered the leftovers and handed off the food to two of the teachers, who carried the pans to the dining hall.

"I should go help," Frannie said. She started to stand, but Alessandro put his hand on her forearm, gently pressuring her to sit.

"Stay."

"But—"

"You set up. It's all right to relax every so often, you know." He aimed a look at her plate. "You don't want to offend Irene by throwing away that coleslaw, do you?"

She tried to ignore the warm strength of his fingers. "Whenever you and I have a moment alone, you tell me to relax. Why is that?"

"You're heard the saying about all work and no play?" A devilish grin lifted the edges of his mouth. "I have the play part of life mastered. I need more of the work if I'm to grow. You, on the other hand, need more of the play. It's good for your mental health."

Her heartbeat picked up when he didn't move his hand. She wondered if anyone else noticed the touch—Chloe in particular had sharp eyes—but Frannie didn't dare look around to find out.

"You've done plenty of work," she assured him. "In fact, I owe you an apology for my attitude on your first day. I couldn't figure out why you were here. I still don't really know why you're here. But you've made a big difference to the shelter. Not just by lending muscle, but by building relationships with the kids."

"You don't need to apologize."

"I didn't think you'd make it this long. In fact, I bet myself you wouldn't make it a week."

He withdrew his hand, but only to cover his heart. "Ouch."

"See? I owe you an apology. So here you go: I'm sorry. I should have looked for the best in you instead of the worst."

"You had every right to be suspicious of my motives for being here." His gaze fell to her mouth for a long beat, then he met her eyes again. "Given my behavior at the palace, you might've attributed it to attraction rather than altruism."

She laughed, but looked at her plate and scooped up the last of the coleslaw. She couldn't let him see the truth…that she *had* wondered, if only for a brief moment. When she finished eating, she dropped her napkin on the plate and said, "My ego's not so big I'd assume you'd fly halfway around the world for me."

He didn't respond, but she could feel him watching her. Before she could carry her plate to the trash, he took it from her. "Come on. You're not on cleanup duty today. You're dancing."

CHAPTER TWELVE

"Alessandro—"

"No arguments." He walked to a garbage can that'd been placed to the side of the gazebo, tossed their plates, then strode back and grabbed Frannie's hand, pulling her to her feet. "I happen to know that you're an excellent dancer."

"You're judging based on what you saw in a ballroom." She glanced at the mass of dancing children, then to him. "This is as far from a ballroom as you can get."

"I'm well aware. Now I'll get to see the full extent of your talent. If you dare." He swung Frannie to the area where Irene, Walter, Pearl, and most of the kids danced and sang along to boisterous pop music. Several of the teenagers whistled and cheered, happy to see more adults joining the party.

The infectious mood of the children and the thumping, rowdy tune sparked a light in Frannie's eyes. "Oh, fine. If that's the way you're going to be…I dare."

Alessandro stepped back in surprise as she whooped, raised her hands over her head, and started singing along with the kids, much to their delight. High-cheeked grins of genuine happiness surrounded him, a stark contrast to the polite smiles characteristic of palace functions or the thinly masked social desperation he witnessed in most dance clubs.

He preferred this. He raised his arms and spun, dancing with the whirling pack of kids.

"Now it's a party!" Johnny called as he, Tehani, and three other teens joined the crowd. "Go, Miss Frannie, go!"

Behind them, Julie's dancing consisted of deep knee bends, which made her shiny black bun bounce on top of her head. She clapped her hands and smiled up at the teenagers as she imitated Johnny, saying, "Go, Miss Fwannie, go!"

"Go, Julie, go!" Johnny called to the little girl.

Ebullient laughter erupted from the toddler as her gaze met his and she grabbed the edges of her sundress to swirl it around her. "I'm go-go-going!"

One by one, kids and adults alike peeled off from other activities to join the dancers, until the entire center of the compound was full. Even Tommy joined in, hoisting one of the toddlers on his shoulders, much to the little boy's delight. Alessandro found himself in the midst of the middle-school-aged boys and girls, singing along as the music transitioned from pop to an edgy, alternative dance tune.

Several songs later, as the adults began to tire, Alessandro found himself face-to-face with Frannie. She'd piled her hair into a messy knot on top of her head and her forehead shone from the exertion of dancing under the bright sunshine.

He'd never seen her look sexier.

"Bet that deep down, you didn't believe I could dance outside a ballroom," she accused, her voice all tease. "Assumed I was all uptight and no let loose, didn't you? Miss Economics….that was *so* wrong."

"I thought I was challenging you to stretch your wings and grow." Against his better judgment, he curled one arm around her waist and spun her toward the very center of the dance area. "I should have known better, given that you're friends with Sophia. She didn't exactly stay out of trouble while she was in college."

"Sophia was fine."

Frannie's hand went to the space between his bicep and shoulder. It felt natural to spread his palm across her lower back, drawing her into an embrace as they continued dancing.

"Maybe by the time you met her. Her first year or two weren't the easiest. She found more trouble than she could handle."

"She'd never lived outside the palace. Maybe she was testing the waters."

"Dangerous waters." He moved his hips in time with hers, keeping the same polite distance between their bodies as Tommy and Irene did while they danced nearby. When the song hit its chorus, he twirled Frannie in a tight circle before catching her in his arms again. He didn't want to talk about his sister. He didn't want to *think* about his sister, or Sarcaccia, or ballrooms. He wanted only to enjoy this moment: the tropical sunshine, the breeze off the Pacific, the lighthearted atmosphere, the radiant woman before him.

Every day he spent with Frannie, he found himself more and more fascinated by her. By the simple things, like the way she circled her fork to corral her coleslaw before she ate it. By the more complex things, like the faraway look on her face as she talked about her upbringing, particularly in light of her parents' divorce. As they danced, warmth filled his chest and he found he couldn't tear his gaze from her face. He couldn't identify the emotion, only that he had a sense of belonging, of attraction that went beyond the physical. Of being *right*.

Frannie's dark, carefree eyes met his. For a split second, her grin widened, then a deeper emotion filled her gaze and her hand twitched against his shoulder. She didn't miss a step, but in that moment, he knew Frannie felt it, too. The sense of belonging, of understanding. Of profound attraction. And, though she quickly masked it, he saw fear.

"Banana cake!"

As Pearl's voice carried through the compound, Walter called, "First piece is mine, and make it a good one!"

Kids stopped dancing and sprinted past them with the force of a typhoon, yelling, "Hurry, banana cake!" and "She's already cutting it!" Even Tommy and Irene quit dancing to rush to the gazebo.

Alessandro became acutely aware of the sensation of his hand at Frannie's lower back. The warmth of her skin carried to his palm through her bright yellow sundress. Reluctantly, he let his hands drop from Frannie's waist. "We're going to be at the back of the line."

"It's all right." Her words were thready from the exertion of dancing. "Pearl made plenty. The whole point of banana cake is to share with as many people as possible."

"Good. Anything that gets such an enthusiastic reaction from Walter deserves to be sampled."

"He drove all over the island to collect enough eggs."

For a moment longer than was comfortable, neither of them moved. He noticed the rise and fall of her breasts as she caught her breath, saw the mixture of trepidation and attraction in her wide eyes.

"I, um, haven't danced like that in quite a while," Frannie finally said. "I suppose I've earned a slice of cake."

He angled his head toward the food area. "Come on."

Frannie smiled and started to turn, but movement at the compound's gate caused him to stop short. Frannie must've noticed it, too, because she paused and muttered, "Uh-oh."

A uniformed police officer raised a hand in greeting. "Have a minute, Frannie?"

She nodded and turned toward the officer. To Alessandro, she said, "That's Joe Papani. It's supposed to be his day off. If he's here, it's important."

"I'll save you a slice of cake."

"With that crowd?"

"If I have to tackle them all. Promise."

* * *

Clouds skittered through the night sky on a warm breeze as, one by one, the adults finished making rounds of the bunkhouse and nursery and made their way to the dining hall. They moved with the exhausted, happy ease of people who'd spent the day outdoors. Though Tommy had doused the fire nearly an hour ago, when the older kids headed to their bunks, the scent of wood smoke lingered in the air and on their clothes.

Alessandro took a seat near Walter, then folded his arms on the table. In his mind, Alessandro could still hear the chorus of the elementary school kids' final fireside song, one about a parakeet who dreamed of becoming a fish so he could swim beneath the waves, and of a fish who dreamed of flight.

He'd have to remember the lyrics to share with Anna, his niece. Though Anna was older than the kids who sang tonight, she'd appreciate the quirkiness of the tale. He smiled to himself as he imagined Anna singing it to her new baby brother, Dario.

It still shocked him that Stefano, who'd been happily single only two years ago, was now married to Megan and a father of two.

"Frannie mention what this is about?" Walter asked. "Tommy told me she wanted all of us here as soon as the kids were down. Part-time employees and volunteers, too."

Alessandro shook his head. "I haven't spoken to her since Officer Papani showed up this afternoon. She told Tommy he was in charge, then left in the officer's Jeep. I didn't see her again until it was time for s'mores. She talked to Tommy for a few minutes, then disappeared again."

"Joe dropped her off about an hour before that," Walter said. "She went straight to her office. Had a bunch of paperwork with her and was on the phone for a while."

"You talking about Frannie?" Pearl slid onto the bench on the opposite side of Walter. "I saw her leave with Joe Papani earlier. Think there's a problem?"

"She didn't seem bothered, so I doubt it," Walter told her.

"No one else seems worried, either," Pearl observed as she took stock of the room. "Even Tommy looks like he spent his day lounging in a hammock."

Walter straightened and his gaze went to the rear of the dining hall. "Here she comes. Guess we'll find out."

Alessandro watched as Frannie bent to ask Chloe a question, nodded, then moved to the end of the long table where the adults had gathered. Though she smiled, he could tell she was running through a mental checklist.

"All here?" She looked around the table, then nodded to herself. "Great. Sorry for the mystery, but I have good news and bad news, and I wanted to discuss both with you before we talk to the kids."

She set two manila file folders on the table, put her hand on the top, then grinned. "Good news first. The Latu family finished the repairs on their grocery store on the north end of the island and started stocking the shelves. They're hoping to open in another week. Yesterday, they moved back into their house."

Irene clasped her hands under her chin. "The twins are going home, aren't they?"

"They are. Even better, so are all three of their cousins. Mr. Latu's sister and brother-in-law returned from the Marquesas yesterday. They're going to work at the store until the Latus can afford to hire back their regular store employees. In the meantime, they're going to move into the Latu's house about a block from the store."

"Those are the Sapani kids?" Alessandro asked Walter, who nodded.

"Both families will fit in the Latu's place?" Chloe asked.

"Seems so," Frannie responded. "The north end of the island had less damage than we did. Sounds like they'll only be under the same roof for a week or two. In any event, day after tomorrow, we'll have five fewer kids here at the shelter. I plan to give them the good news in the morning."

"It'll be a transition for them to go home after spending so much time living and sleeping with their friends," Tommy said.

"Mrs. Latu mentioned that when I talked to her on the phone this afternoon," Frannie said. "Both families wanted to know if the kids could visit on the weekends until more of their neighbors are home. I told her it was a great idea."

She picked up one of the manila folders and looked at Walter. "I have documents that need to get signed regarding their schoolwork. Mrs. Latu's going to take over their schooling until the public school reopens. She heard that the elementary school near them might be opening as soon as October. Can you organize it with the rest of the teaching staff?"

At Walter's nod, she passed him the folder, then put her hands on her hips. "Now…on to the bad news. Several of you saw Joe stop by during the barbecue. He's been monitoring a tropical storm that's formed in the Pacific. Normally, they turn to our north, but this one hasn't yet. It's still tracking in our direction. I'm no meteorologist, but my understanding is that if it doesn't turn north in the next day or so, it'll hit water temperatures that will cause it to increase in strength. It's also less likely to move far enough to the north to miss us."

"How far out is it?" one of the nursery school teachers asked.

"Three or four days." Frannie took a deep breath. "That's why I wanted to talk to everyone in here, after the kids went to bed. You'll notice I closed the shutters so none of them can sneak out of bed and eavesdrop. Even the threat of a storm like this will alarm some of the kids, especially the younger ones. It's likely they'll associate high tides with the tsunami. I'd like to prevent that. They need to understand that this is an entirely different beast. Not only isn't this as severe, we're well-informed and we have time to prepare."

The adults around the table shared looks of understanding. The tsunami had been triggered by an earthquake deep under the ocean floor. The Pacific Tsunami Warning Center had issued an alert for Kilakuru over three hours before the first wave hit, but it took time for word to travel through the community.

"What do you need us to do?" Tommy asked.

"Our top priority is safety. If the storm hits, the greatest impact will be here on the eastern side of the island. The Latu and Sapani kids will be back with their families, which leaves us with fifty-one kids to protect."

She opened the second manila folder and began distributing sheets to the adults. "I'd prefer to remain here at the shelter, but if there's even a remote threat to the kids' safety, we'll evacuate. In that instance, we'll break the kids into four groups, each assigned to three adults. I've worked with Joe Papani to secure shelter for each group on higher ground and outlined the plans on these pages."

The adults fell silent as they pored over the sheets. Alessandro had been assigned to a group with Chloe and Sam Lameko, who taught science and bunked in the room beside Walter's. It didn't miss Alessandro's notice that the kids with severe allergies or other medical issues were all in their group, likely so Chloe could keep an eye on them. Naomi and Remy were also in his group. Frannie had included a list of the essentials each child should pack and directions for reaching their designated shelter. He, Chloe, and Sam were to take the children to St. Augustine's Catholic Church. Judging from the map, it appeared to be the one just visible on the mountain behind the shelter.

"Hopefully, we won't need to do any of this," Frannie said after they'd had a moment to review the information. "The kids shouldn't hear of it unless and until we decide to evacuate. Those of you who are part-time or have homes on the island will see that you aren't assigned to evacuation duty. If the storm is that severe, you'll need to protect your own homes and families. There are plenty of us to ensure the kids are safe."

Heartfelt thanks echoed around the table from the teachers, nursery, and kitchen staff who spent their nights at home. Given that many lost loved ones and had limited possessions in the wake of the tsunami, Alessandro could only imagine their level of concern.

"That brings me to our second priority," Frannie continued. "Over the next forty-eight hours, we need to secure the shelter as best we can. I want each of you to double-check the storm shutters on the buildings where you spend the most time. If there are any issues, let me know. We have wood to cover the windows without storm shutters, but I prefer to wait a day to do that so we don't alarm the kids. In the meantime, Tommy has materials to reinforce the generator shed. Even if we end up staying put, the winds could be high enough to threaten the island's electricity. I want to be sure the generator is secure. Alessandro, could you help him with that?"

"Glad to."

She thanked him with a smile, then turned her attention to the group. "All right. Third priority is to protect our supplies. A lot of people have donated money and goods to the shelter, and we need to be good stewards of their investment.

We'll be forced to leave a lot behind if we evacuate and the less we have to replace afterward, the better. Everything needs to be tied down, locked up, or moved to wherever it's least likely to suffer storm damage."

She turned to the kitchen staff and asked them to pull together a list of what they needed, given that they had the most equipment to handle. Her calm manner reminded him of his own father; Frannie listened to the staff's concerns, made notes of tasks that required her assistance, and offered suggestions to make their work easier. She did the same with the nursery staff, the teachers, and Chloe.

When they finished, she stepped away from the table and smiled. "Now, let's hope for a boring week. I'll keep in touch with Joe as the days progress, and I'll continue to monitor the weather from my office computer. If anyone has concerns or questions, find me. And Pearl, if there's any banana cake left over—"

"You're dreaming," Walter said, which spurred a round of laughter.

"Then let's get our beauty sleep. I'll see you all in the morning. But before we go…a round of applause for the kitchen staff for the amazing work they did today."

They all cheered, then Frannie called for another round of applause for Tommy. "Chloe has declared you a miracle worker," she told him. "The grill itself is beautifully constructed—"

"With help from Alessandro," he cut in.

"With help from Alessandro," she acknowledged. "And the chicken and pork were divine. Thank you. I know there will be a lot of memorable meals cooked on that grill in the months and years to come."

The entire room erupted into cheers for Tommy and Alessandro for their hard work, then the group broke up for the night.

Alessandro stood and wished the others good night, but couldn't bring himself to leave. Maybe the others hadn't seen it, given the confidence with which Frannie set forth the storm plans, but when the cheers faded and everyone started to focus on their beds, her shoulders had sagged.

Once Frannie cleared her papers from the table, she looked up and saw him standing there.

"Hey." The softness in her voice sent an unexpected wave of tenderness through him. She sounded like a woman who'd reached the end of a long, tiring, but satisfying day. "Is everything all right? Did I miss something?"

Her response affirmed that he'd made the right decision in staying behind.

He pointed to the back of the hall. "Your banana cake is in the second refrigerator. Top shelf, behind the pickles."

Confusion clouded her gaze. "What?"

"When you met Joe, I promised to save you a slice of the banana cake. I hid it behind the pickles so Walter wouldn't find it. Or anyone else, for that matter."

Her eyes glimmered and a smile lit her face. "You saved me a slice?"

"Of course."

He was about to offer to retrieve the dessert from the kitchen when a patch of black under her right eye caught his attention. He stepped closer, then used his thumb to swipe the skin there.

"You must've been near the fire at some point." He showed her the dark streak on his thumb. "Soot."

Her fingertips went to the spot he'd just wiped. "I collected the skewers Tommy gave the kids for the marshmallows and put them in the kitchen. One of the handles must've been dirty." Her brow creased as she looked at him. "Was everyone staring at it during the meeting?"

"I doubt it. I didn't notice until now." And he'd been hanging on her every word. His throat tightened at the sight of moisture clinging to one of her lower lashes. "Are you all right?"

She waved off his question and laughed. "I'm fine. Just…I'm overtired and happy to have cake waiting for me."

"Stay right here." He turned and strode to the kitchen, then returned with the cake. "A dose of butter, sugar, and banana before bed should fix everything."

"And eggs," Frannie said as she took a seat on the bench and looked at the cake with the joy of a child looking at a stack of birthday presents. "You can't forget Walter's contribution. I don't want to know how many homes he had to visit to collect enough eggs."

Alessandro set the plate before her, placed the fork alongside it, then fluffed out a paper napkin with a flourish and set it on her lap. He stepped over the bench with one foot and sat sideways, straddling it.

"You're going to watch me eat?"

"I'm going to make sure you eat." He gave the manila folder a pointed glance. "After spending your day doing all that work, you've earned it. I suspected you were smart and capable when I met you at Sophia's party. Now I know you are. I can't imagine anyone better to handle a crisis."

"You'd better not be referring to the storm as a crisis." She knocked on the wooden table for luck. "We don't know how it'll develop."

"Crisis or not, my assessment stands. I'm astounded at how much you pulled together in only a few hours. You found multiple safe shelters, you put the kids into groups that make sense, and you even drew up lists to make life easy for the staff. You're organized and reassuring, and that sets a good example for everyone who lives and works here."

She picked up the fork, then shook her head at him. "It wasn't as difficult as you make it sound, but thank you. You are sweet."

He couldn't help his burst of laughter. "Vittorio would die of shock if he heard you say that."

"Why?"

"I am *not* sweet."

"And you accuse me of not being able to take a compliment?"

"The stories I could tell would rupture your eardrums."

She set down her fork and twisted to face him. "Says the man who walks through the bunkhouse twice a day to check on a stuffed camel, just to keep a little boy happy."

"It keeps Remy from misbehaving, which keeps me from having to deal with him."

"Right." She made a show of rolling her eyes and laughed. "Like the way you were *dealing* with him at the barbecue. I saw you standing behind the grill listening to him. You were completely caught up in whatever he was saying."

"Maybe he was confessing to stealing cookies from the kitchen and I was contemplating an appropriate punishment."

She laughed again and gave him a playful shove. On instinct, he caught her hand. Her laughter faded and her smile faltered. When she looked up at him, the play of emotions in her wide eyes unsettled him.

"Why are you scared of me?"

"Why would you ask that?" Her chin jerked. "I'm not scared of you."

"You are." He said the words quietly. "This afternoon, you gave me that same look when we were dancing."

"There's no look."

Oh, there was a look. As he ran his thumb along the side of her wrist, it intensified. It was fear. And interest. It wasn't the type of interest he'd seen before, when women like Claudine and Sylvie perched on his lap at private parties, nor the type he encountered at palace dinners, when socialites approached him in a cloud of expensive, understated perfume with flirtation in mind.

Frannie's interest was more complex, as if she were trying to analyze her own attraction. And it *was* attraction. He knew with absolute certainty that she wanted him.

So what frightened her? His reputation?

Or was she still upset by his behavior in the library, though it'd happened two months ago?

He couldn't blame her on either count.

He let his gaze travel from her face to the straps of her bright yellow sundress, then down the smooth, lightly bronzed skin of her arm to where he'd captured her hand in his. Gooseflesh rose on her arm. "Does it bother you when I touch you like this?"

"Of course not."

He met her gaze once more, ensuring he had her attention. "I would never hurt you, Frannie."

She leaned toward him, resolve steeling her gaze. Her words were deliberate. "I know that. I'm not scared of you. I don't know why you think I would be."

"Because I want to kiss you right now. I think you know it. I also think you want me to kiss you. That's what scares you."

Her lips parted in surprise, then her chin dropped and she pulled away from him, folding both her hands in her lap.

"Alessandro." An ache tinged her voice as she whispered his name, then she raised her face to his. "I know you're used to flirting with all kinds of women. It's a game and it's fun. I understand that. But I'm the serious, straightforward type. The flirting game isn't one I'm used to playing."

Pain lanced his chest at both her tone and the loss of contact. He took a moment to gather himself, to mentally push down the emotion, then said, "This isn't a game, Frannie. Nor is this the palace library. I'm not going to grab you and kiss you in a misguided attempt to prove a point. In fact, I won't kiss you at all. I just…I don't like seeing that look of doubt in your eyes when I enter a room. I want you to know that when I compliment you, I mean it. When I make a promise, even if it's as simple as promising to save a slice of cake for you, I'm going to deliver."

Her gaze was suddenly shrewd. "That day in the library…what point were you trying to prove?"

He hesitated, realizing what he'd admitted, but there was no going back. "I don't like being measured against Vittorio, particularly when it comes to our roles as members of a royal family. I'll always come up short."

"I did that, didn't I? That was my mistake."

"Yet a little bird told me that you actually said, 'you've gotta be shitting me,' when you saw me walk into the compound with Tommy."

A muscle in her cheek twitched. "A little bird named Chloe, I imagine."

"She found it hilarious, which is why she told me about it, but I suspect you were quite serious. You weren't happy to have me here."

"No, I wasn't." Her face flamed. "But you're not your brother. I knew it then, and I definitely know it now. Not being Vittorio doesn't mean that you're less than he is. In fact, since you arrived here, you've shown that you're much, much more."

Before he could tell her that he possessed a perfectly healthy ego and that he wasn't fishing for a compliment, her fingers went to his knee.

"Anyone who doesn't value your strengths or see your big heart is a fool."

Then she leaned forward and kissed him.

CHAPTER THIRTEEN

If Frannie went strictly by logic, kissing Prince Alessandro Barrali was stupidest choice she could make. But he was right...she did want him to kiss her.

When he'd grabbed her hand this afternoon, told her to forget the party cleanup, and demanded she dance with him, she'd thrilled to the invitation. He'd made her feel alive. Whether he was laughing at Irene's choice of music or swinging the toddlers into the air, she'd been unable to tear her attention from him. He had a knack for showing her how to live in the moment that made her want to spend every one of those moments with him.

Her hours with Joe pushed thoughts of Alessandro to the side, but didn't eradicate them. Even while she'd been on the phone, waiting on hold during her attempts to locate safe shelter on high ground, her thoughts had turned to Alessandro. Then, when she'd entered the dining hall, his presence at the table drew her like a magnet.

He'd paid close attention as she'd outlined the contingency plans for the storm. He'd been the first to study the assignment sheet, had listened intently when others asked questions, and hadn't blinked when she'd asked him to help Tommy with the generator shed. When he stayed behind to ensure she was all right and to offer the banana cake, she'd felt as if he'd seen beyond what she'd said to the group to understand her apprehension about the upcoming storm.

That simple, thoughtful action melted her heart.

She wasn't scared of him; she was scared of herself. How could she not be, when a slice of cake made her choke up?

As she leaned forward and brushed her lips over his, she was more scared than ever. For the first time in her life, what her heart wanted trumped what her brain told her was the proper course of action. She could lose herself to a man like Alessandro Barrali. It had nothing to do with the fact he was from a royal family or that he was wealthy as sin. It had everything to do with the man she was coming to know here at the shelter.

A man who'd return to a robust life in Sarcaccia in September, while she remained here until every child found a home.

She tightened her hold on his knee and gave him one more testing kiss. She'd never made the first move with a man before, but dammit, she wasn't going to regret this, no matter what logic said. For once, she was going to live in the moment, even if he didn't kiss her back.

The hard muscle of his thigh jumped beneath fingertips. A low groan escaped him. He buried his hands in her hair, knocking loose the haphazard bun she'd created while dancing that afternoon, and kissed her back.

It was nothing like the hot, aggressive kiss he'd given her in the library, when he'd trapped her beneath the Morisot and teased her lips with his tongue, daring her to open to him. That kiss left her breathless, confused, and embarrassed. It tortured her in her sleep and made her wonder what she should've done differently... though she constantly changed her mind whether the best choice that day would have been to return his kiss or to somehow avoid it entirely.

This kiss was like a blast of sunshine after a long bout of bone-chilling cold. Soft and comforting, yet all-encompassing. She opened to him, and he angled his head to deepen their connection, warming her to her core with the most tender, romantic kiss she'd ever experienced.

He pulled away, but kept his hands tangled in her hair, holding her forehead to his.

"Frannie." His whisper was dark, a stark contrast to the gentleness of his touch. His chest rose and fell, once, twice...and his breath went ragged on the second exhale. "Oh, Frannie, what are you doing to me?"

It was a chastisement and a warning.

She didn't care; the risk had already been taken.

"Shh." This time, when her lips touched his, he didn't hold back. In a single motion, he pulled her into his lap, his arms locking her in place. He slid one hand along the low scoop of her back, then wadded the fabric of her sundress into his fist and kissed her with a ferocity that left her dizzy.

He was all heat, power, and need. She wrapped her arms around his neck, holding him as firmly as he held her. Her breasts fit perfectly against the hard planes of his chest. She wished she could melt into him and he into her.

Dear God, it was as if she'd been born to kiss this man. Without thought, she moaned into his mouth, her senses overwhelmed by the clean, masculine scent and taste of him. He smiled against her lips, but it was quickly replaced by an all-out assault as his tongue swept hers, sending an intense wave of desire through her.

His hands moved over her spine and a rough sound escaped him. Then he was kissing her neck, her collarbone, her bare shoulders. Slowly, passionately, savoring each new spot as if memorizing her contours. The rough scratch of his jaw dragged along her skin and the sensation nearly undid her. She arched against him in response.

This one moment, this one feeling...it could fuel her fantasies for a decade.

If he carried her to her bed right now, she wouldn't object, though the mental image of crossing the compound with him made her wonder how many times he'd done such a thing over the years, going straight from kissing a woman to bedding her.

She wondered if any of them were special. If *she* were special. Or if he was just alone on a remote island and she was convenient.

His lips teased the sensitive spot behind her ear; a shudder coursed through him, so powerfully she felt it in his fingertips, then she heard whispered words she'd never imagined coming from him. "You are so perfect, so strong, so pure of spirit. *Bella, bella.*"

The beautiful part she guessed he'd uttered before, but there was a poignancy to the way he said it that made her doubt he'd said it quite like that. She was certain he'd never said the rest of it.

She couldn't help but sigh at his heartfelt words. At knowing that this moment was as meaningful to him as it was to her.

His lips met hers once more for a deep, satisfying kiss. Just as she felt his erection against her hip, he relaxed his hold on her and pressed a kiss to her temple before giving her a bittersweet smile. "This is probably not wise, given that Remy could come looking for Humphrey at any moment."

"Or Walter could come in search of cake."

He swept her hair from her face and laughed. "You haven't eaten yours."

"I was busy."

"Too busy for Pearl's banana cake? I take that as a high compliment." He shifted, moving his legs so she slid from his lap to the bench, though he kept her in his embrace. "I think it's obvious now that there's something between us."

"Altruism?" she joked.

"Not by my definition." His brows knit as he studied her. Desire shone in his honey-brown eyes, making her want to lean into him again. "Frannie Lawrence, you are unlike any woman I've ever met."

"And nothing like your type." She said it in jest, but in her heart, she knew it was true. She combed his hair from his forehead. It'd grown in the weeks he'd been at the shelter, leaving him with a rough-around-the-edges look he never sported during his public appearances in Sarcaccia.

"I believe my type is changing. I…I've never enjoyed a kiss like that one." He turned his head and pressed his lips to the soft skin at the inside of her wrist, then took her hands and folded them between his. She didn't miss the scraped knuckles or raw patches of skin along his forearms, likely the result of working with Tommy. "Thank you for making me see what I've missed."

It struck her as the oddest thing to say. His tone made it sound as if he wanted to thank her for passing the salt at dinner. The thought must've shown on her face, because he added, "I'm going home for my brother's wedding soon. When I return, I'll only have two weeks remaining on my term before I head home for good. I suspect my mother suggested I come here because she admires you and wanted me to learn from you. Not to take you to my bed."

"We aren't in your bed."

"No, but not because I don't want you there."

A jolt of pleasure rocketed through her. She pursed her lips, then teased, "If you've never slept with a woman before, you should know it's perfectly normal to be nervous about how you'll perform."

The smile he gave her stilled her breath, it was so sexy. "Now Vittorio would appreciate that comment."

They sat quietly for a few breaths before he said, "I am in awe of you, Frannie. I'm more attracted to you than you can possibly know. If I were a different man, in a different position, I'd beg you to go out to dinner with me. I'd wine and dine you under the stars. I'd treat you the way you deserve to be treated, like the wonderful woman you are."

Her stomach flipped, then sank. She looked to where his hands enveloped hers. "I sense a 'but' coming."

"But," he acknowledged, "I can't change who I am, and I'm not the right man for you. I told you I would never hurt you, and I'm going to keep that promise, just as I kept my promise about the cake. You deserve far better than me, no matter how much we may be attracted to each other."

She blinked. Better than Alessandro Barrali?

He raised her fingertips to his lips for a soft kiss, then set her hands in her lap. "I'm going to go to bed. Alone. It's what's best for both of us. Promise me you'll eat every bite of that cake?"

"I promise." How else could she respond, when he left so much unsaid? She'd never been kissed like that in her life, and she doubted it was mere skill and experience on his part. He'd felt the pull between them as powerfully as she had.

He stood, then strode away from the table. As he opened the door, he said, "Good night, Frannie. Let me know what you need over the next few days and I'll do it. In the meantime, I'll pray for good weather."

The clap of the wooden door against its frame rattled her.

She turned to her cake, picking at the top with her fork before finally taking a bite. It was sweet and decadent, everything she'd expected given Pearl's talents.

It took forever to swallow.

She set down the fork, put her elbows on the table, then pressed her thumbs to the inside corners of her eyes. Once she knew she could restrain her tears, she carried the cake to the kitchen, covered it, and hid it at the back of the second refrigerator, on the top shelf behind the pickles.

She'd keep her promise tomorrow.

* * *

Alessandro swore under his breath when his hammer blow landed right of the nail, narrowly missing the tip of his index finger.

"Break your fingers and you'll be useless to all of us."

Alessandro stepped away, holding the nail in one hand and the hammer in the other. He used the back of one arm to swipe sweat from his brow, then glanced at the afternoon sun. Thick, humid air had settled over the island, a precursor to the storm.

He glanced at Tommy, who continued hammering away on the other side of the generator shed. "If I break a hole in the side of the shed, I'll be worse than useless. Think I'll take a water break. Want anything from the kitchen?"

Tommy shook his head, but when Alessandro returned from the kitchen, he brought two bottles of water and two cookies.

"Pearl?" Tommy asked.

"Of course. Figured you might change your mind about wanting anything if you saw me eating in front of you."

Tommy finished securing the board at the base of the shed, then crossed to where Alessandro had taken a seat on a nearby rock. He swigged half a bottle of water before taking a bite of his cookie. The mechanic grunted in satisfaction, then ate the rest of the cookie as he circled the generator shed, assessing the work necessary to complete their task.

It'd been nearly forty-eight hours since Frannie informed the staff of the possible storm. Sunday had passed quietly. After an early morning mass followed by breakfast, the older kids used the day to catch up on school reading while the adults made discreet preparations. The kitchen staff reworked their menu for the week, front-loading the fresh ingredients to minimize loss, planning for meals that could be packed for evacuation, and locking away dry goods. Storm shutters were checked, benches secured, roofs inspected.

This morning, when the storm hadn't turned, Frannie asked the teachers to mention it during the first hour of class. Thankfully, the kids took the news in stride. The wind rose as school let out, causing many of them to cast their eyes to the sky, but that was the limit of their concern. The afternoon progressed as every other Monday since Alessandro arrived. Most of the students busied themselves with schoolwork in the dining hall, the low hum of their conversations carrying across the compound from the open windows. Those who'd finished occupied the gazebo, swinging their legs from the bench seats and chatting while they waited until enough kids had finished to pull together two teams for kickball. The Latu siblings and their cousins, the Sapanis, had packed their belongings and would depart after dinner.

All was going according to Frannie's schedule. Efficient, predictable, calm.

Alessandro polished off his cookie and rose from the rock. If Frannie could maintain her usual routine, he could do it, too.

"We're nearly finished," Tommy said as he finished his inspection. "I'm happy to handle the rest myself if you want to join the kids or take a break."

Alessandro twirled the hammer and grinned at Tommy. "I'm not as good as the mechanics you're used to working alongside in your shop, is that what you're saying?"

"They're the best or I wouldn't have hired them." Tommy rubbed one of his broad shoulders, glanced at the cloud layer skittering overhead, then looked at Alessandro. "I hope you don't take this the wrong way, but I've been surprised by how competent you are. I expected a European prince to be an indoor person. Not very handy, quick to tire. You're nothing like that. It's been great for me, having you here."

"I'll take that as a compliment." Alessandro couldn't keep the wry smile from his face. "But you'd still prefer to finish the shed alone."

"Did I say that?" Tommy let loose a good-natured laugh.

"Not in so many words."

"It's not what you think." The smile remained on Tommy's face as he picked up his hammer and a fresh board. "You're distracted. I won't ask if it's the storm, the fact we have kids going home with their parents today, or if it's something else. But you were quiet all day yesterday. Today, it took you a full minute to realize you couldn't close the grill properly because the grates weren't aligned. Tools and distraction don't mix."

Alessandro wanted to deny it, but Tommy was too perceptive. "How about I keep the kids from getting into trouble over at the gazebo? I could use a round of kickball."

"They'd love that. I'll be over when I'm done here."

Alessandro packed up the tools he'd used, then tossed his empty water bottle into the shelter's recycling bin as he made his way toward the gazebo. He shoved his hands in the front pockets of his shorts as he walked. Tommy Solofa was a good man. Without being nosy, the Kilakuran had given Alessandro an opening to talk if he needed to…or not.

Even if Alessandro wanted to talk—which he didn't—he wasn't sure he could explain the tumult in his mind.

He hadn't lied when he'd told Frannie his type was changing. If anyone had asked him a year ago, or even two months ago, what he wanted in a woman, he'd never have described Frannie. Yet every time he was in her presence, he found himself transfixed. The first time, at Sophia's party, he'd convinced himself it was because he hadn't been with a woman in months. The second time, in the library, he'd chalked it up to rebellion against her knee-jerk judgment of him.

But day after day at the shelter, when he couldn't help but look up every time she crossed the compound or entered a room, he had no explanation. She drew him as powerfully as the moon controlled the tides. He wanted to know her likes and dislikes, to smell the light verveine soap on her skin. To hear stories about her childhood and moving from New York to Sarcaccia to London. To learn more about her decision to leave a secure job with Jack Gladwell and travel halfway around the world to care for other people's children.

More than anything, he wanted to kiss her again. Every time he closed his eyes, he envisioned her in that split second before she pulled his mouth to hers. It was the most profound, raw, romantic moment of his life. The mere thought of it caused an ache in his lungs that robbed him of breath.

He could have kissed her all night. Slowly and intensely, exploring her, tasting her. Holding her in his arms, feeling the thrum of her heartbeat when he pressed his lips to the base of her throat. Simply listening to her breathe was enough to make him want to throw away his entire life on Sarcaccia and spend it here on Kilakuru.

The urge had nothing do with physical gratification. It had everything to do with Frannie and the way she made him feel.

That thought had entered his mind at the very moment a sigh of pleasure escaped her lips. The whisper-soft, erotic sound of surrender snapped him to reason.

He knew with absolute certainty that he could never be with her. He'd always been the short-term type, one for a roll in the sheets with no emotional attachment.

Here today, gone tomorrow, and he'd ensured the women he'd bedded shared that philosophy.

With Frannie, that wouldn't work.

The instant that realization hit, he was thrown from the most idyllic experience of his life to the most heartbreaking.

CHAPTER FOURTEEN

Alessandro ground his teeth as he stalked across the dusty compound toward the gazebo.

He wasn't what Frannie needed, even if—in that heady moment night before last—she made it abundantly clear he was what she wanted.

Frannie needed stability. She needed love. She needed all the things she gave so willingly to the children.

She needed a man who could make her sigh with happiness for the rest of her life, a man who wouldn't leave her with regrets.

He'd kissed her one more time after hearing that sigh—slow and deep, savoring the last moments he would ever hold her—then mustered every bit of his resolve to pull away. To hold her hands and tell her that she deserved better.

In time, she'd realize he was right and she'd be grateful he'd exercised common sense.

But right now, it was killing him. He couldn't so much as hammer a nail without his mind wandering to Frannie.

He called out a hello to Irene and Mira as he passed the nursery. The two women sat on a small bench to the side of the nursery's front door, chatting. Yesterday he'd inspected the nursery's roof and helped the women make adjustments to the building's storm shutters. The place was as secure as they could make it.

Now the little ones were in the midst of naptime, affording the two women a much-needed break. When Mira waved back, Alessandro noticed the women had a knitting basket between them and that Irene had a ball of yarn and needles in her lap. The colors matched those of an afghan he'd spied in the nursery when the toddlers used it to create a fort under their chairs.

The kids were fortunate to have such care. Hopefully, in the weeks to come, they'd be as fortunate as the Latu and Sapani children and they'd be reunited with their parents or adopted.

He blew out a long breath as he continued toward the gazebo. During the moments he'd spent with Frannie at the barbecue and she'd told him about her upbringing, glossing over the two years she'd spent in Cateri, separated from her father, then casually mentioning her mother's constant travel, he'd wondered if she'd felt lonely or unloved. Perhaps, he'd thought, it was the memory of those emotions that drove her to ensure the children on Kilakuru felt valued and loved.

When she'd pointed out that he'd had a similar upbringing, he'd realized that no, Frannie hadn't felt unloved. But those years hadn't been easy for her. While Frannie hadn't said it outright, the combination of her father's career and her mother's need for travel doomed her parents' marriage.

Frannie would never want a relationship like that of her parents, where she and her partner lived separate lives.

He was bound to Sarcaccia. Much as he traveled to the far corners of the earth, he always returned, and he always would. His mother made it plain that his time on Kilakuru was meant to direct him toward a cause at home. He could only give Frannie the here and now. She wasn't the type to indulge in a short-term fling—or any relationship, he suspected—without getting her heart involved.

He tripped over his own foot, then swore under his breath as he took a stutter step to catch himself. He was losing his mind.

His whole life, he'd been able to spot the long-term-relationship types at a hundred paces. He never flirted with them, and certainly never kissed them, believing that way there be dragons.

He wasn't the man for Frannie. They both knew it, deep down. But accepting that fact proved tougher for Alessandro than leaving her in the dining hall Saturday night.

The kids in the gazebo offered cheery greetings when they saw him approach. He responded with an enthusiasm he didn't feel. "This where everyone's meeting for kickball?"

Tehani spoke first. "It's ten minutes until break time. We'll have enough for two teams then."

"*If* people want to," Johnny added. "We played kickball every day last week, so we're brainstorming different ideas." He ran through what they'd already discussed—volleyball, capture the flag, four square—but as Johnny ticked off the list, murmurs of dissatisfaction echoed through the gazebo.

"You have any ideas?" Tehani asked.

Alessandro took a seat on one of the benches. He made a few suggestions, though he could tell from the kids' faces they weren't excited about any of them.

Mental frustration over Frannie left him craving physical activity. He suspected the kids could use some outdoor time, too, after a day in the classroom, so he didn't bother suggesting any of the board games or art supplies Frannie had distributed over the course of the past weeks. She'd held a few back, but he imagined she'd want those in the event the storm hit and the kids were forced to stay indoors.

Johnny looked to Alessandro. "What sports do you do at home? Any we haven't done?"

"Nothing formal," he told them. "Pickup games, like basketball or *fútbol*, if I'm with friends. At home I'm fortunate enough to have a gym, so I do martial arts there."

"Like karate?" Johnny's chin lifted with sudden interest. "Do you take classes?"

"I did when I was your age. Now I either work out by myself or with an instructor. If my twin brother is home, he joins me. We practice a mix of styles."

One of the girls squinted at him. "Is it true that you and your brother are completely identical? That sometimes even your mom can't tell you apart?"

"My mother can tell pretty quickly, though we tried to trick her a few times when we were younger. I have a scar here" —he indicated the spot under his left eye— "so that's a dead giveaway if anyone gets too close."

"How'd you get it? Was it a fight?"

Alessandro turned to see that Remy had climbed onto the bench behind him. The little boy stood with his toes on the seat and his heels hanging in the air as he gripped the backrest and tried to get a better look at the scar.

"A terrible fight. Violent. Bloody."

Remy's mouth dropped open. "What happened?"

"My brother Vittorio used to own a yellow pickup. Fantastic truck, top of the line. Wide bed with a net in the back, shiny wheels, lights on top. I wanted to use it one afternoon and I didn't feel like asking his permission."

"You stole your brother's truck?" Remy's look of incredulity made it hard for Alessandro to keep a straight face.

"I ran right across our nursery and tried to yank it out of his hands." He grabbed Remy by the shoulders and gave him a light shake, making the boy laugh. "I pulled as hard as I could...and Vittorio let go. I fell backward and smacked myself in the face with the truck."

"Is that true?" Tehani stifled a laugh. "You got that scar because you cut yourself with a toy truck?"

"I did. Vittorio and I were four years old. You should have seen the mess. I bled all over the rug and my clothes."

A chorus of *ewwww* went around the gazebo.

"I was more angry than I was hurt. I didn't want our nanny to know what I did, so I tried to clean up the blood myself. When she heard the commotion and saw the cut, I tried to blame it on Vittorio, but our nanny knew us both well enough to figure out what happened."

"Did you get in trouble?"

"My mother took away my favorite toys for a month. Two weeks for trying to take Vittorio's truck and another two weeks for lying to the nanny about what happened."

"I bet you were mad," Remy said.

"I deserved it. I'm lucky I didn't get more for trying to hide the evidence." He shrugged as he looked around the group. "What was impressive is that my brother wasn't mad at me for trying to steal his truck. He was upset that I got hurt. He started crying and tried to help me clean up the blood."

"Your brother sounds adorable!"

"They were *four*." Johnny shot a look at Tehani, who made the comment, then turned to Alessandro. "I've seen pictures of your brother. He looks tough."

"They're identical twins," Tehani argued. "Which means what you're really saying is that Alessandro is tough."

"And you're saying he's adorable."

Alessandro tried to suppress a grin, but failed. "Tough is about more than looks, but yes, Vittorio is pretty tough. I've taken some hard hits from him in the gym."

"You and your brother fight?" Johnny couldn't keep the excitement from his voice. It caught the attention of the rest of the kids, who'd started their break from homework time and spilled from the dining hall into the center of the compound. "Who wins?"

"We don't fight, we spar," Alessandro said. "It's solely for practice. We're roughly fifty-fifty on who wins. He's technically superior. I'm stronger and take more chances. However, we don't spar that often. Practicing martial arts is more about challenging yourself physically and mentally than it is about winning fights."

"Can you show us?" one of the other boys asked.

"Or teach us?" Tehani's eyes sparkled at the possibility. "Not everything, but a little? I'd love to try it."

"I'm not a teacher. Teaching is an entirely different skill set than—"

At least four or five of the kids interrupted with a, "Please?"

"We promise not to think you're a bad teacher," Remy said.

Every student in the gazebo looked at him in anticipation, even Naomi, who'd tucked into the back of the group. There was no way he'd interest them in volleyball or kickball now.

Behind the kids, he caught sight of Chloe crossing the compound, a first aid kit in each hand. She put them on top of a stack of several identical kits outside the door to Frannie's office.

He started to look away when Frannie stepped out of the office. Chloe said something, then popped the top on one of the kits. Frannie knelt to look inside the plastic container. Her expression was all business, but Alessandro didn't miss that Frannie's hand went to her lower back. He hadn't seen either woman since breakfast, but judging from their expressions, the storm hadn't turned away.

If he could figure that out from a quick look toward Frannie's office, so could the kids. They were smart enough to recognize any change in the adults' routines.

"All right. I'll show you some basics." Perhaps a few of the kids would decide to pursue further study someday. For the short term, it'd distract them from the storm preparations.

With any luck, the activity would distract him from Frannie.

* * *

Frannie looked up from her desk as Walter and two of the other teachers poked their heads into her office. She was about to ask what was wrong, then saw the excitement on their faces.

"You have to see this," Walter told her. "Come quietly."

Unsure what to expect, she followed them outside. Her mind was spinning with a list of what needed to be done now that she'd checked in with Joe and the weather service.

It wasn't until the teachers stopped short that she looked up and realized what was happening. The kids stood in five orderly lines near the gazebo. Each stood with one leg forward, knees slightly bent, hands held in front of them at chin level. As one, they stepped forward, keeping their hands high and eyes forward.

"Is that karate?"

"I don't know," Walter told her. "Some kind of martial arts. I've never seen them so quiet and focused."

"They've been at it for half an hour now," one of the other teachers whispered. "Ever since homework break started. He has them mesmerized."

That's when she spotted Alessandro. He stood near the back of the group, beside Naomi. His voice was so low Frannie couldn't hear what he said, but there was a gravitas to the tone that made it clear he expected his instructions to be followed. The kids moved again, this time, they each kicked their right legs forward.

Alessandro moved to stand in front of the kids. He seemed oblivious to the fact he'd drawn an audience of teachers and kitchen staff. Even Tommy had paused in his duties to come watch.

"He looks like a prince now, doesn't he?" one of the teachers whispered. Frannie agreed. This was the man she'd met in the palace library. A man who moved with confidence, who knew that with nothing more than a look or a simple clearing of his throat, he could draw the attention of an entire room.

A few minutes later, the kids bowed, then clapped their hands as Alessandro declared the lesson finished.

"See, you were great!" Remy told him. The boy's giddiness carried across the compound.

Alessandro said something to Remy, then cautioned the group about the proper time and place for martial arts study, which drew a comment about fighting over trucks from Tehani. Frannie had no idea what Tehani meant, but it elicited a round of laughter from the kids.

"All right. Those of you who still have homework, it's time to return to the dining hall. The rest of you, do you know where you need to be?"

There were nods, then the kids dispersed. As they disappeared from the center of the compound, Tommy began to clap. The kitchen staff joined in, then the teachers standing around Frannie.

"He'll be missed when he goes home," Walter said to Frannie as she began clapping, too.

An image of Alessandro pulling away from her in the dining hall flooded her mind. She could almost hear him saying, *I can't change who I am, and I'm not the right man for you.*

Did he truly believe that? Or was it simply his way of trying to let her down as gently as possible?

She stifled the thought and glanced at Walter as they headed toward the gazebo. "Yes, he will."

Alessandro waved off the adults, then turned to pick up a piece of trash left behind on the gazebo floor. If it was possible for a man with his olive-toned skin to blush, she suspected he would.

Chloe came from nursing station to join the group. "I had no idea you were a martial arts instructor. Frannie would've put you to work sooner if she'd seen what you can do."

"I'm not," he said after he flicked the stray paper into the trash can. "I told the kids that I studied several types and they asked for a lesson. All I did was explain that in most martial arts traditions, the goal is to avoid fighting in the first place. Then we went through a few kicks. I'm surprised that they took to it."

"They all looked happy," Chloe added. "As long as no one ends up in the nursing station, it's fantastic."

Alessandro turned his attention to Frannie. "What's the word on the storm? Any updates?"

She glanced around the circle. Nearly all the adults were present, but the kids were in the bunkhouse and dining hall. "I've been watching all morning and just got off the phone with Joe. The storm has turned, but not enough to miss us completely. Unfortunately, it's picked up strength. The winds are nearly high enough to categorize it as a typhoon."

"When will it hit?"

Leave it to Tommy to get to the heart of the issue. "The outer rain bands will be here by tomorrow afternoon. It's hard to say how bad it'll be, given that it's turned slightly north, but with the higher wind speed I want to evacuate in the morning, just to be safe. I was just about to call the adults together to let everyone know. The kids can sleep in their own beds tonight. We don't have enough vehicles to evacuate them all at once, so we'll go youngest to oldest. The adults who are last to evacuate will be responsible for locking down the bunkhouses. We'll secure the school tonight, then the nursery and kitchen after breakfast tomorrow morning."

"I'll spread the word to the rest of the staff," Chloe told her.

"I'll tell the kids tonight at dinner," Frannie said. "I've given each group a name. I thought we could have them make evacuation group flags tonight to inject some fun in the process. I want this to feel completely different from the tsunami. Like they're going on an expedition."

"We have plenty of art supplies, so that won't be a problem," Irene said. "That's a good idea."

"With any luck, the evacuation will be for nothing and all we'll have is rain and some downed palm fronds." She checked her watch, then asked Tommy about the generator shed.

"Finished. Power shouldn't be a problem. I have a few more windows to cover, but those will take less than an hour."

Everyone else reported that they'd completed their tasks. Frannie thanked everyone for their hard work, then they dispersed to their usual afternoon assignments.

When she stepped into her office, she heard footsteps behind her. She turned, expecting to see Chloe, but Alessandro stood inside the office door.

"What's up?" She tried to sound casual, though the mere sight of him in her space sent her heart racing. It was the first time they'd been alone since he'd kissed her in the dining hall.

Correction: since she'd kissed him.

Either way, she'd thought of little else, even when dealing with storm preparations.

He stepped closer. "I reread the evacuation plan this morning. As I was working with the kids just now, it occurred to me that you left out an important piece of information."

She had? Frannie frowned, then walked around her desk to pick up her copy of the plan. "What?"

"You."

His tone sent a wave of foreboding through her. "What are you talking about?"

Alessandro moved to the side of her desk, boxing her between the desk and the wall. "You're not assigned to any of the evacuation groups. Where will you be?"

"Here." Before he could protest, she told him, "I'll be fine. If the forecast changes for the worse, I'll head to the church where you, Sam, and Chloe have your group, since it's the closest. In the meantime, I'll be here to watch over the shelter and to serve as a central point of contact."

"Frannie, you can't. I know you want to protect what you've built here, but what can you possibly do once the storm hits? You can't walk around the compound fixing things in the middle of the wind and rain."

"I'll be safely indoors." She tapped the cinder block wall behind her. "These walls are solid. If it looks like the tide will be higher than predicted, I'll evacuate, too. Even then, I doubt the water will come this far. This storm isn't the tsunami."

"Frannie—"

Her lower lip jerked. She knew he saw it, and it galled her that he could see how his nearness affected her. "You know why the kids call me Miss Frannie? Because I'm the boss. I make the decisions."

"I have a right to be worried about you."

"No more than anyone else. You don't see them in here arguing, do you?"

"They probably haven't realized what you're planning."

She ran her hands over her ponytail, then adjusted it so it sat higher on her head. "They trust my judgment and know I'll be responsible. I've been in constant contact with Joe Papani. I told him my plan. He'll give me the heads-up if he thinks I should leave."

"How will you get anywhere?"

"I can get a ride with Joe. The police will be patrolling the main road throughout the storm. They'll be driving past the shelter at regular intervals. If Joe doesn't have time to run me to the church, I'll have him drop me at the station. It's on slightly higher ground than the shelter and a little farther from the beach. I'll be fine."

"Did he agree with your plan?"

"He understands."

Alessandro braced a hand against the wall, his fingers resting only a few feet from her head. "That's not agreeing."

Her face heated as he stared down at her. She counted backward from three to try to regain her equilibrium. Then he surprised her by leaning in.

She shook her head and shifted. "Alessandro, I don't understand you."

CHAPTER FIFTEEN

"Nor do I understand you."

Alessandro curled his fingers where they pressed into the wall over Frannie's head. The woman drove him insane. All controlled energy and confidence and those damned dark eyes with the upturned edges.

Yet as she held his gaze and insisted on staying put, the lines of propriety that stood between them began to blur. Despite the fact it was the middle of the day, the temptation to kiss her was even stronger than it had been in quiet of the dining hall on Saturday night. Now he knew how earth-shattering it felt to have her in his arms. All he could think about was wrapping his hands around her shoulders, pulling her spectacular body against his, and capturing her full, soft lips in a kiss that'd buckle her knees. A kiss that'd show her what she meant to him. A kiss to convince her not to put herself in danger.

Except.

He blinked, even as he saw the attraction burning in her eyes. A kiss would go nowhere. It certainly wouldn't change her mind about evacuating.

Frannie was a woman who valued substance. He'd known it the moment they'd met at the Christmas party, and that opinion was reinforced as he became better acquainted with the people she'd hired here at the shelter. To a person, they were solid, moral, and dedicated. Maybe he'd developed substance over the weeks he'd spent working here on Kilakuru, but it wasn't sufficient. Not for her. She deserved more, a man who'd remain with her for the long haul, and Alessandro never made a promise he was incapable of fulfilling.

He couldn't walk away from Frannie Saturday night with a grand speech about his unsuitability, then turn around and kiss her now. Not unless he wanted to make their situation even worse.

He shook his head, as if doing so might loosen desire's grip on him. "All I'm saying, Frannie, is that I want you to be safe. You mean a lot to me."

"I'll be safe." Tentatively, without breaking eye contact, she put one hand on his chest. "What I really don't understand is this" —she flexed her fingers against the front of his shirt— "between us. How you could say you're not the right man for me. I'd understand completely if you believe that *I'm* not right for you, given your family and position—"

"That's not the case. At all."

"Then?"

She was torturing him. "It won't be long before I return to Sarcaccia. That's reason enough for me to stay away from you." How did he phrase this without sounding like an ass? "I also have a reputation."

"So?"

He moved his hand from the wall and covered hers, which still lay over his heart, but only long enough for him to remove and release it. "The reputation is well-earned."

"Again...so?"

He gritted his teeth. He didn't want to talk about this. Not now. To put distance between them, he moved to sit on the edge of her desk. "You must not follow the gossip columns. Or Sophia told you very little about me."

He expected her to argue, to say once again that his reputation didn't matter. Instead, she grinned and said, "Oh, I've heard plenty. Read plenty. Remember, I asked you about your travels at Sophia's Christmas party."

"I'm not talking about my reputation for climbing mountains or going on safari."

"I know that. I expect there's far more to your reputation than even the tabloids know." Her expression sharpened, as if she were staring into his soul. "I wonder, though, if you've been drawn to wild parties or remote places so you aren't constantly reminded of your role in the family."

"Parties are fun. Period. And I travel because I enjoy it. There's the opportunity to climb and dive, though I most value meeting people with different lives and experiences. It keeps my brain functioning on all cylinders."

"And you can't get that enjoyment or stimulation at home because you're locked into a backup position. You're not permitted to do what Vittorio does, despite being raised with the same training, the same education. You accomplished a lot during the months he was in Argentina. I suspect you enjoyed it."

"Enjoyed it?" He gave her a look of utter disbelief. "Ever try living another person's life? I wouldn't describe it as enjoyable. I had to stay in Vittorio's palace apartment. Sleep in his bed. Wear his clothes. I had to *be* him. Do you have any idea how difficult it was to act as if I were that dull for that long?"

She smiled at his description of Vittorio, but it faded quickly. "For most people, the hard part wouldn't be taking on someone else's life, it'd be forgoing their own. Months on end where you couldn't talk to your friends, all of whom thought you were gone. How many weddings or funerals or other celebrations did you miss? How did it feel when you couldn't congratulate a friend on an accomplishment because you weren't supposed to know?"

She didn't give him a chance to answer, but pushed off the wall and spread her hands wide as she spoke. "The more time I've spent around you, watching the way you interact with the kids and the staff, the more certain I am that you're not wired to be a spare to the throne. You crave involvement. You want your actions to have meaning. You want to go to bed at night feeling as if you've accomplished something with your day. Something more than the ribbon-cutting at a new office building in Sarcaccia. Parties, women, gambling…my guess is that you've pursued those activities as aggressively as you have for the challenge of it. Once you had a taste of Vittorio's role, though—much as you hated having to adopt his personality—you knew what you'd been born to do."

"Except I wasn't, Frannie." He gave her a look meant to shut down any argument. "Don't try to make me into something—someone—I'm not. I make no excuses for my reputation. If it was reported in the tabloids, I likely did it. And for the record, Vittorio is an excellent crown prince. Sarcaccia couldn't hope to have a better man on the throne."

"I didn't say he's not. I'm only telling you not to sell yourself short. You are every bit as intelligent and as able as your twin. And maybe you do have constitutional limitations on what you can do, but that doesn't mean you can't make an impact." She paused, then her eyes narrowed. "You never did tell me why you came here. Now I think I know why."

"I came because my mother sent me."

"Sent you or suggested you come?"

"Does it matter? Either way, Queen Fabrizia doesn't take no for an answer."

"One is a punishment. The other is a challenge." Her lips curved into a sultry smile. "And I suspect you've found plenty of ways to say no to your mother over the years, or you wouldn't have the reputation you do. From what Sophia has told me, Queen Fabrizia would have locked you in your palace apartment if she could have."

"Which circles right back to my reputation. If it doesn't concern you, it should."

She flipped her hand in a dismissive wave. "Have you ever driven a car while under the influence? Or done anything while drinking that could put another in harm's way?"

"Of course not."

"I didn't think so. Gambled more than you could lose? Or gambled with someone else's money?"

"No. Nor have I cheated. Nevertheless—"

Her brow lifted. "And did you make promises to any of those women? Treat them poorly? Allow them to have expectations that you had no intention of fulfilling?"

"No. The women I've dated" —he grimaced— "not even dated. The women I've…."

"The women you've…let's say, kept company."

"Kept company, then. They were always women who I was positive wanted nothing more from me than a brief, good time." In other words, women who were nothing like Frannie.

"If you were consenting, single adults and no one was hurt, why should that bother me?"

"It could harm the reputation of the shelter."

She openly scoffed at that. "You wouldn't have come to work here if you believed that."

"Working here and getting romantically involved with the shelter's director are two different things."

She contemplated that, then said, "Your use of the word 'involved' is fascinating."

"Frannie, don't—"

"This place was named the Sunrise Shelter for a reason. A sunrise is a symbol of optimism. A new beginning. Perhaps that should apply to more than the children who live here."

He rose from the desk. None of this mattered. The bottom line was that if Frannie knew him, the *real* him, the man who slept with a famous Italian journalist one night and sat in the back of a dark club with a beautiful Armenian tour guide in his lap the next, she'd know better than to kiss him again. She'd risk too much.

"I'll do whatever you say," he told her. "As you said, you're Miss Frannie. You make the decisions. Just be sure you're making those decisions with your eyes wide open. You underestimate the danger you're in, and if you're not careful, you'll get hurt."

As he strode to the door, she called out to his back, "Are you talking about staying here during the storm? Or about you?"

"Both."

* * *

The nursery school kids were the first to leave the Sunrise Shelter the next morning.

An hour after breakfast, they marched from the nursery to the compound gates wearing paper crowns they'd made the night before and carrying their group's colorful banner. The older kids stood in the center of the compound and cheered for the toddlers as they made their way to the waiting cars and trucks. None of the kids seemed bothered by the evacuation.

As Frannie had intended, the entire event carried an air of celebration, as if they were teams heading out on a camping trip or similar adventure. The kids were far more concerned with how their banners held up in the breeze than with the impending storm.

Tommy, Irene, and Mira were assigned to the toddlers. Each drove a vehicle and carried another adult in the passenger seat who'd then bring the vehicles back to the shelter to transport the next group. Frannie had worked out the driving arrangements so that, at the end of the day, three of the four groups would have a car or truck at their shelter. One of the part-time volunteers who lived near the fourth shelter planned to drive there once his own house was secure, then spend the night so they'd have a vehicle and an extra set of hands in the event of an emergency.

All and all, she couldn't have asked for an easier evacuation.

Once the toddlers were loaded and ready to go, Frannie walked to the driver's window of Tommy's truck.

"Good luck," she told him as she waggled her fingers at the happy kids in the back seat. "Call on the office landline if you need anything."

"I will," he promised. "My cousin was at the community center yesterday and said the director was looking forward to hosting the little ones. I gather he has a couple of surprises for them." He mouthed the words, "a tent and a parachute for play time."

"Sounds like you'll have fun, then."

"We should. In the meantime, let us know if you evacuate. Be on the watch for more roaches and snakes. They like to come up from the beach when the tide is higher than usual."

"Thanks for the warning." She patted the side of the truck, then watched as Tommy led the convoy toward the western side of the island and the community center that would serve as the toddlers' shelter site.

The older kids finished packing while waiting for the vehicles to return, then lined up their backpacks in the dining hall. Kickball and volleyball games started, but stopped once the wind began to gust. Though the sun remained out, the kids decided they'd rather relax indoors. Over the next three hours, two more groups departed. Walter went first, along with two women who served on the kitchen staff. About an hour later, Pearl and the two teachers who lived in the girls' bunkhouse departed with the second group. The final group, which was under the care of Alessandro, Chloe, and Sam Lameko, enjoyed a simple lunch in the dining hall, then helped lock away the dining hall items and pull the trash barrels into secured areas.

"We're going last because our banner's the best," Frannie heard Remy tell one of the other kids as they walked toward the front of the compound, where Alessandro and teachers from two of the earlier groups were due to arrive with the vehicles. Once the final group was safely at St. Augustine's, the teachers would drive two of the vehicles onward to their respective shelters. The last vehicle would remain at St. Augustine's.

"We're going last because St. Augustine's is the closest evacuation site," Sam told Remy, gesturing toward the mountain behind the shelter, where the church stood. "But since you let me help with our team's banner, I agree with you that it's the best."

"I love that it's a rainbow made of everyone's handprints," Frannie said as she moved to walk beside Remy and Naomi. "It'll be a nice keepsake to hang in the classroom when everyone returns."

Remy beamed. "It was my idea. I didn't think anyone would like it."

"But they did."

"Yep!"

Beside Remy, Naomi nodded and smiled. Frannie's insides knotted at the sight. Frannie returned Naomi's smile, but only for a moment before she looked away. She didn't want Naomi to see the tears that sprung to her eyes at the sight of the little girl's mouth curved into a happy grin.

In all her time at the shelter, Frannie had never seen Naomi smile like that. Before, it'd only been at celebrations, like when the kitchen staff brought out cake for a birthday and everyone sang. Occasions where everyone wore at least a polite smile.

This smile came from the heart. From a place of joy.

She felt Alessandro's presence before she turned and saw him walking behind her. He wore the same cargo pants and light shirt as the day he'd arrived. Like that day, he also carried his backpack slung over both shoulders.

"You look ready to go," she told him.

He nodded, then slowed his pace in a manner that hinted that he wished for Frannie to walk beside him, out of earshot of the kids.

"Naomi smiled at you."

There was a tenderness in Alessandro's voice that brought tears to the surface once more. She fought them back and said, "I can't tell you how happy it makes me. There's hope."

Alessandro's gaze went to Naomi, who walked next to Remy. "There's always hope. Speaking of which" —he turned his attention to Frannie— "you can still evacuate with us. Call Joe, let him know, then hop in my car. You'd have to sit with a kid in your lap, but it's not far."

"You know what I'm going to say."

"I do." He stopped walking, compelling her to stop, as well. "I don't like it. It makes me sick inside. Promise me you'll come to the church if the forecast worsens. If you can't reach Joe, call the church. I'll come get you."

"There's no need to worry. I'll use good judgment and will keep in touch with all four shelters and with Joe."

His features tightened. "Frannie."

She knew what he wanted to hear. "I promise."

He wrapped an arm around her shoulder, kissed her roughly on the temple, then strode to through the compound's gates to where Chloe and Sam stood with the final group of kids, waving to the cars that were pulling up to the shelter.

Frannie exhaled. Realizing her hands were shaking, she jammed them into the front pockets of her shorts before walking to the gates. As she had with the earlier groups, she walked to the front vehicle—in this case, it was Tommy's truck with Sam behind the wheel—told them to have a good time, then sent them off with a wave to the kids. She didn't look directly at Alessandro, who drove in the car behind Sam.

Chloe paused and rolled down her window when she came alongside Frannie. "You have everything you need in the office?"

"I do. Everything's locked down and the weather report hasn't changed since this morning. I'll be fine."

Chloe gave Frannie a thumbs-up, then turned on the car radio. As Chloe pulled away, Frannie heard the kids singing. She waved until the car rounded a corner, then walked into the compound. She closed the gate, then flipped the bar to secure it on the inside, just as she did each night when darkness fell.

When she reached the door to her office, Frannie turned and looked across the silent compound. Storm shutters or boards covered every window. Where the volleyball net usually stood, there remained two holes for the posts and the traced outline of the court. The gazebo was empty, the courtyard trash cans removed. Every door was closed and locked. Behind the bunkhouse, the transplanted palm trees flexed with the wind, their fronds waving at the clouds that rolled overhead. Even the chatter of Kilakuru's birds had ceased, as if they, too, had taken cover in advance of the storm.

It was the most alone Frannie had felt in her life.

CHAPTER SIXTEEN

Frannie barely heard the phone over the music blaring in her office.

She shoved the pile of papers she held in her lap to the side, then rose from where she sat cross-legged on the floor to click off the music before she grabbed the receiver.

"Hello?"

Joe's familiar voice came over the line, first with the usual greeting, then, "You been watching the weather?"

She glanced at her computer screen, where the latest radar images appeared. "Have it open on my desk right now. Lost Internet for a while this afternoon, but it's back now."

Now that evening was falling, the storm looked like a giant pinwheel, taking up most of her screen. One edge obliterated the view of Kilakuru; only text on the screen and a dotted outline made the island's location apparent. "If it goes out, I'll turn on the emergency radio, though I can tell just as much from listening."

"The wind is deafening here at the station. The chief just called us in from patrol to keep from getting blown off the roads." She heard voices near Joe, then Joe said something to another officer before he came back on the line. "Our last car is on its way to the station now. Want me to have them swing by and get you, or are you good?"

"The wind hasn't damaged the shelter at this point and high tide isn't until morning, so I'm good. I've spent the evening cleaning out my office. I don't get the opportunity to do that with fifty-plus kids running around." It also took her mind off being alone…and off Alessandro.

Joe's booming laugh made her smile. "I figured you'd opt to stay put. Everything looked solid when I drove by the gate about an hour ago. And I'm not at all surprised that you're cleaning your way through the storm."

"If your office had as much filing to do as mine does, you'd clean, too."

"Probably." There was more noise on the other end of the line, then Joe said, "Chief says that the cell service is out over most of the island. It'll probably disturb your beauty sleep, but given the spotty Internet and electricity, I'm going to call your landline every hour to check in. I want to make sure you're up to date on the tide reports. If you don't get a call, it means the phone lines are out. If it's safe enough to drive, assume I'm coming to transport you to the church or the station. I don't like the idea of having you there with no communication."

"Understood, but don't take any risks. I doubt the tide will come this far inland."

Joe agreed, then promised to call again in an hour.

Frannie took the opportunity to open the office door and peek outside. As the door swung on its hinges, a wet, broken palm frond hit Frannie's legs, then blew across the empty courtyard. The sky, darkened to an ominous gray despite the fact it was only six p.m., spit water sideways, dampening her cheeks. She shielded her eyes to get a better look at the buildings. The edges of the gazebo's grass roof lifted in the harsh wind, but the roof itself remained tight. All else remained still and solid in the face of the storm. No boards appeared loose, no doors popped open. Beyond the compound, only the treetops at the very bottom of the hillside remained visible, their fronds whipping back and forth. The rest of the hill and the church were lost in a dense fog.

She shut the door, then flipped the deadbolt to ensure it stayed closed. "Well, now we're in for good," she said to the empty room. After one more glance at the radar and a few clicks to read the latest update on the tide, Frannie called each of the evacuation locations to check on the kids. Confident all was well, she turned on the music and settled in to finish her filing. It wasn't her practice to keep the volume so high, but it was the only way to hear the lyrics over the howling outside.

She'd just answered the ten p.m. check-in call from Joe and placed the last of the kids' updated health forms into the appropriate folders when the overhead bulb flashed once, twice, then the room went dark and the music cut.

She looked at the ceiling and saw nothing but black. "You had to do that at the very moment I finished, didn't you?"

She'd expected to lose electricity, but stupidly left the flashlight out of reach on the desk. Extending her hands in front of her to keep from crashing into her chair, she crawled across the office. The combination of the wind and rain pounding against the storm shutters and door gave Frannie the impression of being trapped in the pitch-black belly of a ship. Her fingers connected with a desk drawer and she rose slowly, then felt around the top of the desk. She could only imagine how loud the wind would get; the storm wasn't due to peak until midmorning.

Before she could wrap her hand around the flashlight, the generator kicked in, illuminating the lone overhead bulb. She sent a quick thank you skyward for the generator's efficiency, then turned on the computer. Once she confirmed that the Internet was out, she powered down, unplugged the computer, then switched off the outside lights. The less work the generator had to do, the better. After doing a last pass through the office to ensure everything was clean, she opened the supply cabinet to grab the emergency radio. Might as well take it to her room and get some sleep while she could.

Tomorrow morning, she decided, she'd tackle the supply cabinet. She'd been so busy the past few weeks that speed had trumped neatness while shelving inventory. Between her regular shipment and the boxes from Alessandro, the cabinet was filled to capacity.

"It's a good problem to have, Frannie," she mumbled to herself as she moved a box of expense forms to search for the radio. She searched shelf by shelf, shoving aside binder clips, reams of paper, and other office supplies. When she came to the Scotch, she took out the bottles and set them on the floor, then felt around the back of the cabinet until, at long last, she located the radio. She reached for the bottles, then realized she'd only taken five from the cabinet…yet she hadn't seen or felt the sixth.

Crouching, she took a long look at the contents of the shelf that held the Scotch. No sixth bottle.

"No way," she muttered. "No way did you take one."

After the heartfelt conversation they'd had that night, she couldn't envision Alessandro breaking the rules. It went against everything she'd discovered about him…against everything she'd tried to convince *him* were his best qualities.

She located the radio, replaced the bottles, then closed and locked the cabinet. When she organized it tomorrow, it'd show up. Chloe and Tommy knew where she kept the key; it was entirely possible that one of them moved the bottle while looking for another item.

Frannie waited for Joe's next call, then lay in bed listening to the rain slash against the storm shutters and tried to focus on the image of Naomi's sweet smile instead of a missing bottle of Aberlour.

* * *

Alessandro paced the darkened, empty vestibule at St. Augustine's and tried to tune out the heavy rain that pelted the church's roof and thick wooden doors. The children, spread out in sleeping bags in the church's ground level community rooms, were somewhat insulated from the sound. Even if they weren't, it didn't bother them. To the kids, the evacuation had taken on the tone of a camping trip. They'd used the afternoon to listen to the echo of their own voices raised in song in the church's spacious nave, then played games in the downstairs rooms. The priest had joined them in a game of charades, then provided giant easels for three raucous rounds of Pictionary, which lasted until bedtime.

The electricity went out about an hour after the kids went to bed. Not that they noticed or cared. Every one of them was sound asleep within minutes of their heads hitting the pillows.

Even Remy, with Humphrey tucked tight under his chin, didn't stir.

By two in the morning, when sleep remained elusive, Alessandro had slipped out of the boys' area, past Sam Lameko's sleeping form, then climbed the stone steps to the vestibule. He'd checked his cell phone, then powered off the device when he saw he didn't have a signal.

He couldn't stop the worries flooding his mind. Was Frannie awake? Did she have power? He assumed not, though hopefully the generator kicked in as Tommy promised it would. He also had to hope the buildings at the shelter stood as strong against the high winds as the church.

Alessandro wandered into the church's empty nave. Two large candles burned near the altar. Otherwise, the space remained dark. He could barely see the outlines of the pews. Sarcaccia's royal family, as with most of the country's citizens, was Catholic, and Alessandro took solace in the fact that the church had offered shelter to the children for the duration of the storm.

He said a quick prayer of thanks, then made a slow, exploratory walk around the church, peeking into its alcoves and admiring the artwork, before returning to the vestibule and taking a seat on one of its spartan wooden benches. He'd barely settled when he heard soft footfalls on the stone staircase. Chloe appeared moments later, clad in shorts and a zip-up hooded sweatshirt crumpled from having been slept in. A tie at the back of her head captured her hair in a messy knot.

"You're up early." Her whispered words were barely audible over the storm. "Or very late."

"Very late."

She took a seat on the bench beside him, then interlaced her fingers, stretched them over her head, and yawned without bothering to cover her mouth.

"Why are you up here at this hour?" he asked. "You should be sleeping."

"So should you." She finished her stretch, then sighed and propped her elbows on her knees, leaned her chin into her palm, and twisted to look at him. "I came up here because those girls snore and I'm used to sleeping alone in the nurse's station where it's nice and quiet. I assume you're awake because you're concerned about Frannie."

"You aren't?"

"I'm an Aussie. 'No worries' is in my blood." Her brows lifted. "That being said, I do worry when it's warranted. With Frannie, it's not."

Alessandro raised a finger toward the roof. "You do hear that, don't you?"

"High ceilings make it louder." She leaned back, then stretched her legs in front of her and rolled her ankles in slow circles. "If it makes you feel any better, Frannie called Father Jacob to check in before the kids went to bed. She spent the evening cleaning her office. She was in a great mood because her filing was nearly finished and she can finally see her entire desktop. She has plenty of food, she has a flashlight and an emergency radio, and she told me that Joe's calling her every hour for a status report."

Alessandro swiped his hands over his head. Relieved as he was by the update, he couldn't shake the fear that Frannie could be in danger.

"If Tommy or I were running the shelter, we'd have made the same choice as Frannie," Chloe assured him. "The food and medicine aren't just expensive to replace, doing so takes a lot of time. If medicine is available in an emergency because someone stayed at the shelter to goose the generator, it's worth the risk. A *small* risk. And if Frannie's using her precious time alone—the first time alone she's had in months—to get organized, it means she's fine. That's Frannie being Frannie. The time to worry is if she's not acting that way."

Alessandro laughed, then looked sideways at Chloe. "I suppose you're right. Though why she can't kick back and relax with a book, I don't know."

"Because she's Frannie Lawrence, that's why. After a while, her neuroticism becomes endearing. Probably because people like the two of us need someone like her to keep us on the straight and narrow." Chloe shot him a mischievous grin. "Left to my own devices, I'd find plenty to do besides clean."

He gave her a look of open skepticism. "This from the nurse whose space is so clean the kids could eat off the floor."

"The kids will eat off any surface. That's how they end up in the nurse's station in the first place," she replied. "By the way, you were unloading the cooler from Sam's car and missed seeing Remy holding the bag of communion wafers this afternoon. Sam gave Remy the stinkeye, and Remy put them back on the shelf so fast, you'd have thought he'd picked up a spider. He claimed he'd only picked up the package to read the label and see what they're made of."

"Quick thinker, that kid."

"That's when Father Jacob brought out the coconut bars and told the kids he had easels for Pictionary. Not sure the good priest knew how close he came to losing his communion wafers."

"My guess is that any priest who deals with children has had their share of lost wafers."

"And wild Pictionary games." Chloe smiled at the fun they'd had that evening. "Father Jacob didn't mind how boisterous the whole affair became. I suspect he was having as good a time as the kids."

At Alessandro's nod of agreement, Chloe stood. "They'll be boisterous in the morning, too. The wind and rain will get more intense before it stops. Sam and I will need you, which means you need to get some sleep."

"I'll do my best." He was confident Sam and Chloe could handle anything, whether he helped or not. But Frannie versus nature's power? He wasn't so sure.

He smoothed his hand over his jaw, then looked up at Chloe. "This storm is worse than predicted. Don't tell me it's not...I know it is. If Joe has any issues contacting Frannie, or if there's any indication she's in trouble, I'd like to take Tommy's truck to get her. I'd feel better. We might not have power, but the place is plenty warm and there's candlelight."

"It's downright cozy if you ask me."

Alessandro must have let his surprise at her comment show, because she laughed and stuck out a hand to pull him from the bench.

"Oh, come on, Alessandro. The kids see this as one giant escapade. Follow their lead. They're not afraid. They're not thinking of the tsunami. The ocean isn't scaring them tonight the way it often does. And they're only here instead of holed up in the bunkhouses because Frannie is being extra cautious. She won't do anything to put herself in harm's way. She knows that the kids need her. We all need her. So close your eyes and listen to the rain and think of how awesome nature's power can be." She tapped her forehead. "It's all a matter of perspective."

"Until someone gets hurt."

"No one is getting hurt." She put her hands on his shoulders, then spun him to face the stairs that led to the room where the boys were sleeping. "Dream happy dreams until the boys wake you to ask about breakfast. I'll call Frannie in the morning for an update and you'll see that you've worried for nothing."

He thanked Chloe for the reassurance, but as he lay on the floor of the community room alongside the boys, listening to the windows shake with the violent wind, his last thought was, *I'll believe it when the storm is over.*

Chapter Seventeen

Alessandro knew the moment he saw Chloe enter the community room the next morning that either Frannie was in trouble, or that Chloe hadn't reached her.

Chloe didn't appear concerned; if anything, the nurse's smile was broader than usual as she walked in from the direction of Father Jacob's office and greeted the kids. But when Chloe spied Alessandro pouring cereal at a table with Naomi and two other girls, Chloe promptly turned and went to the opposite side of the room, closer to Sam, and joined his breakfast group.

Alessandro recognized the avoidance maneuver. He'd seen his brothers and sister do it often enough at their family dinners, casually taking the seat farthest from their parents whenever they wished to avoid being cross-examined.

He passed a milk pitcher to one of the girls, told the group he'd be right back, then moved to take the empty seat nearest to Chloe. When the kids faced the other way to talk, he took the opportunity to lean in and ask, "Now do I worry?"

"Not yet."

Unwilling to have the kids overhear, he angled his head toward the door and urged Chloe to follow. Once outside the community room, she relented.

"She didn't answer the phone."

"Maybe she went outside to secure a door or check the generator shed."

"I waited five minutes, then tried again. When she didn't answer the second time, I rang Joe at the police station. He answered on the first ring. Said he spoke with her at six this morning."

"That was two hours ago. Wasn't he planning to call her every hour?"

"He has. At six, she was still in bed and had no plans to go outside, but she didn't pick up at seven. He thinks the line must be out."

Foreboding swept through him. "I should go get her. I'm sure she's perfectly safe, but if the situation changes, there's no way for her to call for help. Or for Joe to warn her if the tide looks like it'll be higher than anticipated."

Chloe shook off his concern. "There's no need. Joe's watching the radar and says there will be a lull between storm bands any time now. He plans to drive by the shelter then. If her phone is still out, he'll bring her to the station or up here. Cell service is down everywhere and he'd rather not have her at the shelter if she doesn't have a way to contact anyone."

"Can he get inside? I assume she locked the gate behind us."

"Joe has a key. He promised to call from the station in an hour with an update."

Alessandro glanced toward the stairs that led to the church vestibule. He was tempted to go upstairs, where he could get a better look at the weather and gauge the situation. He hated the idea of waiting. Joe sounded like a reliable man, but he wanted to ensure Frannie's safety himself.

"All right." He could be patient. Frannie made a decision, and if everyone else could respect it, so should he.

An hour and a half later, after playing card games and helping one of the girls fix a broken bracelet, he waved to Chloe, who'd ducked into Father Jacob's office. When she approached, he asked, "What's the word?"

"No word. Now our phone is out." Chloe shot a look at Sam, who nodded, before she turned to Alessandro. "I just took a look outside. It's not too bad, but I can't say how long the lull will last. The most intense band of wind and rain is still due. My guess is that Joe's using this break to bring her here."

"But it's only a guess."

"Yes." Chloe withdrew a set of keys from her pocket. "You're welcome to take the truck. There's only one road from here to the shelter, so you won't miss Joe and Frannie if they're on their way up. If you make it all the way to the shelter, inform Joe. But if the wind picks up or you run into mud, or if there's even a question—"

"Understood."

* * *

Frannie rolled over, pulling her pillow with her. Between the endless roar of the wind, the drumming of rain against the roof, and the hourly calls from Joe, sleep had been fleeting at best.

She curled into her sheets, then groaned as she realized it had been a while since she'd heard from Joe. The phone would ring sooner rather than later.

Shoving the pillow aside, she blinked at the clock on the face of the emergency radio. She pulled it closer, then looked again.

Joe's call was nearly an hour overdue. Either that, or she'd slept through the ringing of the phone. That didn't seem plausible, given that she'd cranked the ringer to maximum volume and left both her bedroom door and the door that separated the office from the back hall wide open.

Reluctantly, Frannie sat up, pulled on her sneakers, then made her way to the office. Though it was morning, the combination of the shuttered windows and the storm made it feel like midnight. She'd just reached her desk and picked up the receiver to check the phone when she heard her name called, followed by pounding on the office door.

"Joe?"

"Yes!"

She hurried to admit the police officer. Though he wore a slicker and hat, he was soaked.

"How long have you been out there?" she asked after she shut the door behind him. Before Joe could answer, she added, "Stay put. I'll get you a towel."

While Frannie strode to the hallway to grab a spare towel, Joe took off his hat and set it near the door. "About a minute. I was afraid you were asleep."

"I was." She returned and handed him the towel, which he used to wipe his face. "I slept right through your call. I'm so sorry. I didn't want you to have to come out in this."

"Not your fault," he assured her. "All the phones on this road are out. I stopped by the Falupi house on my way here. They're sheltering fifteen people."

"Everyone all right?"

"That house survived the tsunami, so I'm not worried about it surviving this." He patted the outside of his slicker to keep water from dripping all over the floor. "As you'd expect, they're having a grand time. When I arrived, the whole family was playing rummy under flashlights they'd tied to the ceiling. Mrs. Falupi even made banana cake before the power went out."

"Of course she did." Banana cake was the answer to every gathering on Kilakuru, no matter the weather.

"The storm's going to pick up again soon," Joe said. "There won't be phone or Internet until at least tomorrow, when crews can get out to do repairs. I'd like to take you to the church so you're not cut off."

"Any change to the forecast since last time we talked?"

"If anything, the winds have picked up. Tide shouldn't come this far in, but my guess is that it'll be close."

"How's the road right now?"

"It was fine from the station to here. We'll see how far we get up the hill. If we can't make it, you can hole up at the station. We have a couple empty beds in the cells. They're nicer than they sound—clean bedding, a decent mattress—and I promise not to lock you in. You might want to bring your own pillow, though. Oh, and you'd better not be afraid of cockroaches. They're coming up from the beach." He spread his hand to indicate the size of the roach. "I saw one on the Falupis' front porch that made me hesitate. If they're at the Falupis' house, they'll be at the station."

Frannie laughed at the idea of staying in one of the island's cells. They were likely as comfortable as her room at the shelter; she couldn't imagine they saw much use. The cockroaches were part of life anywhere in the tropics. She gestured toward her room. "I packed a bag, just in case. Let me change clothes and grab my toiletries and we can go. Five minutes, tops."

Much as she wanted to stay and keep an eye on the shelter, she didn't want to worry Joe. She wouldn't be able to go outdoors to monitor conditions during the peak of the storm, and with the phone out, there wasn't much she could do to coordinate the evacuation groups when it was time to return. She just hoped the generator kept doing its job to preserve the food and refrigerated medicines.

Ten minutes later, they passed the police station. Joe slowed and flashed his lights. The dispatcher, whose office was at the front of the building, waved back. "They'll contact the evacuation sites and let them know you're with me."

She thanked him, then refrained from small talk so Joe could concentrate on the road. What constituted a lull in this storm would be considered a downpour on any other day. The car shimmied with the force of the wind, and Frannie noticed Joe kept both hands on the wheel to keep the cruiser steady. A mile past the police station, the road doubled back and twisted uphill, toward the high point where St. Augustine's stood. Beyond the guardrail on the passenger side, a river of muddy water carried debris downhill. At several points, Joe was forced to slow to cross over areas where drainage channels that ran beneath the road overflowed.

"It'll dry out in a few days," Joe told her as they passed a broken branch that had landed on the guardrail. "We had rain like this once about eight years ago. Engineers reinforced the road afterward to keep it stable on days like today, when the earth can't absorb the water as fast as it falls."

She looked sideways at him. "This is fun for you, isn't it?"

"It's a cop thing. We all crave a certain level of excitement. Shakes up the routine."

"We're literally shaking."

He turned a jaunty smile her way. "Awesome, isn't it? Though I'll hate it tomorrow when this blows over and the flying insects emerge."

"You have a strange sense of fun." Frannie enjoyed lying in bed and listening to the sound of rain hitting the roof as much as the next person, but this was something else.

They saw the downed tree blocking the road at the same time. Joe slowed to a stop.

"Unless you have a chainsaw and the urge to use it in the middle of a storm, we're not getting by that," Frannie said.

His gaze swung from the battered trunk toward the mass of earth and exposed roots on the other side of the dented guardrail, where the tree had ripped from the ground. "Let me call it in so the road is blocked off at the top. On our way down, we'll stop at the turnoff to set out warning flags."

He radioed the station, then told Frannie to stay put. "I have orange tape in the trunk. I'll tie it to the tree so it's visible in case someone misses my warning flags. I'll be right back."

"I'll have the towel handy." She'd thrown it over her head as they'd walked from her office to Joe's cruiser. It wasn't dry yet, but it was better than nothing.

Joe was behind the cruiser, digging in the trunk when headlight beams cut across her line of vision. She squinted through the water blurring the windshield, then tossed the towel onto Joe's seat, lifted the hood of her raincoat, and climbed out of the car.

After taking another look toward the headlights, she cupped her hands around her mouth and called to Joe, "That looks like Tommy's truck," then ducked her head against the rain and jogged toward the tree.

The truck stopped on the other side, clear of the branches that littered the wet, muddy road. Joe came up behind Frannie, orange tape in hand, as the driver put the truck in park and opened the door.

"Alessandro? What are you doing?" She raised a hand to shield her eyes from the rain. "Where's your coat?"

She felt like a mother scolding a child, but he wore only a T-shirt and shorts, both of which were quickly getting drenched. His sneakers were already saturated from the water cascading down the roadway. Even so, his grin lifted her spirits.

"Joe was having trouble reaching you, then our phone went out. Thought I should check on you before the storm gets any worse."

"We were headed to the church," Joe said as he tied the orange tape around the tree, then looped it through the branches to alert anyone who approached.

"Climb over." Alessandro waved Frannie toward the guardrail, where the trunk lay closer to the ground. "I'll drive you the rest of the way."

"I'll get my bag," she said, then hurried to the cruiser. She slid on the wet roadway and nearly fell, but managed to catch herself on the hood of the cruiser. She retrieved her bag from where she'd stashed it between her feet for the drive, then left the towel behind for Joe, figuring it was the least she could do. Once back at the tree, she handed her bag to Alessandro, then clambered over the thick tree trunk with a boost from Joe.

"Stay safe," Joe told them. "Report in when you can. Either the chief or I will drive by the shelter once the storm passes to ensure it's secure."

She thanked him, then hurried to the passenger side of the truck. Once inside, she did her best to shake the water beaded on her jacket to the floor, rather than soak the seat.

Alessandro, on the other hand, didn't seem bothered by the dampness. In fact, he seemed energized by it. He shifted in his seat, intentionally making a squishing sound, then grinned with the enthusiasm of a man heading to a party who couldn't wait to step on the gas and get there.

She shook her head at the ridiculousness of it, then leaned forward to turn on the truck's defogger so Alessandro could see to turn the vehicle around on the narrow road. "I can't believe you came out in this storm without rain gear. What would Queen Fabrizia say?"

"She'd be appalled, but I can't wear it if I didn't pack it when we evacuated. And even if I had, it's raining so hard I doubt it would serve its purpose." He openly studied Frannie's legs and shoes, both of which were soaked. Now that she sat in the dry truck, she realized her shoes squished, too.

Alessandro flashed his headlights at Joe, signaling that they were leaving, then turned the truck. Joe did the same, then headed downhill.

Frannie turned to grab her bag from the back seat. As she did so, she asked, "If you didn't pack rain gear, what did you pack?"

"Toothpaste. Underwear. Magic kits. The essentials." He frowned at her as she stretched so she could see more of the back seat. "What do you need?"

"My bag. Where did you put it?"

He braked. "I thought you had it. I hooked it on one of the tree branches while you were climbing over the trunk so I'd have both hands free to help you down if you needed it."

"I'll run and get it."

Alessandro reached to unbuckle his seat belt. "No, I left it there. I'll get it."

"Again, you're not wearing rain gear. I am." She opened her door and hopped out before he could.

As she half-walked, half-skated down the hill, the wind blew with such ferocity it took Frannie two hands to catch the edges of her hood and ensure it stayed over her head. A small branch bounced across the road in front of her, then smacked into the guardrail and flipped over it. She spied her bag, nabbed it from the branch near where she'd climbed the trunk, then looped the strap over her shoulder and turned to make her way to the truck.

It didn't surprise her to see Alessandro waiting by the passenger door. She suppressed a smile at the thought that, though his mother wouldn't like to see her son standing in the rain without proper protection, Queen Fabrizia would approve of his chivalry.

Frannie was halfway to the truck when she lost her footing. Her hands and knees hit the ground at nearly the same time, but the mud and water covering the surface of the road cushioned the fall. She pushed to stand just as she realized that something sharp pierced her shin when she'd fallen. She heard Alessandro call her name, but was on her feet again before he reached her.

"You're bleeding."

She glanced down at her palms, which were muddy, but otherwise fine. Her knees were similarly muddy, but she could see two distinct trails of blood running down the front of her leg.

"The water's making it look worse than it is. I'll clean and bandage it when we get to the church." She walked to the passenger door, though he hurried ahead of her to open it.

"Careful getting in," he said, putting one hand under her elbow to ensure she didn't slip again. Though it was unnecessary, she appreciated his concern. Once settled, she leaned down to inspect the injury. It didn't look bad; it looked like two punctures rather than scrapes or cuts. She must've hit a branch or pointed rock when she fell. She opened her bag to see if there was anything she could use to wipe up the mess.

"That's not just water making it look worse," Alessandro said once he was in his seat. "Pick up your leg. Let me see."

"You drive. The wind's picking up and so's the rain."

"Not until you've stopped bleeding." He reached across the cab and wrapped one hand around her muddy knee, then lifted.

"Alessandro—"

"Let me see."

His tone left no room for argument. Slowly, she raised her knee higher, then spun on her tailbone. He frowned, clicked on the truck's interior light, then stretched to grab a tissue from a small packet wedged between the seats and used it to blot the skin around the wound. Grim lines formed at the edges of his mouth as he leaned closer.

"It's nothing a warm shower won't fix," she insisted, though the spots were beginning to throb.

"I don't think so." He pressed the tissue to the area beneath the wound to stop the blood from running down her leg. Sharp pain radiated from the two punctures, causing her to wince.

He met her gaze. "Frannie, I don't want to alarm you, but this looks like a snake bite."

CHAPTER EIGHTEEN

"I'm sure it's not a snake bite. You're imagining things," Frannie told him. She swatted his hand away to look for herself. Wouldn't a snake bite hurt worse? Wouldn't she have seen a snake?

Though, given the mud and water flowing down the hill, maybe she wouldn't have. She could barely see through the windshield, even with the wipers going.

She shifted her leg so the dome light shone directly on the injury. She had to admit, at least inwardly, that the bloody holes—distinctly shaped, identical in size, and spaced less than two finger-widths apart—looked like a snake bite.

Alessandro's hand curled around her calf. "I'm not imagining things. Now that it's in the light, this looks worse than I thought."

"Let me keep pressure on it while you drive." She forced a calm tone, though she grew increasingly worried as she studied her shin. "I didn't see a snake anywhere. It's just as likely I fell onto a branch or some other sharp object. Chloe will know for sure. Better to let her handle it."

Alessandro stared at the wound for a moment, as if weighing his options. His fingers tightened around her calf for a moment, then he released her and twisted to reach into the back seat.

"I brought my things in case I couldn't make it back up the hill. I have a hand towel you can use to cover it. It'll be better than the tissue."

"Thank you." She hated to stain his towel, but at least she wouldn't have to argue with him about whether to drive or try to treat the injury here.

He pulled his backpack into his lap, then began rummaging through it. The distinct clink of glass striking one of the buckles made her look up. At the same time, he blanched.

She realized why as he withdrew the hand towel and shifted his arm to block the contents of his bag from her view.

A sickening lump formed in the pit of her stomach as she took the small gray towel and pressed it to her shin. After he returned the backpack to the back seat and put the truck in gear, she said, "You took a bottle of Scotch from the cabinet."

She could hardly breathe while waiting for his response. When that response finally came, it was wholly unsatisfactory.

"I have a bottle of Scotch in my bag, yes. But I didn't take it from your office."

A million angry responses formed on her tongue and died. What could she say?

She stared at the rain-soaked road. The drops hitting the roof and windows made it sound like they were trapped inside a giant metal drum.

"I assume from your silence that you're upset. I wish I could explain, but to do so would break someone's trust. They'd be deeply hurt." His voice sounded strained, though how much was because he regretted taking the Scotch and how much was regret she'd caught him with it, she didn't know. She wasn't sure she wanted to know.

"Frannie, I know this sounds crazy, but I gave my word about what I'd do with this bottle. I didn't want to leave it behind in the bunkhouse, not knowing when we'd return, or even who'd return first. It's in my bag specifically so the kids won't find it."

She dug her fingers into the armrest. "You promised me you would follow the rules. No alcohol at the shelter, and you *know* that includes when you're with the kids for the evacuation. Worse, you've apparently had it in the boys' bunkhouse, which is the last place it should be." She could continue, but what was the point?

Talk about breaking someone's trust...he'd broken *hers*. "I thought we had an understanding."

"We did. We do. I haven't opened it. I won't open it. But I can't return it to your office, either. Please don't ask me to." His fingers brushed her thigh. "I'll explain as soon as I can, but I need to keep that bottle safe. It will mean the world to someone."

She jerked away. "Keep your eyes on the road."

A wave of bitterness surged through her. She'd allowed the moment in her office to mean more to her than it should have. She'd been gullible. Naive.

And if it hadn't been for that moment of bonding in her office, would she have dared kiss him?

"Frannie, I—"

"Please. First things first. Let's get out of the weather, then I can have Chloe look at my leg" —she was careful not to say bite— "and we'll see where things stand. I'm sure Chloe and Sam have been busy with the kids. They'll need our help."

She didn't want to hear excuses. She didn't want to argue about returning the Scotch to her office. She didn't want to feel like a nagging parent. She didn't want to feel the anger that caused her head to pound.

She turned toward the window and thumbed a tear from the corner of her eye when Alessandro wasn't looking.

Most of all, she didn't want to admit to herself that the sight of a bottle in a backpack broke her heart.

* * *

Alessandro drove like a bat out of hell, if one envisioned hell as waterlogged, rather than fiery.

He gritted his teeth each time he was compelled to slow for a curve or to keep the truck from slipping on the clusters of wet leaves and mud that caked the roadway. Much as he wished Frannie hadn't seen the Scotch, it paled in comparison to the horror he felt at seeing her leg.

Kilakuru had snakes. Some harmless, some not. Tommy had assured Alessandro during his first days on the island that snakes were rarely seen, preferring to shun humans. But in the middle of a muddy rainforest road, snakes didn't expect to see humans, let alone have a human fall on them.

He pressed the gas and covered what would've taken five minutes to drive in perfect weather in less than four. He parked the truck alongside the building, close to the rear entrance, then turned to Frannie. Her forehead was puckered as she stared up at the dark building, as if her mind were elsewhere.

"Frannie?"

"When did you lose electricity?" The rain fell thick and fast against the windows, making it difficult to hear her, even after he cut the engine.

"Last night."

She didn't move. "Me, too. Generator worked. Kicked in perfectly. Lights were only out a few seconds. I assume the kids were all right with their flashlights? Everyone's worked?"

"They were fine." He didn't care about the generator. Or the flashlights. "Let's get inside."

She blinked, then straightened in the seat. "All right."

Frannie opened the door before he could get around to help her. She'd tied the hand towel around her shin, but it slipped as they ducked their heads against the rain and entered the church. Sam was waiting for them just inside.

"Saw you parking the truck. How'd you get here so fast?"

"Joe was already on his way with Frannie." Alessandro gestured toward Frannie's leg. The top of the towel had turned an ugly brown-red with blood. "Where's Chloe?"

Sam grimaced at the sight of the injury. "I'll have her meet you in the choir room. It has the most light and it's away from the kids."

"I know where it is," Frannie said.

Sam spun to find Chloe. Frannie set her bag on the floor, then peeled off her rain jacket one arm at a time and hung it on a hook to the side of the door.

"You seem very calm," Alessandro said quietly. He hadn't wanted to alarm Sam, but surely Frannie realized she needed medical attention as soon as possible.

"I told you, I'm fine."

He ground his back teeth. She wasn't fine. Frannie was always calm, but this was different. She wouldn't even look at him. Then he realized that this wasn't pain or fear; this was disappointment. In him. To cover, she was going through the motions of her role as director. Asking about electricity, hanging her coat on the hook just-so.

So be it. If it kept her distracted from the threat to her health, he could take it.

He followed Frannie to the choir room. Chloe met them moments later, first aid kit in hand. "Glad you made it. According to the radio reports, this next band is going to hit hard. Sam said Frannie's hurt?"

"She slipped in mud walking to the truck," Alessandro explained. "She either hit something sharp or something bit her when she fell. She has puncture wounds."

Chloe patted one of the chairs. "All right, Frannie. Let Nurse Chloe take a look."

Frannie sat in silence as Chloe pulled on a pair of gloves, then cleaned and inspected the wound. "Alessandro, would you mind getting a flashlight from Sam? I'd like more light on this."

Alessandro pulled one from his jacket. "This work?"

She nodded, then gestured for him to illuminate Frannie's shin. Chloe reached into her first aid kit and pulled out a headset with magnifying lenses, then palpated the area around the punctures. Alessandro's stomach twisted each time Chloe's fingers pressed around the injured area.

"No idea what did this?"

"I didn't look," she admitted. "I felt something punch holes in my leg, but I was focused on getting up and getting to the truck so I could get out of the rain and mud."

"Are you feeling any nausea? Difficulty breathing?"

When Frannie shook her head, Chloe said, "Numbness?"

"No."

Chloe moved her fingers around the wound, then up and down Frannie's leg, repeating the question. Each time, Frannie said no. "It's sore right where I'm bleeding, but that's it."

"When I press right here?"

Frannie jumped as Chloe's fingers edged one of the punctures. "That's sharp. Feels like it's from the inside, though. Not from your fingers."

Alessandro moved closer with the flashlight. "It bled a lot. She's had a towel on it since it happened."

Chloe nodded, but said nothing. She took Frannie's pulse, then inspected the wound again before digging in the first aid kit for a pair of sterilized tweezers. Carefully, she plucked at one of the holes, then drew a small, blackened lump from Frannie's shin and dropped it onto a piece of gauze she'd placed on an empty chair. A moment later, Chloe pulled a similar lump from the second wound. She studied both spots again, then cleaned and covered the area.

"I think if we wash those, we'll find they're pieces of glass."

"Glass? That's it?" Relief washed through Alessandro. He hadn't realized how tense he'd been since he first saw the blood on Frannie's shin.

"Probably a broken bottle in the road." Chloe removed the headset and stood. To Frannie, she said, "Bet you thought a snake got you. Made me wonder for a moment when Alessandro used the word *bit*."

"I wasn't sure what I fell on."

"I'll clean what I removed to be sure it's glass. In the meantime, let me know if you have any swelling or pain. I want to avoid infection." She glanced at Alessandro. "So you know for the future, the venomous snakes on Kilakuru are sea snakes. Nonvenomous ones can cause infection with a bite, but are otherwise harmless. Thankfully, the sea snakes are limited to the water and the beach area. Not the hills. In all my time diving around the island, I've only seen two. Both times they were moving away from me. They'll avoid you at all costs."

"Good to know." He'd rather be embarrassed by the mistake than fear for Frannie's life.

Frannie gave Chloe a grateful smile and thanked her for cleaning out the wound, then asked what she could do to help with the kids.

"They're putting together a magic show for Father Jacob, so they're occupied. They'll be happy to see you in the audience."

"I'll clean the mud off my hands and knees, then join them." She glanced at Alessandro for the first time since they'd entered the church. "I'll clean your towel and get it back to you. Thanks for driving me."

Before he could tell her he was happy to do it, Frannie turned and headed for the church's restrooms. The shattered look in her eyes as she spun on her heel cut him to the core.

"So, how soon do you go home?"

Alessandro turned to face Chloe, caught off guard by the question. "Home?"

"Your brother's getting married, isn't he? Spending the night in the church reminded me that you have a huge wedding coming up soon."

"Oh. Yes. The wedding's in three weeks." He wasn't sure why, but Chloe's question made him even more agitated with himself for upsetting Frannie. While he'd known it'd be wrong to hold her or kiss her again as he did that night in the dining hall, he didn't want to leave on a sour note.

If he were honest with himself, he didn't want to leave at all. Chloe's mention of home had made him think of the shelter, not Sarcaccia.

"It's going to be a long flight."

"Halfway around the world." He rubbed a hand over his head. "I'm going early so I can attend family events beforehand. There's a rehearsal for the ceremony, then my parents plan to host Emily Sinclair and her parents at the palace the night before the wedding. The whole family will be there."

Chloe repacked her first aid kit, then carefully picked up the gauze containing the fragments she'd removed from Frannie's knee. "I saw coverage of your brother Stefano's wedding on Australian television. Looked like quite the affair. Is Prince Vittorio getting married in the same cathedral?"

"With all the pomp and circumstance. My parents wouldn't have it any other way for the country's crown prince."

She gave him a buoyant smile. "You'll have to take a lot of photos. Or bring back a newspaper for us."

"I can do that."

Chloe angled her thumb toward the community room, where the kids' voices rose in volume. "Sounds like the magic show is about to begin. Should be good. The rain and wind make for great sound effects."

She snapped the lid on the kit, then tucked it under her arm as they walked out of the choir room. "I have to say, I'm jealous. I love it here on Kilakuru, but the chance to attend a royal wedding or spend a few nights partying in the civilized world sounds divine. Especially your parties."

He wanted to tell Chloe that his parties weren't all they were cracked up to be, but suspected her response would be a well-deserved mocking. He'd had fun. Years of decadent, raging fun. But in the face of Frannie's disappointment—and the bottle of Scotch still in his backpack—partying was the last thing that appealed to him.

He hoped that, eventually, Frannie would understand about the Scotch and would forgive him. But he doubted it'd happen before his time on Kilakuru ended.

CHAPTER NINETEEN

Twenty-four hours later, the high-pitched trill of a phone sent a round of cheers through the community room.

Father Jacob passed his bingo card to Remy, then rose from the table and hurried to his office to answer the phone.

Alessandro glanced across the room at Frannie, whose gaze tracked the priest. Though she maintained her usual competent, cheery demeanor, she hadn't spoken to Alessandro once since their arrival. It was as if he'd been cast from the sunshine into the shadow. Though Frannie's slight was so subtle no one else had noticed, the chill went clear to his bones.

He checked his bingo card as the next number was called out. No luck.

Yesterday afternoon and evening saw the entire island buffeted by deafening winds before the rain finally stopped in the wee hours of the morning. After this morning's breakfast, Father Jacob and Sam took a walk around the premises. They reported that two rain gutters and a downspout on the back of the church had been knocked down and that the rear yard was full of debris, but otherwise the property came through the storm unscathed.

To the kids' disappointment, Frannie announced that they were staying put at the church until she received an all-clear from the police.

"There could be electrical lines and trees blocking the roads," she'd explained to the kids over lunch. "Or the roads could be unstable due to the runoff. We're going to wait until we know it's safe. The minute we're good to go, we'll coordinate with the other evacuation groups and carpool home."

The news cheered the kids, as did the first rays of bright sunshine that broke through the clouds to illuminate the room at the same time Frannie announced the bingo game.

Alessandro's mood, however, shifted from gray to black. The only thing keeping him from confessing all to Frannie was the sight of Naomi with a bingo card in front of her, carefully studying her squares as Chloe called out each letter and number combination.

What he wouldn't give to hear Naomi shout, "Bingo!"

If he told Frannie why he had the bottle, she'd understand. But given Naomi's delicate emotional state, he couldn't risk breaking his word. It'd taken months for Naomi to speak. She'd continued to speak now and then when they were alone. Then, two days ago, she'd finally smiled at Frannie. He suspected she'd feel comfortable enough to speak to Frannie, and maybe to others, in the coming weeks.

How would Naomi react if she discovered Alessandro told Frannie that she'd spoken to him? Or that she'd taken the Scotch? Would her trust be broken? Would it set back the progress she'd made?

He had no way of knowing.

A moment later, Father Jacob returned to the room and waved for Frannie to come to the phone.

"What's the news, Father?" Sam asked after Frannie disappeared into the office.

"That was the chief of police. He says electricity is still out on the entire island. There are quite a few trees down, some carports with their roofs blown off, and minor damage to the marina, but no serious injuries. People took the storm seriously and stayed inside."

"That's great," Sam replied. "Doesn't sound like it'll delay the tsunami recovery."

"No, I don't believe so."

"Any word on our return to the shelter?" Alessandro asked.

"That's what he's discussing with Frannie. Now that phone service is restored, she can coordinate the transportation. There's a tree blocking the road for Walter's group, but the chief says a crew is clearing it now. The other two groups are free to return. However, there are multiple trees down on our road, so we'll see what the chief and Frannie decide."

"If it doesn't look like the trees will be cleared anytime soon, we could take the trail," Sam said. "I'd hate to hike up it, but down isn't bad at all. I've done it before. Of course, we'd need to know it's safe."

"There's a hiking trail from here to the shelter?" Alessandro hadn't heard of it. Then again, he hadn't had the opportunity to explore much away from Sunrise Shelter. He'd been to the marina for a couple of diving excursions and had taken short walks from the shelter to the beach and back with groups of kids. Driving to the church was the first time he'd seen the island from one of its high points, and it had been a matter of hours before the storm set in and obliterated the view. "It was quite the drive up here. Seems like it'd be a long way for the kids, especially if they're carrying backpacks."

Sam shook his head, dismissing the concern. "The trail takes a direct route down the hill instead of following the road. In good weather, it's probably a forty-five-minute walk. My parents used to let my brother and me walk to the village after church when we were teenagers. They'd take the car and meet us at one of the beachfront restaurants for lunch."

"It's a beautiful walk," Father Jacob assured Alessandro. "I've taken it to the beach and back for exercise. The teen group here at the church occasionally cleans sections of the trail as a community service project. It's well-maintained, though I can't say what condition it's in right now. There are sections with wooden walkways that could be slick. And there could be trees down."

"But no threat of electrical wires," Sam said. "Though with any luck, the road will be clear later today and we can drive the same way we came. Let the kids save their energy for cleaning up any debris around the bunkhouses."

"Let me guess, you're talking about the trail?" Frannie came up behind Sam and Father Jacob. She was all smiles, but as had been the case the entire day, she never met Alessandro's eyes.

Sam nodded. "I mentioned the possibility of taking it back to the shelter if the road is blocked."

"Turns out, the road *is* blocked. The police chief knows of at least two spots where it's impassable. One is where I met Alessandro, but there's another tree down closer to the station. It's prevented the patrols from coming this way." She looked at Father Jacob. "The police chief drove by the shelter an hour ago and it seems to be in good shape. Tommy Solofa is arranging to take the other groups to the shelter using the cars he has available. I know we're drawing on your resources here, so I'd like to be out of your way as soon as we can, but I won't know the road conditions for several hours. By then, it's likely to be dark."

"The kids are perfectly fine here, Frannie," Father Jacob assured her. "You brought enough food and we have plenty of clean water."

"We're limited on access to showers, though. You won't want to smell these kids in another day, let alone the adults."

The priest spread his arms. "A church is, above all, a haven for those who need one. We don't discriminate based on odor."

Frannie's responding smile made Alessandro's heart flip. Did she realize how breathtaking her smile was?

"Thank you, Father. It's reassuring to feel welcomed. For your sake, though, I'd like to get out today. It'll make the kids feel better to return at the same time as their friends, and I'll feel better the sooner I can ensure the shelter's put to rights and the kids are in school."

Sam gestured toward the front of the church. "I don't mind making a trek down the trail. Now that the landlines work again, I can call from the bottom of the hill to let you know if it's safe. If I run into trouble, I'll turn around and come back. If the path is clear, it'll take the pressure off the road crews to know we're not stranded up here."

"If you're comfortable doing that, it's fine with me," Frannie said. She hooked her index fingers in the front pockets of her shorts. "I don't want you to go alone, though."

"I'll go," Alessandro said.

Frannie started to accept, then shook her head. "No, it's probably better if there's at least one male and one female here with the kids. Either I'll go or Chloe can. Let me talk to her and figure out what makes the most sense."

Twenty minutes later, it was settled. Frannie and Alessandro stood at the front of the church as, with a skip in her step, Chloe shouldered her backpack and accompanied Sam down the road to the top of the trail.

The moment the pair was out of sight, Frannie turned on her heel and entered the double doors without him.

* * *

Frannie couldn't get back to the kids fast enough.

She sensed Alessandro walking a step behind her before she heard his footfalls on the marble floor of the vestibule.

"I would've bet on you to go," Alessandro said as they took the stairs down to the community room.

"Why?" It came out sounding carefree; she felt anything but. She couldn't talk to him right now. Childish, she knew. But it was *hard*. She needed to calm down. To stop thinking about what she'd seen in his bag. To stop thinking about the fact he'd warned her that he wasn't good enough for her, and that he had a reputation. That he'd earned that reputation.

She hadn't believed him. She hadn't *wanted* to believe him. She wanted Alessandro to see himself as she saw him every day at the shelter: the caring man who helped Tommy build a grill, the man who checked on stuffed camels, the man who crawled around on the nursery floor with kids on his back until they howled with laughter.

The man who, according to Irene, helped one of the toddlers learn to use the potty a few weeks ago, despite the fact there was a mistake that soaked Alessandro as well as the child.

Frannie forced back the notion of Prince Alessandro the Beneficent. All it did was open her gullible, bleeding heart to being stomped.

He moved beside her as they rounded the corner of the stairs. "I assumed, given the particular kids in our group and their health needs, that Chloe would've opted to stay with them."

She shrugged. She'd hoped no one besides Chloe noticed the rhyme and reason behind the evacuation assignments. She wanted the kids with health challenges to know they were safe, but without having their differences highlighted to the others.

"Chloe's heard about the trail since her arrival and been dying to explore it. I told her to take advantage of the opportunity. I'm familiar with the kids' health issues. None is so serious that we can't handle them should an emergency arise, which is unlikely at this point, anyway."

"She and Sam should make good time."

Frannie nodded.

They were about to round the final corner, putting them in view of the kids in the community room, when Alessandro stopped walking. Softly, he said, "Frannie."

"Yes?" Again, she kept her tone light.

"Look at me."

"What is it?"

He waited until she turned to say, "You know what. You haven't said a word to me since we were in the truck."

It took her a solid five seconds to tell him, "It's because I don't know what to say."

"How about, 'Alessandro, I trust you.'"

Those four words made her throat tighten and eyes burn. They were almost as powerful as the expression she'd witnessed on his face as Chloe treated her injury.

He'd looked at her with concern, yes, but there was more. If she didn't know better, she'd have identified it as love. Or, at the very least, attraction.

He added, "I've been here two months. I would hope, at this point, that you can trust me."

For longer than was comfortable, she said nothing, weighing and discarding responses. When she was certain she could keep her voice steady, she said, "You wouldn't be around the kids if I didn't trust you. On the other hand, I won't pretend that what I saw in the truck doesn't bother me. You say you have a good reason. Maybe you do, though I can't imagine what it is. I feel betrayed, both as the director of the shelter and personally."

He opened his mouth to speak, but she held out a hand. "Unless it's a full explanation, I don't want to hear it. I want to focus on the kids. I *need* to focus on the kids. But you should know this: if you break the rules and consume alcohol at the shelter, I'll book you on the first flight to Sarcaccia and I'll drive you to the marina myself to ensure you catch it. I don't care who you are or who your parents are. If that means the shelter's funding is cut off, I'll find it elsewhere."

Disbelief clouded his eyes. "You believe my family would cut off funding?"

"I…I don't want to think about it." She realized her hands were balled into fists and slowly released them. "I want you to follow the rules. And I don't want to talk about this any more."

Her heart pounded so hard she could feel it in the base of her throat. She'd never been good with confrontation. She'd never argued with her roommates at school, and while working for Jack Gladwell had been stressful at times, the atmosphere was a positive one. Collaborative.

Even through her parents' separation and divorce, Frannie had lived in a peaceful household. Confrontation with a person she'd come to care about—maybe even love—rattled her last nerve.

He regarded her, nodded, then said, "I'll follow your rules."

"Thank you. That's all I need to know." She turned away, then jogged down the stairs to catch the end of the magic show.

* * *

The next ninety minutes passed quickly. Tired of being cooped up inside, the kids cheered when Father Jacob located a Frisbee and told them they were free to take it to the grassy area at the side of the church. Alessandro went with them, leaving Frannie and the priest alone in the quiet building. When he excused himself to take a much-needed nap, Frannie used the opportunity to clean the community room.

Thankfully, the space wasn't in bad shape. The children were cognizant of the fact they were guests of the church and had been careful not to make a mess. They'd kept their belongings contained, cleared their places after meals, and thrown away their trash. However, given Father Jacob's hospitality, Frannie wanted to do something nice for him. She started by wiping down the tables and vacuuming. When the kids showed no signs of returning, she scrubbed the windowsills and washed the windows. From there, she moved into the choir room, where she dusted the chairs, the piano, and music stands, then cleaned that room's windows and sills.

Father Jacob would never expect it of her, but it made her feel better to do something constructive. She finished washing the final choir room window when the office phone rang. She hurried to answer, grabbing it on the fourth ring.

"Frannie? It's Sam."

Winded from cleaning and her sprint to the phone, she sat in one of the guest chairs in the priest's office. "Where are you?"

"Believe it or not, I'm standing inside your office. Everything was locked up tight when we arrived, but I didn't have any trouble using your key. Branches and palm fronds have blown in, but on first glance, the place looks great. Chloe's doing a detailed walk-through now. Phone is working, obviously. Electricity is out, but the generator's running like a champ."

Frannie gave a fist pump to the empty room. So many people worked hard to finance and build the shelter; knowing it'd come through a major storm unscathed gave her an enormous sense of relief.

"So, the big question. How was the trail?"

"Surprisingly clear. Chloe and I tried to look at it from the kids' perspective. There are some slick spots, but you'll recognize those when you approach them. Otherwise, there's one long section about two-thirds of the way down where the wooden walkway is buried in mud. We tied a pink sock to a tree just above where it starts. Look down on the ground when you get to the sock and you'll see where we marked a path through the trees to take you around it."

The idea of Sam and Chloe tying a pink sock to a tree made her smile. "Sounds like you think we could come down that way without too much trouble."

"As long as you have the light, you'll be fine. The kids would probably enjoy it. However, if you were to come today, you'd need to leave soon."

She checked her watch. It was over three hours until sunset, but Sam was right. With the dense foliage of the rainforest, the trail would be dark sooner than that. Bugs could be an issue, too. "I'll call the police station for an update on the road and let you and Chloe know what we decide."

Sam told her he'd stay within hearing range of the office phone, then added, "We were able to see the road from a few spots along the trail. I'd be surprised if it's clear before tomorrow night. The same mudslide that covered the trail crossed a wide section of the road. The crews will have that to contend with in addition to the trees."

"And that means taking advantage of Father Jacob's good will longer than I'd prefer."

There was noise on the other end of the line as Chloe returned to the office and reported water damage inside the schoolhouse, though the repairs and cleanup needed were minor and all the other buildings were in good condition.

Just as Chloe finished, Frannie heard Alessandro return to the community room with the kids. She ended the call, then dialed the police station. It took only a thirty-second update to determine that the road from the church wouldn't be clear for at least another day or two. Decision made, she let Sam know, then went out to the community room to talk to Alessandro. Before she could say anything, he waved her over to a corner for a private word.

"We cleared the grassy area behind the church before we started throwing the Frisbee. Figured it was the least we could do for Father Jacob. I wasn't sure where to have the kids put all the downed branches and waste, so it's stacked beyond the tree line."

A flush tinged his cheeks from the exertion, but he seemed invigorated. She peeked at the kids as they gathered around the community room table with cups of water. They also seemed energized by their outdoor time.

"Thank you," she said, focusing on Alessandro. "Father Jacob will appreciate that. He's taking a nap, but I expect he'll be down shortly. We can ask if he'd like the stack moved. In the meantime, do you think the kids are up for a hike down the hill?"

His grin made her want to forget that she'd seen the Scotch in his bag. "If you were to suggest it, they'd jump to go. It wasn't easy to convince them to come inside for drinks. I take it the road is blocked?"

"Worse than when we came up. If we go today, though, it needs to be soon."

"I'm willing to help pack the kids and carry the first aid kit. We can load the sleeping bags, cooler, and games in the truck so they're out of Father Jacob's way, then come back for the truck as soon as the road is clear."

"Sounds like a plan. Thank you." She took a deep breath. This was the Alessandro she'd come to rely on at the shelter. The one who saved her the last slice of banana cake. "Okay. Let's do it."

CHAPTER TWENTY

Father Jacob joined Alessandro near the community room windows as the kids cleared their cups from the table. Frannie stood near the front of the room, waiting for the kids to finish so she could inform them of the plan.

"Thank you, Alessandro, for all the work you and the kids did outside," the priest said. "I saw you from my window. That was an enormous help."

He told Father Jacob where he'd stacked the debris and offered to move it, but the priest shook his head. "I have parishioners who volunteer to help me with landscaping every so often, and that's where we put it."

The priest aimed a purposeful look in Frannie's direction. "Since your arrival on the island, it seems you've taken good care of our Frannie, too."

"Frannie takes very good care of Frannie. She doesn't leave much for the rest of us to do."

That brought a soft smile to the priest's face. "True, true." A beat later, he added, "Sam tells me you've made a great contribution at the shelter and that the kids relate well to you. Their parents aren't here to tell you, so I will: thank you. What your family has done for Kilakuru is changing their lives for the better, and the fact you came here personally to work speaks to your character."

He didn't feel worthy of the praise. The priest must've sensed his discomfort because the older man put a reassuring hand on Alessandro's arm. "I think, when you return home, you'll find it has made you better, too."

Frannie called for the kids' attention, then announced that they'd take the trail back to the shelter to meet the other groups. As the kids chattered with excitement, she said, "First, we pack. Do an inventory of everything you brought to make sure it's coming back with you. Your toiletries, pajamas, clothes, everything. Items that are too big to carry will go in Tommy's truck and will come down when the road opens. Once we're packed, Father Jacob will lead us in a quick prayer, then it's time for a kid sandwich."

"I'm the ham!" one of the boys yelled, to which one of the girls grumbled, "You were the ham last time."

Another boy said, "But he's the best ham."

Then everyone started speaking at once.

"I call cheese!"

"You're sooo cheesy."

"Total cheese."

"Naomi should be the tomato."

Naomi made a face, and the girl who'd spoken said, "You're not chicken or turkey. You want cool cucumber?" At a shake of Naomi's head, the girl frowned. A beat later, she brightened. "How 'bout sprouts?"

At Naomi's nod, the girl called out, "Naomi's sprouts! I'm the tomato!"

Alessandro had no idea what they were talking about. Father Jacob smiled to himself, as if enjoying a great joke, then moved away to help the kids gather their belongings.

A few minutes later, as the kids took turns using the facilities and Frannie did a walk-through of the church to ensure nothing was left behind, Naomi moved alongside Alessandro. "Call rye," she whispered.

He blinked. "Rye?"

She nodded. When the kids were back in the room, he said, "I call rye."

Frannie snorted and the kids started howling with laughter.

Before Alessandro could ask what he'd done, Father Jacob called on everyone to bow their heads to give thanks for the lack of storm damage and to ask for a safe return journey to the shelter.

Alessandro glanced sideways at Naomi. She shot him a mischievous grin, then looked down at the floor and folded her hands.

* * *

"No one's going to explain a kid sandwich to me, are they?" Alessandro groused as he loaded the sleeping bags into the back of Tommy's truck.

Frannie found a spot for a bag filled with the leftover paper plates and cups, then locked the truck. Much as she'd love to tell Alessandro the kid sandwich was intended to keep him as far away from her as possible for the sake of her sanity, she didn't want to admit how much he'd been on her mind.

"It's my way of ensuring the kids' safety when we're walking. An adult first, kids in the middle, and an adult last. No one gets ahead and lost or left behind." She smiled at the sight of the kids waiting on the front steps of the church. "Once I called it a kid sandwich, it took a life of its own. They all want to be cheese or ham, because they think it gives them an excuse to be goofy."

"They need an excuse?"

"You tell me, Mr. Rye." She shot a sideways look at him. "What made you call rye? Was it Remy? He'd be the one I'd predict would tie together w-r-y and r-y-e."

"Nope, though I wouldn't put it past him." His gaze went to the little boy. "On that note, we should make sure he has Humphrey."

Frannie nodded, then went to Remy to check on the camel. Once all was in order, they thanked Father Jacob for opening St. Augustine's to them, then waved goodbye and headed down the hill toward the marked trail.

As Sam promised, the walk was a pleasant one. The rainforest canopy kept the sun from beating down on them, and the humidity left over from the storm seemed less oppressive with cool trees surrounding them. Birds tittered overhead and leaves blew on the never-ending island breeze. Otherwise, the only sounds were the soft footfalls of the kids walking along the hard-packed trail and sporadic giggles or chatter as they pointed out sights along the way.

Frannie walked in the front, keeping her eyes peeled for slippery spots, particularly on the sections where the dirt path gave way to elevated wooden walkways. As the kids grew more comfortable, their voices became more buoyant, their laughter more free. She listened, enjoying the happy banter and occasional sounds of roughhousing as someone bounded over a root or smacked a friend with a fallen leaf.

Alessandro's voice came to her ears. She couldn't hear what he said, but one of the girls responded, "You have a sister though, right?"

"I do. Her name is Sophia. I also have a half-sister named Lina, but I've never met her."

"Do you want to meet her?" The question came from Remy.

"Yes, but I'll leave it up to her. My family is pretty famous. It can be hard to meet people in private, at least when I'm in Europe. She might not want that kind of attention."

"Maybe she could come here," one of the girls said.

"That would be quite a trip," he replied. "If she's interested, it would probably be easier to meet her after I return to Europe."

"It'll be sad when you go," Remy said. "Miss Frannie will miss you."

"So will Humphrey," one of the other boys added. "*Humphrey* thinks you're cool."

"Stop it," Remy yelled, which sent the kids into gales of laughter. The group quickly quieted. Frannie suspected it was either because Remy started thwacking a branch against the trees as he walked, warning them that their teasing wasn't appreciated, or because Alessandro had given them a look meant to silence them.

For all his playfulness with the kids, she noticed that Alessandro had become a good disciplinarian when it was warranted.

"I think you'd like my sister Sophia," he said, distracting the group from Remy and his branch. "She's very good at board games and cards."

"Better than you?" one of the girls asked.

"Much better, but I'd never admit it to her. She's the reason I learned about the shelter. Sophia went to college with Miss Frannie and they became friends. Then Sophia invited Miss Frannie to a Christmas party where I had the chance to dance with her, and she told me about Kilakuru."

"You danced with Miss Frannie at a party? Was it at your palace?"

"It was."

A chorus of *wooooo* rose from the kids. Frannie understood how Remy felt; she wished she could grab his branch and start whacking trees, too. She missed the next sentences as they rounded a corner and took a steep downhill turn that required everyone to use nearby tree trunks for balance, but a moment later she heard one of the boys ask when Alessandro was going home.

"I volunteered for three months. I'm going home in a couple of weeks for my brother's wedding, but then I'll return to finish my time here. I have about three weeks or so at the shelter after the wedding."

"That's not very long," Remy said. Frannie heard a far-off thunk in the trees; apparently Remy had thrown his branch. "Can you stay longer?"

"I'd like to, but I don't know if it's possible."

"Hey, what's that?" One of the boys jogged past Frannie to reach for a low-hanging tree branch with electric pink fabric attached to it. "Is that Chloe's sock?"

"Looks like it." She'd wanted to hear more of the conversation between Alessandro and the kids, but it was forgotten in the rush to the sock.

"Here's the detour!" Remy pointed to the ground, where branches and volcanic rock had been placed to frame a path that led slightly uphill.

Frannie led the group along the uphill path. Sam and Chloe's markings were excellent. It wasn't long before the group crossed over the mudslide—thanks to strategically placed rocks they could use as stepping stones —and were back on the main trail. They hadn't gone far when Alessandro stopped the group and approached Frannie.

Facing away from the kids, he whispered, "I need to go back. Can you take a water break?"

"What's wrong?"

"Look behind me."

She glanced at the kids. Most were standing at the edge of the trail, looking at a small waterfall that was just visible on the downhill side. Remy, however, stood away from the group, his eyes filled with unshed tears.

"He dropped Humphrey?"

Alessandro nodded. "The camel was sticking out of the side pocket of his backpack. I saw Remy stuff Humphrey inside his sweatshirt after the kids teased him, but now he doesn't have it. If you take a water break, I can go back."

"It could be a long way."

"I climb mountains, remember? You'd be surprised how fast I can cover a trail like this. Tell them we forgot to get Chloe's sock and I'm going back for it while they rest for a minute."

He dropped his pack near her feet, then took off. There was no sign of urgency in his movements; he was quick and light on his feet as he disappeared into the rainforest, heading back uphill.

"We forgot Chloe's sock," she told the kids when they turned away from the waterfall. "We can take a break here while Alessandro gets it."

"Let's time him!" one of the boys called. Predictions were made and those who had watches started counting the minutes.

Less than fifteen minutes elapsed before she heard Alessandro coming down the trail. When he rounded the corner nearest them, he waved the sock over his head. "Got it!"

There was a whoop as one of the girls was declared the closest to guessing the correct time. Alessandro asked Remy if he'd carry the sock in his backpack, then he carefully tucked the sock and Humphrey into the largest pocket.

"We'll go as soon as Alessandro gets a drink," she told the group. "Get your things together. We'll be at the shelter in another twenty minutes or so."

"How far did you have to go?" she whispered when Alessandro retrieved his pack.

"A few minutes beyond the sock. Not too bad." He took a long drink from his water bottle, then a self-satisfied grin lifted his mouth and lit his eyes. "If they knew how far I went, they'd be more impressed with my time."

"Thank you." She peeked to ensure the kids weren't listening, then added, "Most people would've been annoyed at having to go back. You're better with the kids- -and more patient with them—than you give yourself credit for."

"For these kids? I'm happy to do whatever it takes. That doesn't make me a saint." He gave her a long, meaningful look before turning to the kids and calling out, "Time to move! Kid sandwich!"

* * *

The next two weeks passed in a blur. Electricity was restored two days after everyone returned to the shelter, though the generator did its job in the meantime. The kids helped clear the compound of debris, classes resumed, and—once the road was clear—Sam and Tommy retrieved Tommy's truck from the church. Pearl, being Pearl, sent cookies along for Father Jacob.

Alessandro and Tommy spent two days repairing the water damage done to the schoolhouse and reinforcing a section of the roof to prevent future problems. Boards were removed from windows, trash cans returned to their usual spots, and the volleyball net raised. Walter accompanied Johnny and Tehani to the police station each afternoon to do college research, since Joe was kind enough to offer use of the Internet until Frannie's computer was back online.

The kids went through the days following the storm on an adrenaline rush. During afternoon free time and evening hours at the fire pit, stories tumbled out of them about their time away from Sunrise Shelter. Even the nursery school kids wanted to talk about their "adventure."

Frannie's contact with Alessandro was largely limited to the dining hall and during group activities in the evening. As always, Alessandro sat with different groups of kids at each meal, though she noticed he took the time to speak to Naomi at least once each day.

Try as she might, Frannie couldn't keep her heart from soaring every time she heard his laugh, spied him crossing the compound with a textbook under his arm, or spotted him refereeing a kickball game. When Pearl mentioned making an extra batch of cookies to send back to Sarcaccia with Alessandro when he left for his brother's wedding, Frannie smiled and encouraged the surprise. On the inside, however, she grieved at the thought of his departure. She even felt a twinge of disappointment when Chloe and Alessandro went for a dive early one morning. Not because she was jealous, but because she knew she'd miss watching Alessandro interact with the kids at breakfast, and there were only so many breakfasts left.

He'd changed from the man who'd walked into the compound unsure about his ability to deal with children. Now, he thrived on his work with them. Each time she saw him laughing with a child or giving them a fist bump for tackling a tough homework assignment, it warmed her inside. It even made her wonder if he'd given thought to becoming a father himself.

She had to face the facts: if what she felt for Alessandro wasn't love, it was close. At the very least, it was a case of deep infatuation.

A couple of days before Alessandro was due to depart, Frannie invited the nursery school kids to join the older ones in the dining room near the end of homework time to make an announcement. Two of the girls, an eight-year-old and a six-year-old, would be leaving with their parents the next day. Kilakuru's temporary hospital was hiring for the first time since the tsunami, and their parents had secured jobs. They'd arrive from New Zealand in the morning. To celebrate, Frannie announced that there would be kiwi, mango, and papaya at dinner. "Before you tell me that's boring…it's going to be set up like a dessert bar," she explained. "You can mix the chunks of fruit yourself, then you'll choose from five different flavors of honey to put on top."

The announcement of the honey prompted whoops of joy from the kids before they scattered.

"Honey?"

Frannie jumped at the sound of Alessandro's smooth voice behind her. When she turned, he flashed a smile so charming her heart leaped to her throat.

"You've been holding out on all of us," he accused. "Since when do we have five flavors of honey?"

"Jack Gladwell was in Hawaii on business last week. He sent a huge box of flavored honey." She didn't reveal that he'd also sent macadamia nuts, some of which Pearl planned to use in Alessandro's cookies. "I thought it'd be the perfect way to celebrate. Much as I love these kids, the best days are when they leave."

"May they all be so lucky." His expression grew more serious, and in a low voice he asked, "Will you be in your office tomorrow night? After the kids go to bed?"

"Of course."

"After lights out, I have something for you. Wait for me."

Before she could respond, he turned and followed the kids out the door.

* * *

Frannie tried to concentrate on her paperwork, but found herself reading the same paragraph over and over without comprehending it.

The bunkhouse lights were extinguished precisely eighteen minutes earlier.

She smoothed her ponytail and tried to ignore the fear knotting her throat. Alessandro hadn't said why he needed to see her, but she had one guess, given that his boat was scheduled to leave in the morning.

The clues were all there. The dozens of times she'd looked out her office window during the past two weeks to see him glancing at his cell phone. Since service was restored, he'd received messages nonstop. The effort he made to tie up projects. The one-on-one time he spent with Remy, Naomi, and the other kids who needed it most.

Saying he "had something" for her. Since he asked to meet her after lights out, he wanted privacy.

Please, don't be his notice.

A wave of yearning hit her with such force she put her hands to her stomach. He'd said he wasn't right for her. When she saw the Scotch, she believed him... for a few days. But since their return to the shelter, she'd only seen the Alessandro she'd fallen for. The man who winked at Pearl and befriended Sam, Tommy, Irene, and Walter. The man who picked up on the humor of a kid sandwich and dealt with toddler messes without blinking.

The man who gave her a kiss on a dining hall bench that was unlike any she'd experienced in her life. The man who'd treated her with care when he thought she'd been bitten by a snake, and whose adoration was plain on his face while he'd watched Chloe pull the glass from the puncture wounds.

It was that look on his face—after their kiss, and after she'd been so upset about the Scotch—that confounded her.

She shouldn't trust him, given that he had the Scotch in his bag and that he'd essentially warned her he'd break her heart. He flat-out told her he was no saint.

But deep in the marrow of her bones, she did trust him.

She propped her elbows on the desk and forked her fingers through her hair to massage her scalp. If he was giving his notice, she'd be gracious. She'd pretend it was all right, even though it wasn't. She exhaled, then muttered, "It doesn't make sense."

"Am I disturbing you?"

Her head snapped up. Alessandro stood in her doorway, filling the space. Over his shoulder, he carried the same backpack he'd had his first day at the shelter. When she waved him in, he swung it in front of him.

It was full.

"Not at all. I tend to talk to myself when I'm working." She gestured to an empty chair near her desk and smiled, proud of herself for sounding relaxed.

"I won't be long." He approached, but dropped his backpack onto the chair instead of taking a seat. He shifted back on his heels and shoved his hands into his back pockets. "You know I'm leaving tomorrow."

She gave a slight nod. "It's going to be a long trip. What time is your plane?"

"Eight in the morning. Tommy advised me to take the five a.m. boat from the marina to make it to the airport in time. He even offered to give me a ride."

"I'm not surprised."

"He's a good man. It's an insane hour to get out of bed, even for someone used to being up all hours with the toddlers."

Alessandro glanced at his backpack then swiped a hand over his jaw, the day-old stubble making an audible scrape. A streak of dirt on his forearm caught her attention.

Before he could speak, she raised a finger in a silent request for him to stay put, then retrieved a washcloth from the bathroom and handed it to him. "For your arm."

He glanced down, then scrubbed the area harder than necessary. Despite being born to world of polite conversation, he suddenly seemed as uncomfortable as she did. "Tommy and I drove to St. Augustine's this afternoon to help Father Jacob replace the broken downspouts. I haven't had a chance to shower."

She ignored the mental image that sprang to her mind of Alessandro in a hot shower. "I'm sure Father Jacob appreciated the help."

"Wish we could've done it sooner."

He handed Frannie the washcloth, which she set on the edge of her desk. Small talk couldn't cover the palpable tension simmering between them. She'd die a slow death if she didn't rip off the bandage and get the pain over with.

She conjured a smile. "You said you had something for me?"

"I do." He angled his head toward the backpack. "I'd like to leave that with you."

"Won't you need it?"

"The clothes I wear at the shelter aren't exactly appropriate for a wedding. The sum total of my packing list for the trip home is my toothbrush, toothpaste, and a book for the plane." A small muscle leaped at the corner of his mouth. "The Scotch is in there. It'll be safer in your office than in my room."

"It was safe here in the first place." She raised a hand, checking her attitude. No sense in it. "I'll keep an eye on the bag."

"Thank you."

She swallowed, hating to raise the topic, but needing to. "Family celebrations tend to focus a person on home and responsibilities. Have you considered your plans?"

"What do you mean, my plans?"

"You volunteered for a three-month term here. By the time the wedding is over, you'll only have three weeks left. If the king and queen cross-examine you the way they do Sophia, they'll expect you to address your royal obligations."

The edges of his eyes crinkled. "Let's see…that's celebrations. Responsibilities. Cross-examine. And obligations."

She frowned, which made him laugh. Her confusion mounted. "I don't understand."

"I know you don't." He surprised her by reaching out to cup her cheek. "When you're nervous, your speech gets more formal. You use longer words, you stand straighter. Like you're doing now."

She became aware of the tension in her shoulders. He was right; she held herself more formally when she needed to subdue her nerves. He was making her more anxious with every passing second. It was all she could do not to tremble at his touch.

"You're worried I won't return. Either because I'll be tempted by the ability to enjoy nights out and a tumbler of Scotch whenever I wish, or because my parents will demand I fulfill my family obligations." His thumb grazed her lips, then stilled. "You're right about my parents and the pressure they exert. I've spent a lifetime rebelling against them. But I won't leave Kilakuru before my term ends. Regardless of my obligations at home, I owe that to the kids. I owe that to you."

His eyes searched hers for a long breath, then a second. Frannie didn't move. Didn't dare. Her stomach pitched as if she'd crested the peak of a roller coaster and a rapid, headlong plunge awaited her.

"The challenge isn't in resisting my parents," he finally said, "or even in resisting the Scotch and nights out with friends. It's in resisting you. You've changed my life."

His gaze dropped to her mouth for a long moment. His lips parted and he moved fractionally closer before his hand dropped from her cheek.

On a long exhale, he said, "I'll see you in a week," then strode out of her office, letting the door slam behind him.

CHAPTER TWENTY-ONE

Heat rose in shimmering waves from the asphalt at Cateri's airport. It radiated through the leather of Alessandro's shoes as he approached the uniformed driver parked at the edge of the tarmac. Sarcaccia was known for its warm weather this time of year, but it felt off to Alessandro after his months in Kilakuru. Different humidity, different scent to the air.

Alessandro feigned a polite smile as he greeted the driver. As a member of the royal family, Alessandro had the luxury of skipping customs. Grateful as he was to avoid the crowd in the terminal, he wasn't up for small talk, either. Grit laced his eyes from a lack of sleep, his back ached from the long flight, and, much as he hated to admit it, he missed Frannie and the kids already.

The driver strode to the back of the car to close the trunk when he noticed Alessandro didn't have a bag. Rather than wait for the driver to open the rear door, Alessandro moved to do it himself.

"You're welcome to ride in the front."

Alessandro did a double take, his ears registering what his eyes had not. He looked to the back of the sedan. "Vittorio?"

"I assumed that you, of all people, would see through the sunglasses and uniform. Much as I'd like to attribute it to my talent for disguise—"

"Talent? You?"

"—I consider it symptomatic of extreme jet lag. Even that godforsaken island where you've been holed up must have a mirror. Though, given your appearance, I suspect the place is without a proper barber."

It's not godforsaken, he wanted to retort. *And I'm not holed up.* Instead, Alessandro walked around the car, slid into the passenger seat, and waited for Vittorio to put the car into drive.

"What possessed you to come to the airport dressed like that? Did the entire staff resign?"

"It's a wonder they haven't, given Mother's obsession with wedding details. Yesterday it was a fixation on the carriage I'm taking to the ceremony, of all things." Vittorio's mouth twisted as he adjusted the rearview mirror. "I wanted time alone with you. It may not happen at the palace between now and the wedding. If I'd simply taken a car, photographers and reporters would've followed me to the airport. I've never seen them so thick. It's worse than when Stefano and Megan married."

The palace and cathedral were surrounded by media trucks in the days and weeks before their younger brother's wedding. Alessandro couldn't imagine where more could park.

"Never would've believed you'd be so starved for my company." Alessandro looked sideways at Vittorio as his twin guided the luxury sedan along the marked road that bordered the tarmac, heading toward the airport's security gate. "You must be desperate. Should I be concerned? Is there trouble in paradise?"

He asked knowing full well there wasn't. He'd never encountered two more compatible people than Vittorio and Emily.

"No trouble of that sort, though I do have what I'd call a problem."

Alessandro raised a brow, waiting for Vittorio to continue.

"I have no best man."

Alessandro used one hand to shield his eyes from the sun as Vittorio passed through the security gate and guided the car onto the road that would take them to the palace. "Your wedding is the day after tomorrow."

"I'm well aware, but you didn't give me the opportunity to ask before you jumped on an airplane to Kilakuru. Felt like a question that should be asked in person." Vittorio looked at him and smiled. "I'd be honored if you'd serve as my best man."

Alessandro stared at his twin for a long moment. "I assumed you'd asked Massimo or Stefano."

"That's a terrible response," Vittorio said. "Who raised you?"

Alessandro couldn't help but laugh as they entered the heart of Cateri, with its winding, cobblestoned streets and medieval architecture. "The answer is yes, of course." He slanted a look at his twin. "You have a lot of faith in my ability to pull off a bachelor party. Tomorrow's out, since we have the family dinner, which leaves tonight."

"I don't need a bachelor party. Or want one, for that matter."

"Why else would you have me as best man? Aren't I known for parties?" He said it with a lightness he didn't feel. Spending the night carousing in a Sarcaccian bar or on board one of the Barrali family yachts didn't appeal in the slightest.

Alessandro smiled to himself at that thought. The night he'd met Frannie at Sophia's party, when he'd stood at the bar wanting nothing more than to indulge in a glass of Scotch and a romp with a curvaceous blonde, he wouldn't have believed it, but he was suddenly far more willing to dance with Frannie and a pack of rowdy children in the hot southern Pacific sunshine than dance with scantily clad women in the darkened nightclubs of southern Europe.

If banana cake was involved, all the better.

"I don't discount your social talents," Vittorio said. "I ask because I can't imagine anyone else standing by my side when I marry Emily. If not for your sacrifice—for the fact you gave up five months of your life to give me breathing room—I'd never have met her. Nor would I have had the strength to take the risks I did to prove to her that she should marry me. You're quite good at that, you know…encouraging people to stretch beyond their imagined limitations."

The compliment touched Alessandro, but he wasn't comfortable saying so. Vittorio had needed that time away; Alessandro had only done what was necessary.

He shifted in his seat, then raised a hand in greeting to the familiar gate guard at the rear entrance to the palace grounds. "I haven't spent much time around Emily, but it's obvious to me that she understands you and loves you. She's excited to marry you. That has nothing to do with me and everything to do with who you are."

"And wanting you by my side has everything to do with you. Don't discount what makes you who *you* are. It's more than being the main draw of every party." Vittorio rolled the sedan into its designated spot in the palace's underground parking garage, then groaned as he cut the engine.

"What?"

Vittorio looked in the rearview mirror, then jerked his thumb over his shoulder. "Mother switched our carriages. I'm switching back as soon as I can find a way to do it without putting the staff in a bad position."

Alessandro climbed out of the sedan, eyed the gilt carriage, then tapped one hand on the roof and looked across at his twin. "Let your best man handle it. Mother hasn't seen me in months. She's less likely to get angry with me."

"Don't count on it."

"I'll promise her that I'll use that thing" —he glanced back to where the antique carriage, a family heirloom, was parked— "when I get married."

A burst of laughter erupted from Vittorio as they walked toward the elevator that would carry them to the palace's living quarters. "Mother will tell you it doesn't count if she's not alive to see it."

"Stefano, Massimo, now you…who's not to say I'm next?"

Alessandro's phone buzzed as the words left his mouth. A glance at the screen revealed a flirtatious text from a Greek heiress who'd arrived in Sarcaccia to attend the wedding. Alessandro pocketed the phone, but not before Vittorio caught sight of the message.

"You next. Did you suffer a head injury on Kilakuru that I should know about?" Vittorio started to say something else, then held up a hand, cutting off his own statement. "Never mind. I don't want to know. Let's take the staff corridor and find lunch before the family descends on us. Chef Fournier promised me made-from-scratch pizza and I intend to collect."

"Sounds delicious." Pizza from the palace's new chef ranked right up there as one of life's greatest delights.

It was also the perfect distraction from Alessandro's sudden mental image of Frannie sitting beside him in the antique carriage, holding a bouquet of flowers and wearing white as she beamed with happiness.

From the depths of his soul, he wanted her. He knew he'd always want her. But he was a Barrali, and as tied to this island and all that the palace represented to its people as she was committed to the children of Kilakuru and their shelter. Worse than that, he'd lived a life of debauchery. If Frannie were faced with the reality of his existence prior to his stint on Kilakuru—the nights of gambling, women, alcohol—she'd be repulsed. She might say she wasn't bothered, but it was easy for her to ignore reality when they were in the middle of the South Pacific with no paparazzi, no twenty-four hour news cycle, and none of his acquaintances. Not so here in Sarcaccia. Some women—like that Italian journalist—would have no problem spinning his reputation to their advantage, were they to step out with him publicly.

Not so Frannie. Aside from the months Alessandro had spent in his brother's role, he'd lived a life that was the antithesis of Frannie's virtuous one.

The look he'd seen in her eyes when he'd left his backpack in her office…to let go of her and walk away, rather than pull her body to his and bury his face in her hair, was as painful as summiting Everest without supplemental oxygen.

The shelter changed him. *She'd* changed him. Despite that, he was everything Frannie didn't want or need.

With a last, long glance at the elegant carriage, he turned to celebrate his brother's bliss.

* * *

Late the next evening, Alessandro leaned against the wide windowsill in the living room of his parents' palace apartment, gave his Aberlour a slow swirl, then let the liquid burn a happy trail down the back of his throat.

He'd slept in this morning for the first time in months, then rolled over in bed and clicked on the television coverage leading up to tomorrow's wedding in Cateri's main cathedral. True to Vittorio's description, the airport had been jammed for days, restaurants were booked solid, and even tiny hostels on the far side of Sarcaccia had been turning away reservations for months. Thousands—if not hundreds of thousands—of people already lined the streets of the capital, staking out their spots to watch the carriages drive the wedding party to and from the ceremony. Far more media—and more tourists—crammed the island than in the days leading up to Stefano and Megan's wedding fifteen months earlier.

He'd sighed and clicked off the television.

After the peace of Kilakuru, the television, the endless pings on his cell phone from friends and acquaintances, and the flurry of invitations to private parties registered as chaos to Alessandro's brain. Standing in the quiet of the massive cathedral during this afternoon's wedding rehearsal provided only a temporary respite. The moment he'd stepped out of the gothic structure, his phone lit with more calls. He'd ignored them all. Invitations—salacious or otherwise—could wait until he was home for good. Today, he wasn't in the mood.

He took another sip of his Scotch, gratified by tonight's focus on family time.

Now that dinner had concluded, the Barrali clan, Emily, and Emily's parents—who'd traveled from Oregon earlier in the week—enjoyed conversation in front of the fireplace. The relaxed atmosphere was a stark contrast to the formality of the palace itself or the pomp and circumstance that would dominate tomorrow. And, despite the large number of people in his parents' apartment, the room was far more peaceful than anywhere else Alessandro could be on Sarcaccia.

Emily's parents had married in their forties and Emily was their only child. "The happiest kind of surprise," Mrs. Sinclair said over dinner as she smiled in her daughter's direction. With that, Mrs. Sinclair and Queen Fabrizia hit it off immediately, each curious about the challenges the other faced when it came to raising children in their unique circumstances. They now sat in armchairs near the fireplace, sipping wine and chatting. Prince Stefano, King Carlo, and Mr. Sinclair occupied a sofa and talked sports. Everyone else drifted between the massive antique sideboard, where the staff had set out an array of after-dinner drinks, and the windows, where the night view of the palace gardens triggered discussion amongst the royal siblings of whether or not to go for a walk.

The couple of the moment, however, remained separate from the group. Vittorio and Emily stood behind one of the room's two sofas, leaning toward each other as they spoke. Vittorio's hand was at Emily's waist, but the manner was caring instead of possessive, and Alessandro could tell from Emily's expression that she didn't need the gentle touch to understand how Vittorio felt about her. They were a team. Inseparable.

Alessandro took another sip of his Scotch as he discreetly studied them. Their relationship fascinated him. Each was used to being the center of attention upon entering a room—Vittorio as crown prince, and Emily as the executive producer and host of a popular travel show called *At Home Abroad*—and each was used to being in control. Alessandro would've thought their worlds would be in conflict. He'd always pictured Vittorio marrying a woman with a great deal of fortitude, yes, but one who preferred to stay out of the limelight. A woman more like Frannie.

Yet if anything, being together strengthened both Emily and Vittorio. They respected each other. They relied on each other. Seeing them now, Alessandro couldn't imagine Vittorio with anyone *but* the dynamic Emily Sinclair.

Someday, Emily would make a wonderful queen. She'd navigate palace politics with the same grace and insight as Queen Fabrizia.

Alessandro turned his gaze out the window, taking in the view as soft lights illuminated the garden's fountain. Marriage wasn't a topic he'd considered at length, though on the brief occasions he did, he'd imagined he'd end up with a model. An actress. Possibly a member of another royal family or one with a great deal of wealth. A woman used to the spotlight, who moved in his circles and thrived on a busy social calendar. A woman who wouldn't blink at his reputation, as long as she knew he'd be faithful in marriage.

Yet he'd fallen for a woman who'd left behind her college friends and a position that allowed her to rub elbows with a billionaire for a social circle consisting of children and shelter volunteers.

Frannie was the most compelling person he'd ever met. Her laugh, her penchant for order, and her quiet, yet confident management skills…she intrigued him to no end. Like his mother, Frannie possessed the ability to note the mood of those around her without having to be told and to adjust her interactions with them. Unlike his mother, however, Frannie never used that skill for her own advantage. It was always to the benefit of the other person.

With the kids at Sunrise Shelter, especially, Frannie's ability was a great gift.

Alessandro took another long sip of his Scotch. She made him want to be the very best version of himself. Not because he was bored, as he'd been that day on the *Libertà* with Claudine and Sylvie, or even because he needed a challenge. She'd shown him that helping others gave him the soul-deep satisfaction of having contributed to the world rather than taken from it.

Through the window glass, he heard the deep chime of the palace's clock tower marking the hour. He wondered how Frannie would fit in to palace life. She'd seemed perfectly at ease during Sophia's party. While her clothing wasn't as flashy as many of the women, she wasn't out of place. She'd danced with the poise of a woman used to formal events, though without pretentiousness.

On the other hand, Frannie lived a simple life at the shelter, one without creature comforts, and never once complained. He closed his eyes for a brief moment, remembering the expression on her face when he withdrew the plush white robe from the box. Her dark eyes had widened and her lips had parted. Then he'd lifted the card and started to read. Excitement had thrummed through him…and she'd called him Your Highness. Tried to reject the gift as too extravagant, never mind that it was just that, a *gift*. It wasn't intended for practicality, but to be enjoyed.

She'd finally relented and she'd written what he was sure must've been a gracious note to the designer. It'd thrilled him to see her wear it when she crossed the compound en route to the shower house.

The sound of Emily's carefree laughter carried to his ears.

The first time he met Emily Sinclair, at the season finale of her television show *At Home Abroad* a little over a year ago, they'd hit it off. Alessandro admired her work ethic and her easy way with people from all backgrounds and walks of life, from the back streets of Buenos Aires to the palace halls in Sarcaccia.

From the first word he'd uttered, Emily had been able to tell Alessandro from Vittorio.

Just as Frannie had been able to tell, once she'd met them both.

He closed his eyes once more. He couldn't imagine a woman more perfect for him than Frannie. What he wouldn't do to have her in his life. If only—

"Tired?" His sister, Sophia, came to stand beside him at the window. "Or contemplating when you can safely escape to pursue other activities?"

He angled his head to smile at her. "Neither. Just thinking."

"That's a first." She set her wineglass on the windowsill, then used both hands to lift her hair so it fell behind her shoulders. "We haven't had time to talk since you returned home. What do you think of Kilakuru and the shelter?"

"It's wonderful. Unplugged, but never quiet." Imagining the island coaxed a smile from him. "You hear the birds and the wind and the rush of the ocean at all hours. Everyone's friendly. It's a true community. And the kids at the shelter are amazing. I could talk about them for hours. They've been through so much, yet for the most part, they're optimistic. They value their friendships with each other and love the staff. They even love school. They take nothing for granted."

"Well, if that's all." One of her dark brows rose fractionally as she looked sideways at him. "Sounds like you're enjoying yourself."

"I am. It's been good for me." His gaze traveled across the palace's verdant gardens toward the far wing of the palace. The gray gravel of the garden paths, the spray of water from the fountain, the sparkling chandeliers visible in the arched windows of the palace's ground floor…all of it familiar, imbued with a sense of home, yet a million miles from the rough and tumble lushness of the island.

"You have three more weeks there?"

"You've been keeping track."

"Mother has. She always counts the days when you're away."

"When any of us are away." Queen Fabrizia's concern was difficult to hide during Vittorio's long sojourn to Argentina. Alessandro angled a look at his sister as Sophia picked up her drink. "By the way, when I was packing the boxes to send to Kilakuru, what made you suggest the scented soap?"

Her long fingers tightened around the glass. "I don't know. It was so long ago. It's an item everyone can use and it's easy to ship, I suppose. Why?"

Her apparent forgetfulness didn't fool him for a minute. "Why verveine? Why not lavender or honey, since Sarcaccia is known for those?"

She lifted and dropped one shoulder. "Frannie's mother sent it to her while we were at university. I thought she'd appreciate it, plus it's a scent few find offensive, so it's one others are likely to enjoy."

He pinned her with a look. "So you *were* aware that Frannie Lawrence runs the shelter. Funny, you never mentioned her when we packed the boxes."

CHAPTER TWENTY-TWO

Sophia drew back in surprise. "Of course. You didn't?"

He laughed. "Oh, Sophia. Don't pretend. You knew I had no idea. It must have taken quite the conversational gymnastics on your part to help me pack those boxes, yet not mention Frannie and make it all seem completely natural."

Despite being caught, she feigned offense. "That's ridiculous. Why would I lie to you?"

"That's what I'm attempting to determine. It wasn't a coincidence that you appeared at my apartment door to borrow a book at the exact same time I'd requested the staff come to help me pack a shipment to the island. You took the time to inspect my selections—the games, the magic kits, the kaleidoscopes—and were very quick to suggest the soaps and the sports equipment."

"I'm brilliant that way."

"I don't deny that—well, I might to our siblings" —he angled his head toward the center of the room— "but you had those ideas in mind when you arrived. And you knew Frannie would be the beneficiary. The question is why."

"Because she's my friend?"

"And you wanted her to have a meaningful, intimate gift. From *me*. And without my knowing that's what I was doing."

"Believe what you want." Sophia huffed and faced the gardens again. "I think you've grown accustomed to manipulative women. Now you see it in every female who enters your orbit, whether they're manipulating you or not."

"That's not true. Not all women." For the first time in his life, he believed that, now that he knew Frannie and the other women at the shelter. They cared nothing for his title, his wealth, or what physical pleasure he might give them.

Though he hoped Frannie had at least considered the last after the kisses they'd shared.

He set his Aberlour on the windowsill and looked at his sister. "In this case, however, you *were* manipulative. But given Frannie's very happy reaction to the soap, I suspect you were looking out for my best interests. Ensuring my volunteer time began on the right foot, perhaps. If that was the case…thank you."

Sophia narrowed her eyes, refusing to confirm his suspicions, then she softened. "You're welcome."

A wave of laughter rose behind them. Sophia and Alessandro both glanced over their shoulders to see everyone cackling in Bruno's direction. Bruno beamed as if he'd stunned the room with a rare joke.

The queen stood, then announced that the palace chef had set up a dessert buffet in an adjacent room. "I realize that we're all worried about how our clothes will fit tomorrow, but he's assured me it's all delightful and nothing is too heavy. I plan to partake and perhaps enjoy a sip or two of cognac."

"That's our cue," Sophia said, a wily look in her eye. "I talked Chef Fournier into making a tray of meringue with blueberries. I want to make sure I have a few."

"A few?"

"More than a few."

Alessandro offered his arm to escort his younger sister to the buffet, but was stopped by Vittorio. "No, not you, best man. You and I are taking a walk through the garden. Sophia would be happier sharing those meringues with Emily, anyway."

"She eats a lot less than you do," Sophia noted, then gave Alessandro a quick kiss on the cheek before bolting for the adjacent room.

The brothers watched as the women disappeared through the doors leading to the adjacent room. Alessandro cocked a brow at his twin. "You're denying me meringues for a walk in the garden?"

"We can swing by the kitchen later, if you'd like. I asked Chef Fournier to set aside extras of everything in case Emily and I wanted them tomorrow night."

"You're assuming you'll be one of those couples who miss eating on their wedding day?"

"I'm taking every precaution against it."

Vittorio finished his drink, then crossed to the sideboard and left the empty glass on a tray. Alessandro did the same, then spun to follow Vittorio to the garden. The crown prince appeared outwardly relaxed as they descended the wide marble staircase and paused to greet Umberto, the head of palace security, who stood sentry at the base.

"Prince Vittorio, Prince Alessandro. Heading to the gardens for a stroll?"

"Thought we could use the peace and quiet before the pandemonium begins tomorrow."

Umberto, a towering man with a rock-hard jaw and tight, military haircut, graced them with a rare smile. "It's a beautiful evening for it. You may have noticed that, given the number of people in town for the wedding, I've assigned a guard to each exterior door. If you'd like more privacy, I'll have them step inside."

Vittorio waved off the suggestion. "We'll be fine. Thank you, Umberto."

The crown prince's tone conveyed nonchalance, yet as the men exited the palace and stepped onto the garden's gravel path, Alessandro sensed tension within his brother. Vittorio's suggestion that they head toward the benches on the other side of the fountain, away from the guards who manned the doors, confirmed his suspicion.

Whatever bothered Vittorio, he wished to be alone to discuss it.

"I managed to switch the carriages," Alessandro said as they moved out of earshot of the guards.

"Do I want to know how?"

"No."

That elicited a grin from Vittorio before he paused near one of the ornate benches on the far side of the fountain. Water sprayed high in the air, then splashed down into the pool in a steady rhythm. It had a calming effect on the spirit. It also obscured the sound of their conversation.

Alessandro sat on the bench, crossed his arms over his chest, then kicked out his legs and tipped his head to observe the night sky. "Are we to stare at the stars and smile as if you're a carefree groom while you tell me what's on your mind?"

"I'm that transparent?"

"Only to me. Possibly to Mother. I suspect that when she's on her deathbed, she'll confess her ability to read minds."

Vittorio sat beside Alessandro, but kept his gaze on the fountain. For a long minute, he sat in silence. Then he said, "How have you been doing with the children on Kilakuru?"

"Surely that's not why you brought me here."

"Humor me."

Alessandro shrugged, keeping his face angled toward the sky. Briefly, he told his brother about Naomi. Her silence, her sweet smiles, her theft—which brought a snort of amusement from Vittorio—and the day she first spoke. His hope that it would lead to conversation with others. He mentioned Johnny, Tehani, and several of the other children. The rambunctiousness of the toddlers…and the deep respect he had for those who worked in the nursery. "Their energy is boundless," he told Vittorio.

Finally, he described Remy and the boy's attachment to Humphrey. "I worry most for him," he admitted. Though Alessandro hadn't contemplated it until now, Remy's situation struck him as the most dire of all the children. "Most of those who were orphaned will likely find homes as residents return to the island. They have extended families who we hope will eventually take them in. Remy has no one. His extended family is in the Marquesas and hadn't spoken to his parents in years. They have no interest in him."

"He sounds like a wonderful boy," Vittorio said. "Once the economy on the island is stabilized, his situation may look different."

"I hope so. He's able to stay in school and he's well-loved at the shelter, but it's not the same as having a true family. Even he knows it." Alessandro angled his gaze toward his brother. "I assume you're asking about children for a reason?"

"I've wondered if you see yourself as a father someday, given your experience with the children on the island."

Alessandro looked to the stars again. He could pick out Orion's Belt, but few other stars were visible, given the bright lights of the city. "Six months ago, I would have said sure. But it would have been an automatic response. One of those 'someday' answers that means nothing. But now? Yes. They're a pain in my ass sometimes and they're exhausting, but at the end of a day with them, I go to bed feeling perfectly content. I can only imagine what being a father is like."

Vittorio's answering chuckle held an odd note. Alessandro straightened on the bench and frowned at his brother. "Emily's pregnant, isn't she? That's why you're asking about children."

Really, he was the last person Vittorio should talk to if he was worried about how to handle fatherhood. Stefano already had a son and a daughter. He and his wife, Megan, were doing a wonderful job raising them, despite the spotlight on the family.

"No, she's not." He planted his elbows on his thighs and steepled his fingers to his chin, then cocked his head toward Alessandro. "But that *is* why I wanted to talk to you. I should have done it in the car yesterday—I wanted to—but it didn't feel right."

A sense of foreboding crept up his spine. "*What* didn't feel right?"

"There's no way to say this but to come right out with it." He turned on the bench so he fully faced Alessandro. "It's highly unlikely Emily and I will ever have children. The press hasn't discovered it yet, but when she was twenty-three, Emily was diagnosed with Hodgkin's lymphoma. She's perfectly healthy now, thank

God, but at the time, the recommended course of chemotherapy for her stage and type of cancer was one that frequently causes ovarian failure. In her case, it did."

Vittorio sounded matter-of-fact, but Alessandro knew it must've taken his brother—and Emily—a great deal of time to come to terms with such a sad reality.

Before Alessandro could express his sorrow, Vittorio continued, "Emily had eggs harvested first, so there's a possibility. However, the odds aren't in our favor. It's much tougher to have a successful pregnancy from a frozen egg than from an embryo. We've already seen a fertility specialist. Two of them. For us to have a child...well, it'd be close to a miracle."

Alessandro pushed to stand. From birth, Vittorio had been raised to carry on the Barrali line. He faced far more pressure than most crown princes to do so. Under the treaty Sarcaccia signed to gain its independence, a Barrali had to hold the throne. Once the Barrali line ended, the island would revert to Italian control.

Wonderful as Italy might be, Sarcaccians were proud of their independent status.

"I'm so sorry, Vittorio."

"Don't be. I have Emily. I can honestly say that I'm happy, whether or not we have children."

Alessandro stared at the fountain for a moment, then walked behind the bench, braced his hands on the backrest beside his brother, and stared at the water as the enormity of Vittorio's revelation settled upon him. Deep breaths didn't ease the ache in his chest. He felt raw. Scraped out from the inside and left to rot.

"Don't look so maudlin." Vittorio aimed a look toward the nearest door, where a sentry stood watch. "Look as if we're having a relaxed, pre-wedding talk. Bonding."

"It's hard not to be maudlin. I know how much you want children. How much you're expected to have children."

"By the country, perhaps. But not by Mother and Father. When Emily and I informed them of our situation, my bride-to-be actually offered *not* to marry me. She insisted that the country should come first. Of course, they wouldn't hear of it." He looked over his shoulder and grinned. "They knew you could do the job.

They also knew I'd never be happy without Emily. I told them I'd gladly step aside and have you assume the role of crown prince. Permanently."

Alessandro closed his eyes.

From the moment he'd left Frannie on Kilakuru, he'd dreamed of ways he could make right all the wrongs he'd committed in his life. How he could make himself worthy of her. He'd almost convinced himself that if he extended his stay on Kilakuru, he might—might—overcome his past. He hadn't quite believed it, but in his gut, he still had hope.

But now…if he were to become king after his father, would Frannie even have him? He'd be under more scrutiny than ever. And his lifestyle would be nothing like Frannie's.

He tightened his grip on the back of the bench, then released it and moved to sit beside his brother.

"You'd do a great job, Alessandro."

"That's the least of my worries," he snapped, then regretted it. "Not that I should have any worries. What you and Emily must be going through…knowing you may never have children, knowing the reasons may become public—"

"We don't care. We can always adopt. The child wouldn't inherit, but it doesn't matter to me. Falling in love with Emily has changed everything for me. My view of the world—and my role in it—is vastly different than it was before I met her."

Alessandro couldn't help but let out a self-deprecating laugh. Oh, how he knew that to be true.

Vittorio's expression changed. "The world has officially tilted on its axis. You're in love."

Oh, he hated that his twin could read him so well. Still, Alessandro scoffed, "Don't be ridiculous."

He immediately realized Sophia had uttered the same phrase only moments before, when he'd accused her of lying.

"It's Francesca Lawrence, isn't it? The woman you mentioned to me at the Sarcaccia F.C. game we attended after I returned from Argentina? I met her before you went to Kilakuru. She applied to the Barrali Trust for funding." A slow grin spread across Vittorio's face. "You've always liked the name Francesca."

"It's Frannie."

His lips quirked. "Frannie?"

"That's what she prefers."

Vittorio was quiet for a long moment, then cast a sidelong glance at Alessandro. "You don't deny being in love with her. And now you're worried about how my news will affect your relationship."

Alessandro gritted his teeth. No, he didn't deny it. Couldn't deny it. But that didn't mean it was right. "There's nothing to deny because there's no relationship. I'm not the right person for her."

"Ouch. She actually said that?"

"Of course not." Alessandro rolled his eyes. "You, of all people, know my faults. I'm your mirror. Where you're reserved and thoughtful, where you're duty-bound and honorable, I'm...not that."

"You make me sound as exciting as cardboard. Even so, what does it matter that we're not alike?"

"If she married me, she'd regret it the rest of her life."

Vittorio said nothing. Alessandro realized he'd given too much away. It was the word *married*. He should've said something else, especially after making the carriage comment in the garage yesterday.

When Vittorio finally spoke, his words were measured. "You're certain of that, are you?"

Alessandro turned to the window and nodded. "When I first met her, I thought she'd be perfect for you. She's responsible. Dedicated. Of course, at the time, I didn't know you'd found Emily. Who *is* perfect for you."

"From what I recall, you described Francesca—Frannie—as a stick-in-the-mud. And I asked you who used that phrase anymore."

"And I said, 'a stick-in-the-mud like you.' Which is still true. You're a stick-in-the-mud."

"Yet you're in love with a stick-in-the-mud." Vittorio laughed. "I suppose I'll take that as a compliment."

"You're twisted."

"And you don't give yourself enough credit." Vittorio shot him a pointed look, one that compelled Alessandro to face Vittorio as he spoke. "You did more for me in the five months I was away than any man has a right to ask of his brother. You gave up your entire life so I could get mine in order. You never complained, never asked for anything in return. Not only that, you did a spectacular job acting as crown prince. You likely saved hundreds, maybe thousands, of lives by negotiating the safe zone surrounding Abu Kamal."

"Vittorio—"

"You didn't do it for the recognition, either. When you did those things, everyone believed you were me. And you thought they'd *always* believe it was me. We had no plans to come clean. You did it because it was the right thing to do."

"You make me sound like Mother Teresa. I'm not. In fact, I could tell you stories that'd singe your ears. Remember Claudine and Sylvie, the women seated at our table following the Cannes Film Festival a few years ago? That night— "

Vittorio held his hand palm out. "Whatever you're about to say, I believe you. I know all about your rendezvous with that Dutch artist, too. Your reputation is well-earned. But at your core, I know who you are. You're the best brother I could have. The best prince this country could have. You need to trust Francesca to know who you are."

"I know who I am and what I am, the good and the bad. She deserves a different type of man." He hated to admit it, even to Vittorio, but it was the truth. "If I did anything right while you were away, it's because I needed to convince the world that I was you. Much as I know you can be a pompous ass, Sarcaccia couldn't do better than to have you follow our father on the throne. And frankly, I'm holding out hope that you and Emily have children, both for your sakes and mine."

Vittorio snorted. "The throne is the distant future. Francesca is now. Let it be her decision."

Alessandro shook his head, but Vittorio put a hand on his shoulder. "If Emily acted as you're acting now, I wouldn't be marrying her tomorrow. She didn't think she was enough for me."

"Emily is wonderful. No way she's done half the things I've done."

Vittorio grinned and released Alessandro's shoulder. "No, she hasn't. But she knows I'm the crown prince. And she knows the terms of the treaty between Sarcaccia and Italy."

"She also knows you have four brothers."

"Be that as it may, she didn't want to deny me my birthright. What I've been trained to do my entire life. Even if I wasn't a prince, Emily knows how much I want children. She didn't want to deny me that opportunity, either. She was afraid that if I married her, I'd have regrets."

"You talked her out of that, obviously."

"Only because she gave me the opportunity. Thank God she did, because I don't know what I'd do without her. There's no other way I can put this…but my soul lives with Emily. It always will." Vittorio's mouth contorted, then he raised his face to look at the windows of their parents' apartment, where Emily and Sophia could be seen talking and laughing where Alessandro had stood earlier. "Give Frannie that opportunity, Alessandro. Let her decide what she can accept and what she can't."

"It's different." Vittorio's situation was one of birth. Alessandro's was one of poor choices. He wasn't good enough for Frannie, and there was no changing it.

Vittorio pushed from the bench. He glanced at the windows, then turned to face Alessandro. "I want you to think about something. When's the last time you were scared? No need to answer. Frankly, I've never known you to be scared in your life. You stared down the nannies, even when you were in the wrong. You climbed Kilimanjaro with a strained muscle and hid it from everyone. You believed with all your heart that you could switch places with me and fool millions of people. And you succeeded, every time. But now, with Frannie, something scares you. This isn't about what's right for her. It's about *you*. Perhaps it's as simple as a fear of commitment. But perhaps it's that your reputation allows you to be the center of every gathering, yet prevents people from truly knowing you. If no one truly knows you, they can't reject you." He waved a hand. "Whatever it is, you need to face what scares you. Then talk to her."

They'd never had such a personal conversation before. Not about emotions. Not about fear. It unsettled him, especially since it was the night before his brother's wedding. "Vittorio, I appreciate the advice. But my situation isn't like yours."

Vittorio's gaze hardened. "Don't bet on that, best man. You'd be wagering more than you can afford to lose."

Alessandro opened his mouth to argue, but Vittorio had already spun on his heel and strode toward the palace doors.

CHAPTER TWENTY-THREE

The Internet, Frannie decided, was both her greatest blessing and greatest curse. Today she'd experienced both.

From the moment the kids awakened, the entire shelter buzzed with gossip about Prince Vittorio and Emily Sinclair's wedding. Chloe had been the first to pop into Frannie's office and ask to use the computer to check the news. Before long, nearly every adult who worked at the shelter had asked to peek at the coverage, despite the fact Kilakuru was hours ahead of Sarcaccia and the event hadn't even started. Finally, Frannie downloaded photos from a slew of websites and carried a projector to the dining hall so everyone could ooh and aah over the photos of the Barrali and Sinclair families leaving the cathedral following the previous day's rehearsal, then the morning procession through the streets of Cateri for the ceremony. The kids, especially, were taken with the scope of the event.

Throughout the viewing party in the dining hall, one sentence was heard over and over: Prince Vittorio and Alessandro look *exactly* alike!

The response each time was similar: They do!

Or: They're totally identical!

Or: How can anyone tell them apart?

The last was answered more than once with: Alessandro's face is a deeper tan from being on Kilakuru.

The statement was often followed with giggles, though Frannie had to agree. On the surface, it was the only way to tell them apart, especially in photographs. Those photographs, however, made Frannie yearn to see Alessandro in the flesh. He'd only been gone a few days, but it felt like an eternity. She'd caught herself looking toward the boys' bunkhouse each morning, half-expecting to see him strolling toward the shower house with a towel draped over his shoulder. She missed the surety of his walk as he crossed the compound to join a volleyball game. The wicked sparkle in his eyes before he spiked the ball...usually in a way that allowed the nearest child to make the save if they went all-out for it.

Photos—and the Internet—failed to convey the subtleties that made the real, flesh and blood Alessandro...Alessandro.

Finally, at dinnertime, Frannie had declared the viewing party over for the day. She promised to gather photos and video from the ceremony itself to show to the kids the next day.

On the other hand, the Internet provided Frannie with the happiest moment of her entire week. She'd been in the midst of compiling the rehearsal photos when she received a surprise message from Naomi's father, asking if she was available to video chat. During their talk, he told her he'd secured a position with Kilakuru's fire department. The family would be living on a tight budget and staying with relatives for a short time, but he'd booked a flight that would return to the family to the island in less than twenty-four hours.

Naomi was on a science field trip at the beach when the call came, but Frannie assured Naomi's parents that she'd share the good news with Naomi as soon as possible. Tears shone in Mr. Iakopo's eyes when he told Frannie he couldn't wait to hug his daughter. Mrs. Iakopo, who stood behind her husband during the call, didn't bother hiding her tears. They flowed down both cheeks, dripping onto the baby boy in her arms.

Frannie prided herself on her toughness, but when she'd clicked off the chat screen, she'd been compelled to reach for a tissue to wipe her eyes. Of all the children in the shelter, Naomi had been most hurt by having to stay behind while her parents went off in search of employment.

A knock at her open office door that evening made Frannie smile in anticipation. To ensure Naomi had privacy for the news, Frannie asked Irene to tell Naomi to come to the office after dinner ended.

"Come on in, Naomi. If you don't mind, please close the door."

Naomi's dark eyes were wide but unreadable as she turned to shut the door. She only took a couple of steps into the office, then looked from the empty chair to Frannie.

"Go ahead and take a seat. This is all good news, Naomi."

Once the girl was seated—on the very edge of the chair, Frannie noticed—Frannie walked around the desk, moved aside a few papers, then turned and sat on top of it. "Did you have a good day today?"

Naomi nodded.

"Did you like seeing the photos from the royal wedding?"

Another nod. This time, she allowed a hint of a smile to show.

"Well, I'm about to make your day even better. While you were at the beach this afternoon, your parents called. Your father has a job. Best of all, it's right here on Kilakuru with the fire department."

As Naomi's eyes watered and her hand went to her mouth, Frannie added, "Your parents and baby brother will be here tomorrow. They've already booked their flight. They'll arrive after dinner, and you're going to move into your uncle's house until your parents can find a new place to live. There's a small school not far from his house. A few girls from your old school are already in classes there, so you'll even have friends. It's only ten kids right now, but I think you'll like it a lot."

Naomi let out a sob, then tears poured from her eyes and over her hand. Frannie moved from the desk to kneel in front of the little girl.

"I'm so happy for you, Naomi. Your parents are really excited. They can't wait to see you."

Naomi nodded and squeezed her eyes shut. As quickly as Frannie could catch her, Naomi fell from the chair and into Frannie's arms, then buried her face in Frannie's shoulder. Frannie fought to hold back her own tears as she held Naomi and let her cry. Once her sobs slowed, Frannie leaned back, holding Naomi at arm's length. She swooped a palm over the girl's head, then down her back and over her long, thick black braid. "Better?"

Naomi nodded. She took a long, deep breath, then exhaled and smiled.

"We'll have to pack your things. Everyone will be so happy to hear your news. I bet the kitchen staff makes special treats for dinner tomorrow night to celebrate."

Suddenly, Naomi's face fell. "What about Alessandro?"

The sound of Naomi's voice so shocked Frannie she froze for a split second.

Panic flared to life in Naomi's dark eyes, spurring Frannie to respond as if nothing out of the ordinary had occurred. "Alessandro will be happy for you, too. He'll hate that he wasn't here to say goodbye, but you'll see him again before his volunteer time is up. I'll make sure."

Naomi shook her head, then her lower lip started to shake.

"What's wrong, Naomi?" She'd never before asked Naomi a question that couldn't be answered with a yes or no. She hoped now wasn't the wrong time to do so.

"He promised me." Her eyes darted to the supply cabinet, then she quickly looked to Frannie. "He promised me something…for when my parents come."

"And now he's not here."

She nodded, then sniffled. Fresh tears sprang to her eyes, but she swiped them away with the back of her hand.

Frannie stretched to grab two tissues from the box on her desk, then handed them to Naomi. She crouched in front of the girl again, rocked back on her heels and wrapped her arms around her knees. "I'm going to ask you a question. I want you to tell me the truth, even if it's supposed to be a secret." She aimed a deliberate look at the supply cabinet. "Does this promise have to do with a bottle that was in my office?"

The drop of Naomi's jaw told Frannie all she needed to know before Naomi snapped her mouth closed, then nodded.

"Did you take it from the supply cabinet and give it to Alessandro?"

Another nod.

"Did he ask you to?"

A vehement shake of the head. "I heard you tell Chloe it's his special treat. He told me I shouldn't have, because it's against the rules and he couldn't have it."

"But you wanted to do something nice for him."

She nodded, then blew her nose and let out a ragged breath. "It's my parents' special treat, too. Alessandro told me he would keep it and promised to share it with them when they came to get me."

Frannie swallowed the hard lump that had formed in her throat. She could only imagine the emotion that had gone into the conversation.

Naomi had talked to Alessandro.

Likely, she'd been talking to Alessandro for weeks. No wonder he didn't want to break the girl's trust. How must he have felt when Frannie stared him down in the truck and accused him of stealing the Scotch? Particularly after he'd taken the risk of driving down the hill in the storm to get her from the shelter.

Frannie took the used tissues from Naomi, then handed her a fresh one. "Alessandro left the bottle here with me when he left for the wedding. He didn't tell me why, but he wanted to keep it safe. If he promised you he'd share it with your parents, then he will. As soon as he gets back, I'll send him to your uncle's house. All right?"

At Naomi's watery nod, Frannie smiled. "In the meantime, you need to pack. I'll talk to your teachers so they can get everything together to send to your new school. If you're up to it, you can tell everyone. If not, I can."

Naomi wrapped her arms around Frannie's neck and gave her a hug that nearly knocked her backward.

"I can," she whispered.

"They'll be so excited."

Naomi bracketed Frannie's cheeks in her soft hands, then, to Frannie's shock, kissed her on the forehead before sprinting out the door.

Frannie stayed where she was, crouched on the floor, until the sound of Naomi's steps faded. Finally, she allowed herself to roll backward onto her rear, then leaned her head against the side of her desk and exhaled.

* * *

Alessandro waved to the crowd as he escorted his mother to her open-topped carriage, which waited on the cobblestone street fronting Cateri's main cathedral. A few steps back, King Carlo descended the stairs alongside Emily's best friend and matron of honor, Rita Bragna. The two were deep in discussion about the recent season of Emily's show, *At Home Abroad*, which filmed in Sarcaccia. As the show's co-executive producer, Rita was currently scouting locations for the next season and had asked the well-traveled monarch for his advice.

All around them, the air sounded with cheers, high-pitched whistles, and the deep tones of the cathedral's bells, which announced the conclusion of the royal wedding ceremony. For as far as Alessandro could see, people lined the streets, their balloons and Sarcaccian flags peeking out from behind the barricades. Smiles lit every face and many eyes shone with happy tears.

The wedding of a crown prince was a once-in-a-lifetime event.

Behind Alessandro and Queen Fabrizia, near the massive double doors at the top of the stairs, Mr. and Mrs. Sinclair paused for photos with Prince Massimo and his wife, Kelly. Sophia stood nearby with Prince Stefano, Stefano's wife Megan, their daughter, Anna, and their new baby son, Dario.

Alessandro watched as Stefano bent to plant a kiss on top of his daughter's head.

"You seem uncharacteristically joyous," his mother said, keeping her words quiet and face turned toward Alessandro's so eagle-eyed cameramen couldn't pick out her words.

"It's a wedding. Emotional poisoning is a common side effect, is it not?"

"Judging from your expression during the exchange of vows, you began suffering early." She raised a hand to recognize the crowd, then allowed Alessandro to help her into the flower-bedecked conveyance. Once he took the seat beside her, she added, "You were riveted when they pledged to love one another for the rest of their lives. If I didn't know better, I'd have thought you were suffering even before you entered the cathedral."

Oh, he was. From the moment he'd awakened early to meet his brother for breakfast, on through their time in the dressing room before entering the sanctuary, he'd ached for Frannie. To share the day with her. To glance at her while the bells rang, to hear her comments on Emily's stunning gown and the scent of the blooms that filled the air. To witness her reaction to the heartfelt vows.

When he'd heard Vittorio give his oath to Emily in a tone which conveyed the deep fulfillment Vittorio felt despite the likelihood they'd be unable to have children, Alessandro's heart nearly burst.

This, he knew, was true, deep love.

He also knew if he said those same words to Frannie, he'd be as emotional as Vittorio. And as certain. The awareness jolted him. He'd only kissed Frannie twice. Had never walked hand in hand with her, had never made love to her. Yet he was as positive of his feelings as he was that the sun rose to Sarcaccia's east and set to its west.

He pointed out a baby being held aloft by its father, then waved. "What do you think of our carriage, Mother?"

"It's the one I wished your brother to take. My assistant Daniela informed me that you made a switch." The queen straightened in the seat and fluffed her dress, a custom-made silk in a sky blue that flattered her features. "I allowed the change. However…I will not allow you to change the subject."

"Which was?" He paused, pretending to think. "Oh, yes, the wedding. I wasn't aware they planned to use the traditional vows, since they skipped exchanging them at the rehearsal. Not that I expected anything less than a very formal, traditional ceremony from Vittorio."

"Perhaps you're growing more appreciative of the traditional. As I aged, I discovered its value. That which may appear plain, or staid, often has far more depth and meaning. It's what allows the traditional to endure."

Umberto, the palace security chief, sat alongside the driver. At a signal from the queen, Umberto nodded to the driver, who guided the horses toward the palace.

"I suspect you're trying to tell me something, Mother."

She raised her hand to recognize a group of schoolchildren gathered on a balcony, holding signs congratulating the newlyweds, then gave Alessandro a knowing look.

"I have never, in all your years, known you to pursue a woman. It is always you who are the pursued. For your looks, title, and wealth, I'm sure, not any particular facet of your personality" —she said this with a twinkle in her eye— "because most women never see your sense of humor or your intelligence. Or the protective streak you keep hidden away. You hide your best traits from casual acquaintances, which prevents them from being attracted to who you truly are."

Given the cameras lining the processional route, he resisted the urge to roll his eyes. "You are a mother blind to her children's faults. And that is *your* greatest fault."

She sighed, though there was amusement in the sound. "When Vittorio left, it was your idea. You acted as if it were a great game to take on his role, but I know the truth of the matter. It was an act of great love."

He had no answer for that, so he gave none. His mother was skilled at wheedling information by remaining silent, but when she realized he'd admit nothing, she tried a different approach. "I saw you dancing with Francesca Lawrence at Sophia's Christmas party and I knew."

"You knew…what?"

Though the queen continued to smile, he could tell from her shift in position that she was growing exasperated with him. "Francesca is one of those women who, on first glance, appears plain. Traditional. Staid. Yet you danced with her twice when you had every reason in the world to walk away. Your eyes never left her face. You *smiled*, genuinely smiled, for the first time in weeks. You steered her toward the middle of the floor so you could keep her to yourself. You were captivated in a way I've never witnessed, and I've witnessed you with plenty of women."

The horses slowed their pace as the carriage rounded a corner, taking them through the heart of medieval Cateri en route to the palace. The queen tilted her chin to acknowledge a group of well-wishers who'd climbed the wall of a garden so they'd have a view from above the street-level crowd, before speaking again. "Francesca might appear traditional, but she's more adventurous than what one might expect. More independent. When I saw you dancing that night, and I witnessed the look of curiosity on your face, I knew you'd pursue her, given the opportunity."

"So you created an opportunity."

"Oh, no. The opportunity was there, and you made it clear that you were ready for it." She raised a brow and looked at her son. "I merely ensured you knew of it."

"I had no idea Frannie was on Kilakuru."

His mother's smile was all-knowing. Likely because he'd referred to Frannie, rather than Francesca. "She'd mentioned the island to you. Months later, you remained intrigued enough to go. And, you might recall, I told you that you were welcome to extend your three-month obligation if your time at the shelter were to prove fruitful."

"You did. However, I now have responsibilities here." Responsibilities that went far deeper than he'd known before yesterday's talk with Vittorio. He might never ascend the throne—didn't want to ascend the throne—but he owed it to his countrymen to prepare for the possibility.

She angled her head at the uniformed guards flanking the palace gates, then gave a final wave to the crowd before the carriage entered the palace courtyard.

"Happiness often lies behind obstacles. Emily and Vittorio have faced their share, as have King Carlo and I. There comes a time when one must choose the proper course of action. To scale an obstacle, or choose a different path entirely? To pursue the happiness of one's heart, or the obligations of one's circumstances? In a long-term relationship, the question is likely to arise more than once."

The driver slowed the horses, drawing the carriage to a stop under a portico at the side of the palace. The carriage that carried Emily and Vittorio from the cathedral was parked a short distance in front of them, empty now that the newly-weds had entered the palace and were likely making their way toward the balcony, where they'd appear for the cameras and for those gathered on the street in front of the palace.

Alessandro signaled the driver to give him a moment alone with his mother. Umberto looked to the queen for confirmation, then joined the driver near the side entry.

"I assume you're talking about the obstacles you faced when you discovered that Father had Rocco, Enzo, and Lina out of wedlock." At his mother's nod, he drew in a deep breath, then puffed it out. "It was early in your marriage. How did you know your relationship would survive it? That you'd love him for as long as you have?"

"Oh, Alessandro." The queen released an uncharacteristic sigh, then smiled at her son. "I knew within days of meeting Carlo Barrali that he would be the love of my life. Not because of his good looks or his wealth, and not because he was heir to the throne, though all those attributes have shaped the man he is. When we met" —her eyes went glossy— "it was as if I were called to him, as if your father's soul spoke to mine. I simply knew. I'd never again meet a man like Carlo. I never wanted to."

Alessandro spread his palms against the cool, black leather of the carriage seat, then flexed his fingers. His mother's words were eerily similar to those Vittorio uttered last night.

My soul lives with Emily. It always will.

Alessandro had seen the evidence today in the cathedral, when Emily smiled at Vittorio as he slid the ring onto her finger.

The clopping of hooves against cobblestone indicated that the carriage bearing his father and Rita Bragna drew near. Emily's parents would soon arrive in the carriage behind theirs.

The queen flicked a glance the direction of the sound, noting that their time was short. "The difficulty was in knowing whether Carlo viewed me the same way. Once I knew he did, I was certain we could overcome any obstacles in our path. We would love each other, and we'd love the family we created, however that family might be shaped. I believe it's the same with Vittorio and Emily."

"What made you so sure of his feelings?"

"I asked. Then I listened carefully to his answer." The king's carriage stopped behind theirs. The queen brightened, then signaled for the driver to return and open the carriage door. "On that note, it's time to forget obligations and celebrate. I intend to dance to my heart's content." She gave Alessandro's knee a quick pat. "I hope you will do the same."

CHAPTER TWENTY-FOUR

Francesca stared at the bright red numbers on her bedside clock. Nearly one a.m. She closed her eyes and pulled her pillow over her face.

If he arrived as scheduled, Alessandro would return to Sunrise Shelter tomorrow. She couldn't wait. At the same time, she ached at the thought that he'd be leaving again in only three weeks.

If having him gone for a week for his brother's wedding was this painful, what would it be like to know he was forever out of her life?

How hard would these next three weeks be, knowing how hard she'd fallen for him, yet having to keep her distance, since he'd plainly stated that he didn't believe they had a future?

A buzz from the direction of her office cut short the thought. She waited, unsure of what she heard. Then it came again: the distinct sound of the front gate buzzer, which was wired to sound in her office.

She toed into her slippers, then made her way through the office and into the compound. She moved quietly, not wanting the person at the gate to see her until she ascertained their identity.

"Frannie? It's me."

Her heart soared at the sound of Alessandro's voice. She hurried to the gate, then flipped the bar to admit him. Though she kept her voice low, she couldn't hide her happiness. "What are you doing here?"

"Caught an earlier flight, then managed to find a captain who'd ferry me to Kilakuru from the airport."

"But…it was your brother's wedding!" She drank in the sight of him in the muted light as she closed and locked the gate behind him. His face bore the evidence of his long flight. Stubble covered his cheeks and chin, and his hair was as tousled as she'd seen it in a long time, despite the fact he'd apparently gotten a haircut during his time at home. He wore a pair of tailored gray slacks, expensive-looking leather belt and shoes, and a cream-colored shirt that, at one time, had been crisply ironed.

Despite his wrinkled clothes and apparent exhaustion, he looked amazing. She'd missed him terribly. Even more than she'd been willing to admit to herself while tossing and turning in bed, waiting for his return.

"I wanted to get here as soon as I could."

"Why? Did you hear about Naomi?"

Alarm skittered over his face. "Naomi? Is she hurt?"

"No, nothing like that. She's perfectly fine. Happy. She spoke to me the day of your brother's wedding." Frannie couldn't hide the joy in her voice. True to her word, Naomi had also told her bunkmates that she was going home. Word spread through the shelter at lightning speed…both about the fact Naomi was going home, and that she'd finally spoken aloud. "I thought she might be the reason you—"

"You're the reason."

Frannie paused, her train of thought derailed. "What?"

Alessandro ran one hand through his hair as he looked at her. Suddenly, she was aware of the fact she stood in the middle of the compound in a thin nightgown with no bra. "Mind if we speak in your office?"

Not trusting herself to speak, she tipped her head toward the office indicating that he should follow. As soon as she flipped on the overhead bulb, she excused herself, then retrieved her robe from her room. When she returned to the office, she found Alessandro pacing the small space.

"What's wrong?"

He stopped, then looked at her. She couldn't read his expression, but his thoughts seemed weighty. It wasn't like him. When he didn't answer right away, she tried again, "How was your trip home?"

"Other than my family conspiring against me?" He let out an exasperated laugh, then shook his head. "Never mind. The trip was long, the wedding was elegant and heartfelt, and everyone took the opportunity to try to convince me they know what's best for me."

She couldn't stop her smile. "Families will do that. You should've heard my father when I told him I wanted to run a shelter for kids in the middle of the South Pacific. He was supportive, of course, but concerned. He knew how secure I was in my job with Jack Gladwell. He knew if I wanted marriage and kids, I could stay with Jack and have that."

"He was scared for your future."

"Maybe. At least, the future he had envisioned." She thought of Naomi and smiled. The little girl had been beside herself with happiness when she'd left the shelter with her parents and baby brother. "I don't need a specific future when I'm happy in the here and now."

"That's exactly what I wanted to discuss." Alessandro moved closer. "When I met with Mikhail at the palace, I committed to the shelter's standard three-month service term. With such a capable staff, you probably don't need me to stay longer. I'm not sure how much I truly contribute. However—"

"Yes."

Her breath stilled at the electricity that flared in his golden eyes. "Yes?"

"The kids would love it if you stayed." Her voice hitched, and she took a deep breath before adding, "So would I."

His mouth lifted into a slow, sexy grin. "How did you know that was what I wanted to say?"

She shrugged, then returned his smile. "I didn't." She'd spoken without thinking. Only hoping.

"It *is* what I wanted to say." He moved another step nearer. "I can't imagine leaving the kids. I especially can't imagine leaving you."

"I thought you weren't the right man for me. Those were your words."

"I still imagine I'm not." His mouth twisted, then he said, "You've completely ruined me, though. The whole way to and from Sarcaccia, my phone kept ringing with messages from women who wanted to see me while I was home. Or from male friends who wanted to go to parties, knowing we'd all leave with female companions. It didn't work. All I could think about was you." A self-deprecating laugh escaped him. "You've absolutely ruined me for casual sex."

"You, ah, tried? And—"

"No! No." He shook his head, then moved to frame her shoulders with his hands. His gaze dropped to one hand as he slid his palms down her arms, then returned them to her shoulders. When he met her gaze again, he said, "All I could think about was the kiss we shared in the dining hall. About the fact that the entire time I walked behind you when we followed the trail from the church, I watched the way the sunshine came through the rainforest canopy and made shadow patterns in your hair. I thought about how I spend my days listening for your laugh. I thought about the way the kids watch you and the staff relies on you. If you wanted to, you could run the world and do it with your heart as much as with your head. And I realized that you scare the living daylights out of me."

Her throat grew tight. "I do?"

"At Sophia's party, I felt like you could see right through me. I loved talking with you, but more than that, I was impressed with your perception. Then when I saw you again, in the palace library, I saw doubt in your eyes. All my life, I've been used to being compared to Vittorio and failing. You didn't mean to do it, I know. And I reacted badly. Then you questioned me when I stood right here in your office the day I arrived on Kilakuru, I felt it again. But what hurt—what *scared* me—wasn't being compared to Vittorio. It was being rejected by you."

The emotion in his voice nearly undid her. "You're not used to female rejection."

His thumbs pressed into the skin of her shoulders, warming her through the plush fabric of her robe. "True. But in your case, I was scared because I liked you. Not because of the way your eyes tilt up at the edges or because you have a smile any man would love to see turned his way. I liked you the moment you said hello at the bar and zeroed in on the fact I was tired of small talk. You danced like a dream. You asked me the most bizarre questions. You fit in my arms. And you mesmerized me. All that was before I came here and understood the depth of your compassion. Before I fell in love with the fact that you secretly *do* want back copies of *The Economist* and you use big words when you're nervous. Before I realized how truly wonderful and interesting you are."

Her face heated at his words. "I have a confession to make. I didn't approach you at the bar solely to ask about whether Alessandro might be interested in charity work."

"No?"

She gave a slight shake of her head. "When you ordered your Scotch, there was frustration in your voice. As if your mind was on more important matters. There was a rebelliousness in your stance and in your eyes. I loved that. The contrast between the formal, rule-following prince and the man who saw that there are times that formality should be cast aside in order to get things done. Of course, I thought you were Vittorio. But that hint of contrariness appealed to me. It's what I felt when I quit my job to come here. It wasn't what was expected. People flat-out told me I was foolish to leave such a perfect position, and I wondered if I was doing the right thing. But taking the less-traveled road helped me grow. It gave me purpose. When I saw that look in your eyes at the bar" —she swallowed at the admission— "I admired you. I'd always aspired to be that confident. As confident as I may have acted that night, I wasn't."

A wry laugh emanated from him. "You know, when I decided to volunteer here, I thought it was because I needed a challenge. I needed to prove my capabilities. But I've learned that I can find a challenge anywhere. What I really needed was a purpose. *Meaning.* You gave me that meaning, you challenged me to grow, and I've fallen in love with you for it. For who you are. And I was so scared of being rejected that I didn't give you the opportunity to reject me." A divot formed between his brows as he focused on her. "I told you I wasn't the man for you, but that was an excuse. I said it out of fear. I should have taken the risk—"

She thought her heart would burst as she put her fingers to his lips. All she'd needed to hear had been said. More than that, she felt it. He radiated love.

"Shhh. You're good enough. More than good enough. You're everything I could ever want. I'm crazy in love with you." She stretched onto her tiptoes, then shifted her fingertips to his cheek and pressed a soft kiss to his mouth. "And I very much want you in my bed tonight."

His eyes drifted closed, then his arms came around her, tight and possessive, pulling her into a hug that lifted her from the floor. He dragged his lips across her cheek, then murmured, "I don't want to have sex for the sake of sex. I'm done with it. I want to make love to you. Slowly. Beautifully. I want it to mean something. To mean everything."

She wrapped her hand around the back of his head, cradling him to her as he kissed her ear, her neck, then her shoulder. Engulfed by the raging desire and immense love she felt all at once for this man. They stood wrapped in each other's arms for a long time, then finally, he pulled away enough to make eye contact.

"Once, I brought a woman to orgasm without touching her. I simply stood near her and talked her into it. I took her imagination where she wanted to go."

"Braggart." She couldn't help but give him a flirtatious grin. No way would she let him do that to her. Not tonight.

He shook his head, his expression remaining serious. "It worked because I didn't know that woman, not really. And she didn't know me. Nor did we care to. It's symptomatic of every relationship I've ever had." He scoffed at his own words. "They weren't even relationships. I'm telling you this because I want to know you, Frannie. I want you to know me, even if that scares me. If I stay here tonight, I want it to be about that. For the first time in my life, and I believe for the last time, I'm truly, deeply in love."

She bracketed his face with her fingers. "Then know me. And love me. There's nothing to fear."

His mouth came down on hers in a kiss that stole her breath. Minutes later, they'd made their way to her room, having extinguished the office lights and locked the doors behind them.

"It's a twin bed," she murmured against his mouth.

"I don't care."

Then they were on top of her tangled sheets, her robe somewhere on the floor, her nightgown around her waist. Her breath thundered in her own ears as she pulled his shirt from his pants, then slowly undid each button so she could explore his glorious, hard upper body. She wanted to learn his contours, to taste him, to know him as well as she knew herself. Ironically, even as she revealed each increment of bare skin and muscle, then explored him with her fingertips, she felt she already knew him...that she knew how they fit, how compatible they were, how and where to touch him to make him mad with desire. Each movement of her hands over his body drew the reaction she ached to see. She savored each sound, each pleasured flinch, each hazy-eyed smile of satisfaction. Then, when her nightgown disappeared and she was naked to him, he gently rolled her to her back and kissed his way down her body, taking her nipples into his mouth one at a time.

His gentle, slow worship of her body drove her mad with lust even as her heart threatened to burst with love. She thrilled to the gooseflesh that rose along her skin.

"You are heaven," he murmured against her belly. She realized then that he was shaking. So was she.

"Dear God, Frannie. You are my home."

Long minutes later, when he slid one hand to her hip, entered her, and breathed her name, she closed her eyes and whimpered softly, overwhelmed.

Yes, they'd both found home. A safe place, a loving place. A place where they were known. The best place. Forever.

* * *

Frannie stirred just before sunrise.

Alessandro held her in front of him, spoon-style, in her narrow bed, and pressed a long kiss to the top of her head. Her sigh of contentment warmed him to the core.

"Rule breaker," he whispered. He couldn't believe they'd spent the entire night making love right in the compound, only a short distance from the bunkhouses where the children slept. At the same time, it'd felt amazingly right.

Her arms tightened over his, then she wiggled so her back rested fully against his torso. "This from the man pretending to be his twin brother the first time we met."

"I had good cause."

"So do I."

He chuckled at that, then dropped another kiss into her hair.

"Thank you," she whispered, her voice filled with emotion.

"Don't thank me—"

"Not for that," she said as she threaded her fingers through his. "For pushing me to expand my views. And for encouraging me to ignore the rules sometimes. Rules have always brought me security. You've shown me that it's okay to relax when I'm wound so tightly I can't see beyond my mental walls. Not just that it's okay to relax…but *good*."

He nuzzled against her. "In that case, you're quite welcome."

"Speaking of rule breakers," she said, "I need to tell you about Naomi." Frannie rolled over and explained that Naomi's father had secured a position with the island's fire department and that Naomi had gone home. "She confessed to taking the Scotch from my cabinet. She also told me how you reacted when she gave it to you. I promised her you'd go visit and share a drink with her parents."

Alessandro could only imagine Frannie's reaction to hearing Naomi's sweet voice, let alone her reaction to the words themselves.

"Hearing her speak…oh, Alessandro, it was the most beautiful sound." Frannie squeezed his arm. "It was a moment I'll remember the rest of my life. Thank you."

"Why thank me?"

"Because she spoke to you first. You earned her trust, which made her feel safe, then you ensured she'd speak again by keeping her trust when she stole the Scotch." Frannie's thumb moved along his arm in a sweet caress. "I owe you an apology. I should have trusted you."

"Frannie, you did trust me, or you would have demanded I return the liquor to the cabinet."

She laughed, and the sound reverberated through him. He could listen to it for the rest of his life. Her expression turned serious, and he could tell she was about to grovel in earnest. Much as it would feed his ego, he didn't need to hear it. She was already forgiven.

He pressed a kiss to her forehead. "Much as I'm enjoying your rule-breaking, we shouldn't get caught. I'll go across the hall to the room I used when I first arrived. At breakfast, let everyone know you let me in late. They won't question that I stayed across the hall instead of trying to go through the bunkhouse where I might wake everyone. You can tell them I'm sleeping in."

"Wait, you get your beauty sleep, but I don't?"

"You don't need it." He relaxed into her pillow, unwilling to move quite yet. He wasn't sure how they'd make a relationship work in the close confines of the shelter, but they would. He had no doubt.

"You having morning-after regrets?" she asked when he remained quiet, though he could tell from her tone she didn't believe it to be the case.

"Not at all. Just thinking about logistics."

She used her fingers to comb his hair away from his face. "How so?"

"Eventually, I do have to return to Sarcaccia. And on that topic, I need to tell you something private and trust that it will never be repeated." He waited for her nod of acceptance, then explained about Vittorio and Emily. "I hope that it's all for naught and that Emily can get pregnant and carry a baby to term. Realistically, though, it's a very long shot. I need to prepare for that. Maybe I should have told you last night, before we got to this point. But my mind wasn't exactly on my brother."

She spread one hand across his chest. Her gaze followed her fingertips. "You didn't need to tell me at all. It's Emily and Vittorio's business, not mine."

"If you and I want a future, it's your business, too. I know you don't want a relationship like your parents', where—much as they might love each other—their passions mean that they live separate lives. I want to stay with you at Sunrise Shelter until the last child is gone, and I'll do my best to accomplish that. However, I'm beholden to the people of my country. When it's time to go, I have to go. But I need to know if there will be a day that you can come to Sarcaccia with me."

Frannie's hand stilled over his heart, then she looked into his eyes. "That's a lovely invitation."

"Lovely or not, I need you to be honest. If it's not something you can do, I should go at the end of my three months. He covered her hand with his and looked deep into her dark eyes with their beautiful upturned edges. "Staying here, knowing that I can't be with you...it would be very difficult."

"I dream of the day the kids all have homes and don't need me any more. With everything in my heart, I believe that day will come. After that, then, yes. I'd be willing to move Sarcaccia with you. But I can't promise not to spend my time there helping children in need. Their situation isn't what the children face here on Kilakuru, but it's my calling."

He lifted his head from the pillow to give her a soft kiss. "I'd expect nothing less. It's who you are. On the other hand, if Vittorio doesn't have children, and I ascend the throne—"

"That's a big if. Even so, I know you could do it. You've proven how good you could be."

He appreciated her confidence, but there was a bigger issue. "It is a big if. But *if* it happened, I'd want you by my side. It's a lot to ask—you should see all my mother does—and I wouldn't ask it of you unless you were willing to take on the responsibility."

He knew he was putting the cart before the horse, both in planning a possible ascendancy to the throne and a possible marriage. They'd spent only one night together. But, as with his mother and father, and with Vittorio and Emily, he *knew*.

He held his breath, afraid to hear her answer, yet knowing he'd had to take the risk and ask.

"Your mother spends a great deal of time helping teens. She might not live with them, but the support she gives makes a difference. If I can make a difference the way she does, I'd be happy." She shrugged. "It's not a decision we need to make now. But I have a question for you."

He covered her fingers, then drew them to his mouth for a quick kiss. "Yes?"

"This is all new. I realize we've spent a lot of time together since you arrived and have gotten to know a lot about each other, but—and I don't mean to sound insecure...I'm asking this honestly—how do you know you won't get bored with me?"

He wanted to laugh, but the sincerity in her voice stopped him. He didn't take his gaze from hers. "You saw the news when my father announced that he'd had three children with Teresa Cornaro?"

At Frannie's frown and nod, he continued, "Two of them were born at the beginning of his marriage to my mother, one was born before. My father only informed me—and my brothers and sister—a few days before that press conference. But my mother knew about the Cornaro children all along. I've seen my parents' relationship firsthand over the years. They had an arranged marriage, but I know how deeply they've come to love each other. When I was home for Vittorio's wedding, I asked my mother how in the world she'd known it would all work with my father. How she knew she loved him. She said something along the lines of, 'I simply do. I think I knew within days of meeting him. His soul spoke to mine.' That's how I feel when I'm with you, Frannie. As if your soul speaks to mine. I'm in love with you. It's a love I believe can overcome any obstacle." His fingers tightened around hers. "We don't have the obstacles my parents had. God willing, we never will. The worst that can happen is that I become my father's heir. Or we have to figure out how to live on opposite sides of the world for a short time. Can you see a way for us past those difficulties? I know, given the troubles your parents had, it might seem impossible."

She sat up in bed, pulling him with her. Silently, she draped one arm over his shoulder, then tucked her other hand beneath the sheets, where her fingers found his knee. When she met his gaze, her smile was brilliant.

"Have you ever heard the saying about seeing the distance of your headlights?"

He felt himself returning her smile. "You don't need to see the entire road in order to drive in the dark. You need only see the distance of your headlights."

Her hand moved slowly up his thigh. "Exactly. You once asked me if I was bothered by my upbringing, by my parents' divorce or having to move so many times. I meant it when I said I wasn't. None of us knew what the future held, but because my parents gave me love and security, I only needed to see as far as the headlights shone. That sense is what I want to give to these kids. But most important, it's what you give me. It's why, even when you left me in the dining room and said you weren't the man for me, I had hope, deep in my heart, that we'd find a way, even if I couldn't see it in that moment."

Her hand eased farther up his thigh, though when he glanced down, the sheets obscured the movement. "You are amazing." And he was so, so lucky.

She leaned toward him, slowly, until her nose touched his. "I have every confidence that we'll find a way to reach our destination, even if we can't see the road right now. If you believe that, too, we have nothing to fear."

Her hand shifted higher just as his mouth found hers. They made slow, romantic love until her bedside alarm rang, then, with a final kiss, he darted across the hall.

EPILOGUE

Two Years Later

Frannie picked up a handful of seed pods that had fallen from the palm trees surrounding the compound, then tossed them in the organic waste bin. Now that the trees—some planted, others transplanted—were strong enough not to require staking, they generated seed pods by the dozens. Having to clean up every time she walked across the compound was a fair trade for the shade they provided.

She shielded her eyes and angled her head to watch as the trees bent with the breeze. Kilakuru would always bear scars from the tsunami, but the trees were a sign of the island's healing.

On that thought, she pushed through the door to the dining hall.

Music pumped through speakers strategically placed in the corners of the dining hall as kids and adults alike danced under the spinning overhead fans. This afternoon, Frannie and Alessandro had pushed the tables to the room's outer edges in order to create a makeshift dance floor. Paper chains made by the kids the day before now hung over the doorway and the refreshment table. Even Chloe, visiting from Australia on an extended diving trip, had come to the shelter this morning to help decorate.

The energetic beat reminded Frannie of the night she met Alessandro at Sophia's Christmas party, but little else resembled that affair. This was all island verve, sandals, and red punch, rather than wealthy Europeans dressed to the nines and sipping champagne.

"This is quite the celebration. I've never seen the kids so happy," Tommy said as he came to stand alongside Frannie. "I've never seen you so happy."

She ladled a cup of punch and handed it to Tommy. "Probably because I've never been so happy."

Tommy's grin broadened. "Four kids in one week. Hard to believe. You're going to miss them, I bet."

"They aren't going far. The Luani kids will be here on the island with their parents, now that their home has been rebuilt. Their mother is going to run her beauty salon from their house until their father's pharmacy opens. After that, she'll move into space at the back of the pharmacy building."

"She'll do big business. You didn't know her before the tsunami, but her salon was always full."

"Irene told me she's very good." Irene had waxed poetic about Mrs. Luani's talent since Frannie first arrived on Kilakuru. When Irene heard the Luanis were moving home, Irene urged Frannie to book an appointment immediately or risk having to wait a long time.

"And Walter tells me the Tolangi sisters were adopted. Is that true? Irene hadn't heard anything about it."

Frannie nodded. With few children left at the shelter, Irene had found a permanent position elsewhere on the island and Tommy was days away from reopening his auto repair shop. They'd both fallen behind on shelter gossip. "They're going to live with an aunt and uncle who've moved back to Kilakuru. They're thrilled."

"So it's true. That's wonderful!" Irene said, coming up behind her brother. "What's the plan once they move out? Surely you're not keeping the place going with one resident?"

Frannie schooled her features to keep from betraying her emotions. "Remy's needs haven't changed. I've always told the kids that the shelter would be their home for as long as they need it, and I'm going to stick to that."

"It'll be hard on Remy, being alone," Tommy said. Lines of concern crisscrossed his brow. "Especially with Johnny gone. He's always looked up to Johnny."

"Johnny's been great about keeping in touch with Remy, and Remy understands that going to California was the best thing for Johnny's future." Ever since Johnny was awarded a scholarship to attend college in the United States, Frannie kept close tabs on Remy and his reaction to the situation. So far, all had gone well. It helped that Remy witnessed the regular communication between Tehani and Johnny since Tehani left to attend college in Fiji the year before.

"Remy's matured a lot since moving into the shelter. Even so, it'll be difficult for him to be the only one here," Irene said.

Choosing her words carefully, Frannie told them, "You never know when there'll be children in need. We could end up with new residents next week. That's why Jack Gladwell named this the Sunrise Shelter. It's a place of optimism. Of new beginnings."

Frannie smiled as she saw Alessandro greet the Iakopo family, who'd been invited to the celebration. To Irene and Tommy, she said, "In the meantime, once the hospital opens down the street, we'll offer a portion of our beds to families who want to be near their loved ones. I expect there'll be a lot of kids coming in and out. Plenty of company for Remy, should he want it."

Both Irene and Tommy looked doubtful, but Frannie was saved from further comment when Alessandro signaled for her to join him.

"We'll talk more later," Tommy said, his gaze following Frannie's to where Alessandro now climbed onto one of the benches to call for the crowd's attention.

Frannie crossed the room and took Alessandro's proffered hand, then joined him to stand on one of the wooden benches. Alessandro waved to Sam, who was in charge of the music, and Sam fiddled with the speakers so the music gradually faded. Slowly, everyone in the room turned to Alessandro and Frannie.

"Thank you, everyone, for coming to our engagement party," Alessandro said. "Are you having fun?"

A scream rose from the kids, while the adults looked up at the couple with beaming faces. While Alessandro and Frannie fought to keep their relationship private for as long as possible, those who worked at the shelter figured out that they'd fallen hard for each other within a few months of Alessandro's return from Prince Vittorio's wedding. And everyone knew the story of how Alessandro proposed. First, he'd faked an emergency at the gazebo. When Frannie arrived, she'd been directed on a treasure hunt. She'd ended up visiting the spots they'd most enjoyed in their two years together on Kilakuru, with the children stationed at each location to hand her clues to her next stop. She'd even been compelled to drive to St. Augustine's, where Father Jacob handed her a map that led to the shelter. In the end, Frannie found herself in the nurse's station, in the very spot where she'd been standing when she'd first spied Alessandro entering the compound with Tommy and had uttered a curse word to Chloe.

Alessandro had waited for her beside that window. He asked if she wanted to swear at him. After she gave him a playful swat, he'd knelt in front of her, told her he wanted the treasure hunt to be her last adventure without him, then asked Frannie if she'd marry him. Of course, she'd said yes.

"Many of you have probably heard the rumor that I'm a prince in some faraway land," he said, which resulted in a roar of laughter. "You've been good enough to treat me as you do everyone else who lives here at the shelter, as a friend."

"Whether you deserve it or not," Walter called from the back of the room.

"We know who took the last cookie from the dining hall yesterday," Sam added. "It wasn't me."

Frannie laughed, knowing it was likely true. Pearl still worked at the shelter, the last of the full-time dining hall employees. Just as she had on the day Alessandro arrived on the island, Pearl made sure to give him a cookie or two whenever there was a fresh batch.

Alessandro put his arm around Frannie's shoulders and pulled her close. "I'm not admitting anything." He looked down at Frannie, winked, then looked to the crowd. "As I was saying, there's a rumor that I'm a prince. I hate to say that it's true, but it is. And as a prince, I'm expected to have a very fancy wedding ceremony in a cathedral on my home island of Sarcaccia."

"That sounds terrible," Tommy called over the crowd.

"I'm sure Frannie and I will hate every moment of it," he replied. "We won't have any red punch and Sam won't be able to DJ."

"Oh, stop," Frannie whispered. "Get to the point."

"That being said, once the ceremony on Sarcaccia is over, we plan to come here for a second ceremony, one that everyone can attend, right here at Sunrise Shelter. You're all invited."

A chorus of cheers rose through the room. After one more long look at Frannie, Alessandro told everyone, "We would, however, like to bring one person with us to Sarcaccia to attend the wedding. We'd like this individual to be part of the ceremony."

The room grew quiet, then Frannie searched the room until she saw Remy standing on one of the benches near the rear of the hall. "Remy, we'd very much like you to be our ring bearer."

Silence reigned for a moment, then pandemonium erupted. "We'll cover all your expenses and you'll have a place to stay at the palace," she assured him once the noise subsided.

"You'll also fly back here with us afterward," Alessandro said. "What do you say?"

Remy nodded and grinned, then jumped from his bench and sprinted through the room. It took only seconds for him to jump onto the wooden bench beside Alessandro and Frannie, then hug each of them.

"Thank you, everyone, for throwing such a wonderful party for us," Alessandro said. "Now get back to dancing!"

With a whoop, Sam started the music. Alessandro and Remy jumped from the bench, then Alessandro grabbed Frannie by the waist to swing her to the floor. Instead of joining the crowd of dancers, Alessandro turned to Remy and said, "Why don't you walk outside with us for a moment?"

"Sure."

Alessandro smiled as he led Remy away from the boisterous confines of the dining hall, toward the shelter of the gazebo. Though an island breeze blew through the compound, as always, the heat reflecting off the hard-packed dirt made walking across the open area akin to standing on top of a barbecue grill. Once they were settled on the benches, Alessandro looked to Frannie.

Her heart pounded in her throat as she turned to Remy. "The trip to Sarcaccia should be a lot of fun. It'll give you a chance to get to see what Alessandro's life is like away from the shelter."

A wide smile lit Remy's face. "Thank you for asking me. I…I'm really excited." He looked at Alessandro, then Frannie. "Ever since I found out he was from Sarcaccia, I've read everything I can find about it. You remember when you set up the projector in the dining room and showed the photos of Prince Vittorio's wedding? It looked completely different from Kilakuru. It was amazing."

She smiled at the memory. "If you'd like, you have the chance to live there someday." She waited a beat, then said, "After Alessandro and I are married, we would very much like to adopt you."

Remy's mouth dropped into a silent O. Frannie felt tears springing to her eyes as she watched the expression on the face of the boy she hoped would become her son. "There are more hoops to jump through here on Kilakuru, but we've already cleared it with your relatives on the Marquesas. It's entirely up to you."

"You can take your time to think about it," Alessandro said. "You *should* take your time. It's a big decision and there's no rush. The offer to go to Sarcaccia and serve as our ring bearer stands either way."

Remy's eyes squeezed shut as Alessandro spoke. Finally, he opened his eyes and nodded, then enveloped Frannie in a big hug. She could feel the tears streaming from the corners of her eyes, but she didn't care. Her world existed in this moment, in this gazebo.

"Thank you," Remy said once he released her. He looked from Frannie to Alessandro. "I would love to be in your wedding. And I don't need to think about it. The adoption part, I mean. My answer is yes."

"Are you sure?" Frannie fought to keep her voice steady. She desperately wanted him to say yes, but knew he hadn't had much time to process it. "I don't want you to feel pressured. Don't do it because you feel like you have no other choice."

Remy sucked in his lower lip. She hadn't seen him do that in almost two years…since soon after Alessandro came to the shelter. "I don't want you to adopt me because you feel sorry for me."

"We want to adopt you because we love you," Alessandro said. "We've told you all along that we consider everyone who lives and works here at the shelter a family, but you're special to us, so special we want to make that family permanent. That being said, it's up to you. If you decide you'd rather not, we'll still be here for you. Frannie and I will live here at the shelter until everyone has a home or is old enough to pursue either college or a full-time career on their own."

Remy's gaze flicked between them, then he smiled. "I'd be your son?"

"Legally, yes," Frannie said. "However you want us to describe you, and the way you refer to us, would be up to you. If you were to call us Mom and Dad, we'd be thrilled. If you're more comfortable with Frannie and Alessandro, that's fine, too."

Remy rocked on his heels and considered that. "I think my dad would tell me to call you Mom and Dad. If he knew he couldn't be here for me, he'd have picked you to raise me. He would've liked you a lot."

"That's a big compliment, Remy. Thank you. I know he meant the world to you."

"You should visit Sarcaccia before you make a firm decision," Alessandro said. "At some point soon, Frannie and I will likely need to move there. If we adopted you, we'd make it a point to visit Kilakuru frequently, but both of us have family in Sarcaccia, and I have duties there. We'd need to know that you'd be comfortable living there."

Remy's dark eyes creased in concern. "If we moved to Sarcaccia, what would happen to the shelter?"

"Walter's teaching job at the shelter is only part-time now that most of the kids have transferred to other schools," Frannie said. "It's not enough for him to live on, and the other schools on the island aren't hiring right now. I was planning to ask him to take over my job. He'd be great at it, and it'd mean he could stay here on Kilakuru if that's what he wants."

"He wants to marry Pearl," Remy blurted out. "He'd stay."

"He does?" Frannie couldn't be more shocked. "How do you know that?"

"I heard them talking about it behind the bunkhouse last week. They don't know I heard. Walter told Pearl they need to wait until they both have steady jobs, but said that when that happens, he's going to sweep her off her feet and give her lots of babies." Remy couldn't hide his amusement at the last part.

"Well, we should make sure that happens no matter what." Alessandro's voice made it clear he was as surprised by the news as Frannie...and just as delighted by it.

"My decision is made," Remy said, his voice sure. "Even if you didn't want to adopt me, you're the closest thing to parents I've had since my dad died. Wherever you live, I want to be."

"All right." Alessandro stood, then put a hand on Remy's shoulder. "Let's keep this between us for now, all right? There's a long process to go through when we return from Sarcaccia. Once we're a few steps into it, we can surprise everyone."

"They're going to love it," Remy said. A cheer from the direction of the dining hall caught his attention.

"Go ahead." Frannie stood and smiled at Remy as she wrapped her arms around Alessandro's waist. "We'll be there in a minute."

Once Remy disappeared through the doors, Alessandro said, "Think he'll keep it quiet?"

"I think he will." Remy had always been good at keeping his own counsel, except in one instance. "If you don't count Humphrey."

"Humphrey moved from his bed to the nightstand," Frannie said. "Don't know if you noticed that."

"I have. Humphrey hasn't left the nightstand in months. I think it's a good sign he doesn't need his camel with him."

Alessandro pulled her closer. She leaned her head against his shoulder and marveled again at how well they fit. When he'd come home from Vittorio's wedding and told her how he felt, she didn't think she could love him more. But she did, every day.

"This will be quite the adventure." His voice held a note of contentment that made her heart do a slow flip. "I'm glad we're tackling it together."

"You're not scared of the future? There are still a lot of unknowns."

"Not at all. Whatever happens, you and Remy are my happily ever after."

She turned into him and gave Alessandro a kiss full of promise. When they finally broke apart, he took her hand to stroll to the dining hall and join the party.

"Dance with me?" he asked.

"Always."

Acknowledgements

Many thanks to Isabella, owner of the original Humphrey of Dubai.
Remy wouldn't be the same without you.

Other Titles By Nicole Burnham

The Royal Scandals Series

Christmas With a Prince (novella)

Scandal With a Prince

Honeymoon With a Prince

Christmas on the Royal Yacht (novella)

Slow Tango With a Prince

The Royal Bastard

Christmas With a Palace Thief

The Wicked Prince

More Royal Scandals titles will be available soon. For updates, please subscribe to Nicole's Newsletter at www.nicoleburnham.com.

ABOUT THE AUTHOR

Nicole Burnham is the RITA award-winning author of over a dozen novels, including the popular Royal Scandals series. All About Romance declares, "Nicole Burnham gives life to a fictional kingdom and monarchy that feel as though they could be real" and "gosh darn it, Nicole Burnham is good…readers should definitely check her out."

Nicole graduated from an American high school in Germany, then obtained a BA in political science from Colorado State University and a JD/MA in international relations from the University of Michigan. She lives near Boston, spends as much time as possible at Fenway Park, and travels abroad whenever she can score cheap airfare.

Nicole invites you to visit her website and subscribe to her newsletter at www. nicoleburnham.com.